The Day After Never

Havoc

Russell Blake

ISBN: 978-1982935566

Published by

Reprobatio Limited

Cry "Havoc," and let slip the dogs of war

— Julius Caesar, William Shakespeare

Chapter 1

The Chinese amphibious transport dock ship *Yimeng Shan* was anchored several hundred yards off the Smith Cove waterway, its lights glimmering in the predawn fog that enveloped Puget Sound. The ship had arrived a week earlier and disgorged a fighting force of eight hundred and seventy-five Chinese marines, as well as a host of military engineers to assess the state of the city's infrastructure and the port facilities. They'd secured Harbor Island without a fight and established a base, where they'd staged their invasion troops in anticipation of making a push to seize the city.

After a week of sending out patrols to test the defenders' strength, that night the Chinese troops had been given the order to move.

Gunshots echoed across the water as they secured the wharves across from Harbor Island. The commander had specified that the areas vital to Chinese interests were to be prised from the control of the warlord who ruled the city, and once they'd established another defendable base downtown, the marines could mop up the enemy fighters at their convenience.

The presence of a warship and a large invasion force in plain sight on Harbor Island had achieved the desired psychological shock and awe, and the civilian prisoners the patrols had captured reported that the warlord's gunmen had left the city in droves. So far resistance from the remaining fighters had been largely ineffective, their attacks amateurish and disorganized, and the Chinese were now battling for the waterfront and working their way toward the downtown area.

A dozen leather-clad bikers had tried to stop the Chinese at the Harbor Island bridge, but a few skillfully targeted mortars had blown their sandbagged bunker to pieces. By the time reinforcements arrived from the city, hundreds of Chinese had already poured across the bridge and were shooting it out with the vastly outgunned warlord's fighters, who showed no stomach for battle against a disciplined, well-outfitted enemy.

Flames licked at the night sky from warehouses and big-box outlets, where the locals had lost skirmishes as they'd tried to halt the onslaught, and now the Chinese marines were working their way inexorably north in grim silence, their orders to neutralize anyone who put up a fight. So far their offensive under cover of darkness had appeared to have taken the defenders largely unawares, which surprised the Chinese given the Americans had had a week to prepare themselves.

Shots rang out from a brick building by the rail yards, and a soldier screamed as slugs ripped through his chest. The man tumbled forward, and his rifle clattered against the asphalt as he hit hard. The marines around him spread out and ran for cover, their weapons trained on the building. Each soldier carried three hundred rounds of ammo, which was all they had been allocated for the offensive, so they held their fire until they could spot a target. Almost as one they raced toward a tangle of abandoned cars that clogged the deserted street.

The fog had reduced visibility to under thirty yards, so to hit anything, one had to be close. More shots barked from the building, and the squad leader signaled to three of his men and pointed at the muzzle flashes emanating from a window on the second floor. The men took off, zigzagging to the building entrance, their boots pounding on the pavement as bullets rained down around them.

Two of them stopped just short of the entrance and fired up at the window while the third freed a grenade and lobbed it through the opening. The blast sent a shower of debris and flame into the street, but the soldiers continued into the building, leading with their assault rifles. The lead soldier indicated the doorways along the hallway, and the trio methodically made their way along the corridor, pausing at each room and sweeping the interiors with their weapons.

The building had long ago been gutted by looters, and all that remained in the rooms was debris and refuse. It took the soldiers five minutes to pronounce the area clear, and then they hurried to rejoin their platoon as gunfire from the boulevard reached them through the fog.

The defenders were barricaded in a warehouse near the railway, and at least two of the warlord's snipers had taken cover on the far side of the block in a bell tower, where they'd cut down an attempt to flank the warehouse. Six marines lay wounded or dead in the middle of the street after having been caught in the open by the sharpshooters.

The squad leader barked orders to his men, and a pair of them ran back toward the bridge as the rest laid down covering fire. They melted into the fog, and the squad leader instructed the troops to stop shooting until he gave the signal to open up again.

An occasional shot rang out from the tower or the warehouse, but they missed their targets. The squad leader waited patiently, knowing there was a good chance that enemy reinforcements would arrive at the warehouse before his men got back, but they'd be forced to make an impossible choice – either expend a ton of ammunition and men to overwhelm the warehouse with no guarantee of success, or do as he'd done, and send the fastest runners to the temporary base by the bridge for serious ordnance.

When the men returned, the squad leader grunted his approval and whispered to them. They worked their way to the front of the formation and took up position behind the husk of an old brick building, from where they could sight on the warehouse without being picked off by the snipers.

The first of the antipersonnel rockets they'd brought from the base streaked from the launcher straight toward the row of windows where the shooters were hiding, and detonated with a whump that shook the ground. The bell tower was the recipient of the second projectile, which vaporized the upper section and collapsed half of the rest.

The squad leader was ordering his men to move on the warehouse when more rifle fire pocked the walls around him. He ducked, fished a small radio from his belt, and called in a report to the ship. A voice answered, and he made his request, which was approved a minute later as his men exchanged volleys with the defenders.

"Hold your fire," he called out. "Don't throw away rounds you'll need later."

The Chinese fire died, and he waited, eyeing the second hand of his mechanical watch impatiently as time crept by.

A series of muffled booms sounded from the island. He listened for the telltale whistle of incoming mortar rounds and was rewarded a moment later by the expected sound.

The warehouse roof exploded with geysers of flame as the 120mm shells detonated across its surface. A second salvo of white phosphorous projectiles finished the job in a series of blinding flashes, leaving the building a smoldering ruin.

The squad leader was already in motion before the roar of the explosions faded, leading his surviving thirty men forward toward their ultimate objective: downtown Seattle.

By morning, the fog had burned off and been replaced by an oily haze from the burning buildings that dotted the skyline. The Chinese occupation force had successfully contained the waterfront and downtown district and was in the process of creating an armed perimeter in case any of the locals decided to play hero. An occasional gunshot rang out as squads went block by block to mop up stragglers, although they'd taken the city with surprisingly little effective resistance, which had been a pleasant surprise after hearing the reports of the decimation of the Oregon contingent's warship.

Several hundred of the warlord's fighters had been captured or wounded; they were being held in one of the large sports arenas, watched over by guards with assault rifles and a machine gun nest strategically located in the bleachers. A group of Chinese officers entered the stadium and made their way down the steps to where the field commander, Major Ling, waited with his men.

The major snapped to attention as they approached, and the two officers in the lead returned his salute as they faced him.

"At ease, Major," said General Song, the ranking officer and new military governor of Seattle.

"Yes, sir," Major Ling replied, and relaxed.

"You suffered forty-seven casualties?" Song asked. "How many hurt?"

"Another eighteen."

General Song nodded at the news and turned to where Colonel Wei stood to his right. "See to it that our wounded receive attentive care and are kept comfortable."

"Yes, sir," Wei said.

Song addressed Major Ling again. "You'll be happy to know that Hamilton, the warlord who controlled Seattle, was killed in a skirmish east of here no more than an hour ago."

"That is good news. Congratulations, sir."

"It is you who deserves the credit. Your offensive drove him and his henchmen out of the city. Good work, Major. I'll see to it that you receive a commendation."

"Thank you, sir."

The general looked over the prisoners, some of whom lay on the ground, while others stood glaring at the Chinese. The enemy fighters were a filthy bunch, ragged beards and long hair the norm, their arms covered with tattoos and their faces adorned with piercings and prison ink.

"Quite a collection, aren't they?" General Song said, more of a statement than a question.

"Yes, sir. We were fortunate that they were as disorganized as they were. Apparently they've grown accustomed to preying on the population and weren't expecting to confront a trained force."

"They look like the criminals they are," Song agreed.

"What do you want to do with them?" Major Ling asked.

The general thought for a long moment. "Don't waste

ammunition. Bayonet them and leave their bodies for the buzzards. It will serve as a warning to the citizenry that to oppose us is to die."

Colonel Wei edged closer to the general. "Perhaps we could use the stronger ones as slaves? There is much to be done, and we'll need manpower."

Song shook his head. "No. We must send a message to any still out there. They will receive no mercy. We'll get our slaves from the peaceful locals. These scum are responsible for the loss of forty-seven good and honorable men. They will pay for their crimes in the most expedient manner possible. Organize a bayonet squad and make quick work of it," he ordered, and turned.

"Yes, sir," Ling said, and watched the brass climb the stairs and disappear from view as they went to inspect the rest of the troops.

Ling had no issue slaughtering the warlord's fighters. There was no Geneva Convention at play, and whatever the military governor decreed had the weight of law. He studied the prisoners, whose wrists were cinched behind their backs, and called over his subordinate Captain Ma.

Ma hurried to the major, who leaned into him and spoke in a low voice. The captain's eyes widened when the major finished, but his expression was stony when he nodded to Ling.

Half an hour later, hundreds of corpses littered the playing field, and a lake of blood stained the grass. Swarms of flies so thick they appeared to be black smoke descended on the bodies to feast, and the stench of bodily fluids was overpowering when the breeze blew from the sea. Seagulls wheeled overhead, and several landed and hopped over to an appetizing body and went to work on its eyes with their razor-sharp beaks. Ling watched for a minute and then turned to his gathered men.

"Leave the gates open for anyone who wants to come and see what happens to those who oppose us. I suspect the enthusiasm of the lazy Americans for more fighting will be nil."

"If the reports are correct, many in the city will view us as heroes after years under the rule of these animals," Ma said.

"Perhaps. But you are to treat any residents as enemies of the

Chinese state until proven otherwise. We are not here to win hearts and minds. We have a job to do." He took a final glance at the carnage and managed a tight smile. "I'm sure the gates of hell will be busy today with this bunch."

Chapter 2

Ulysses Granger and two of his trusted men crept toward a collection of dwellings that had been set up on the grounds of the Rocky Mountain Laboratories. The residents had obviously felt safer behind the high-security barrier fence that encircled the area while they scavenged for anything of value in the sprawling complex. Old trailers and campers were scattered haphazardly near the main building, a monstrous black hulk in the moonlight. Ulysses's nose wrinkled at the noxious aroma from a sewage trench on the far side of the squatter camp, and he grimaced at his subordinates, his eyes hard.

They'd been watching the camp for two days and were confident that they wouldn't be disturbed on their foray into the main building if they did so at night. All of the activity they'd noted had been during the day, and the camp's security consisted of a pair of bored guards armed with shotguns at the gated entrance. Ulysses had scaled the twenty-foot-high wall an hour earlier, halfway to the barricaded rear exit, which the squatters left unguarded, no doubt because the wall and tall gate were impassible.

Which they would have been for most.

But Ulysses and his men weren't *most*. They'd come prepared with homemade grappling hooks and rappelling cord and were now making their way to the building, their boots soundless in the tall grass. All three gripped AR-15s and wore plate carriers and looked far more like commandos than the top echelon of a popular religious cult whose doomsday orientation had attracted a regional following among survivors seeking an explanation for the ongoing misery of their post-apocalypse existence.

Ulysses slowed as he approached the camp and signaled to his men, who spread out. They didn't expect to meet any resistance at the late hour, but were taking no chances. The squatters had followed the same routine both nights – sit around a central fire for the evening meal and then head off to bed as the flames burned out. Now, five hours after nightfall, nothing was stirring among the trailers, and with the guards' attention focused outward, the men drifted through the camp like phantoms.

The laboratory entrance had once been fortified with bulletproof glass and massive steel plates, but since being abandoned, the entry had been breached, and the main door yawned open like a dark mouth. Ulysses guided his men inside, stepping around piles of debris. He strode with obvious purpose, his lips moving as he counted his measured steps. Once through the lobby, he turned left after twenty-nine paces and led them into a long hallway, where he paused and cranked the charging handle of a small LED flashlight.

They continued down the corridor until they reached the end, where Ulysses pointed to a set of double steel doors. "That's it," he whispered, and his men nodded in unison. They approached the doors and could make out scarring from where the scavengers had hacked at it with axes and pry bars, to no avail – the doors remained shut, solid as the side of a mountain.

Ulysses handed the nearest man his rifle and shrugged off the straps of his backpack. He set it down at the side of the doorway and withdrew a plastic tub as his companions stood guard. He next removed several small ceramic vessels that looked like flowerpots cut in half, and painstakingly affixed them to the union of the doors, directly over where he knew from studying the blueprints that the locking bolts were located. He then opened a coffee can, filled the vessels to the brim with dark powder, and inserted a sparkler into each.

"Get back," he instructed in a low voice, and his men hastened away as he fished a disposable lighter from his pocket. He flicked it to life and lit the three sparklers in rapid succession, and then hurried away as they flared.

The homemade thermite ignited moments later, and all three men winced at the blinding white flame that hissed from the door. The adhesive melted in a nanosecond, and the pots fell to the floor, but the heat from the chemical reaction had done its job, and molten metal streamed in rivers down the steel plates.

The men were deep enough in the building that the sound of the clay cracking on the linoleum floor wouldn't be heard in the camp, but they still waited, frozen in the darkness, as their eyes adjusted, weapons pointed down the long corridor as they listened for any hint of movement from outside. After half a minute, Ulysses cranked the flashlight again and moved to the doors, which were still steaming, the metal pooled on the floor glowing orange. He pushed against the one on his right with his boot, and the door groaned and opened several inches. He tried again, and it moved another foot and then swung wider as its hinges creaked in protest.

"We're in," he said. "Stay here. If anyone comes to investigate, you know what to do."

The men followed him into another corridor and stood like bookends on either side, guns at the ready. Ulysses continued along the hallway until he reached a junction, where he turned left. He cranked his flashlight again and spotted three more metal doors, the farthest one to a stairwell that led down two stories into the class 4 bio-lab area that was his final destination.

He made his way down the steps and used the thermite to cut through another security door. Once in the basement, he hurried to a vault with hazmat suits hanging on racks on one end and a series of airlocks on the other. Ulysses eyed the suits with satisfaction – all was exactly as described by one of his acolytes as he'd lain on his deathbed.

Ulysses continued past the chamber to another security door emblazoned with a biohazard decal, and after melting its bolts, pushed past the steel slab and entered another vault – this one filled with miniature green metal canisters. Another crank of the flashlight, and he read the series of letters and numbers on each, whispering the syllables reverently until he found the one he had come for.

The government had officially ceased the development of chemical and biological weapons decades before, but, in spite of treaties committing to destroying stockpiles of the agents, had kept samples, ostensibly for research – the reasoning being that it was impossible to design effective antidotes and countermeasures without access to the agents in question.

The lab was home to a host of nightmare pathogens so virulent that they could only be safely studied in a handful of class 4 facilities like this one. But the designers of the lab had never factored in the long-term failure of the power grid, and after a year of continuous operation, the generators had run dry, and the lights – and safeguards – had gone dark.

As with many of the fail-safe systems designed to act as redundant backups, nobody had envisioned the world reverting to medieval conditions for a sustained period, which had left the lab a cemetery for the most horrific agents the world had ever known.

Ulysses wasn't interested in the Marberg or Ebola or smallpox secreted behind yet even more impenetrable doors – steel so thick it would require a plasma torch to cut through. His interest lay in the more mundane agent his dying worshipper had described: one of a number of highly toxic nerve agents that had been weaponized as an aerosol that killed within moments of release.

He removed the canister and hefted it, the metal surface cool to the touch. Heavy for its size, it contained enough neurotoxin to kill thousands nearly instantly, yet was small enough to fit in his backpack. Ulysses studied the top of the canister's innocuous threaded lip, to which a dispersal nozzle could be fitted – he'd already secured several from a hospital, where oxygen bottles of similar design had lain abandoned among the skeletons.

It was hard to believe such a small, seemingly innocent container could kill a stadium's occupants, but the dying man had been clear that it could do that and more. After so much senseless death, the man had wanted to unburden his mind in his final moments and had willingly violated his oath to take his secrets to his grave.

Which had provided Ulysses with both an idea and a purpose.

He adjusted the backpack and, when he was sure the canister was safely ensconced and protected from an inadvertent blow, slid the straps over his arms and retraced his steps to where his men were waiting, unaware of his reasons for wanting to enter the lab and unquestioning of his motive. Ulysses was a prophet, a messiah figure for those in his flock, and his actions were those of a divine messenger.

A smile crept across his face and a giddy light danced in his eyes. Anyone who'd seen it would have gazed into the soul of madness, but there was nobody around to witness the eerie transformation from his usual placid expression. He allowed himself the moment of triumph, muttering as he walked along the hall, his voice a guttural growl as he mouthed nonsense words in a language of his own invention. Speaking in tongues – a sign of divine inspiration, he'd told his followers, who had believed, just as they believed everything else he'd fed them, fueled by a fever that burned as bright as a solar flare. What he hadn't shared with them was that before the end times, he'd been diagnosed as having schizophrenia and had been on a steady diet of medication to control his hallucinations, a fact he'd never shared with anyone, not even his son Elijah, who was the closest person to him on the planet.

Ulysses laughed out loud and then stifled the sound with his hand. It wouldn't do to be talking to himself and laughing like a maniac in the dark. His men, loyal as they were, might begin to question his decisions, which he couldn't afford.

He had far too much work to do.

Important work nobody else had the courage or stamina for. Work that he'd been saved by God to see completed, just as that same God had sent the dying man to him, seeking absolution and understanding, and in so doing had delivered unto Ulysses the tool he required to fulfill his destiny.

He would be the rider of the pale horse prophesied in the Good Book, the angel of death who would be the instrument of the final reckoning.

Ulysses took several deep breaths and, when the giddiness he felt was under control, began walking toward the stairwell again with the determined steps of a prizefighter approaching the ring for a title bout.

Chapter 3

Amber Hot Springs, Colorado

Duke walked his horse to where Elliot and Sierra were standing by the thermal plant, Luis and John trailing behind him with a column of overloaded horses in tow. Sierra held Eve's tiny hand and smiled as they approached. Elliot shielded his eyes from the sun with his hand and nodded to Duke.

"Be careful not to leave a trail," Elliot said.

"Of course."

Elliot looked the pack animals over. "You have enough to make a decent start?"

"Should be plenty. With enough ammo and spare guns, I can own the world. And there's always gold to prime the pump, right?"

Both men smiled at Duke's confidence.

"You figure two days' ride?" Elliot asked.

"'Bout that. I may be back for a reload once we've set up camp." Duke shook his head. "Too bad we couldn't have stayed in the old place. It had a lot going for it."

They'd discussed staying put in Duke's last trading post, but now that Shangri-La had moved another hundred miles north, it was too far from that location to make sense as a trading hub for the enclave. They'd pored over maps to identify promising sites and had narrowed it down to several highway rest stops on the main road between Pueblo and Colorado Springs, which was now an enclave run by neo-Nazi fundamentalists. Duke had selected the most desirable weapons and barter items he could get his hands on to kick-start the business, and he and Luis as partners had agreed to set up another trading post at a more practical distance from the new Shangri-La.

Luis frowned, and his facial tattoos creased with the expression. "Hope the transmitter makes it. It looked kind of iffy."

Duke patted his shoulder. "Elliot's wirehead gave it the once-over. Good as new." He walked to Sierra and hugged her. "Tell Lucas to come by whenever he gets back from his little vacation."

She smiled. "I will."

Duke knelt in front of Eve. "You take care of yourself, princess. Keep that brother of yours out of trouble."

She held his gaze with unblinking eyes so blue they seemed to glow in the sunlight. "I'll do the best I can. He doesn't always listen."

"Where is he?"

"Off with some kids."

"Do your best, and help your mother."

Eve nodded solemnly. "I will."

He straightened and shook hands with Elliot. "We'll check in once we're settled. Good luck with all this."

"Thanks. We have our hands full, but we'll manage. No real choice before winter hits, is there?"

"You should think about places that don't get buried in snow half the year."

Elliot smiled. "I'll make a note of it. But this isn't so bad. Plenty of fishable lakes within a day's ride. There's river water just down the hill and hot springs for power generation. We could have done worse."

"No question. Talk to you in a few days."

"Good luck."

Duke saddled up, and Luis and John followed suit. "Thanks."

Elliot watched the riders disappear down the trail and looked around the hot springs, where homes were being built and life was going on.

They'd managed to survive in spite of the best efforts of some of the most dangerous groups in the country, and had thwarted the virus with their vaccine against all odds. Deep snow and the challenges of rebuilding their community in a new place might have seemed daunting to many, but to the residents of Shangri-La they were par for the course. Their vision of a peaceful outpost of civilization, where everyone worked for the greater good and respected the rights of others, was a powerful one, and they'd proven they were willing to do whatever it took to protect and nurture it.

Elliot sighed and turned to Sierra. "How's your place coming?"

"It's coming. We've had a lot of help, for which we've got you to thank."

"Lucas made a hell of a sacrifice taking the vaccine west. It was the least we could do to repay that."

She looked away. "I hope he comes home soon. I need him here."

"That makes two of us. He will. He's one of the toughest and most resourceful men I've ever laid eyes on."

"I hope that's enough."

"Me too."

Chapter 4

Newport, Oregon

Lucas slowed Tango with a squeeze of the reins, and the big horse came to a stop. Jeb, Mary, and Rosemary did the same, and Ruby called out from the back of the procession.

"Are we there? Is that Newport?"

Jeb nodded. "Yep. You can smell the cooking fires. Just over that rise."

Lucas glanced back over his shoulder at them and adjusted his hat to better shade his eyes from the morning sun. "I'll take a look. Stay here."

He goaded Tango forward, and the stallion trotted up the incline until Lucas had a good view of the town below. Plumes of smoke rose from the chimneys of many of the small homes, and he could pick out people making their way along the streets with bundles in hand. Lucas was about to turn to tell the others it was safe to follow when the distinctive snick of a lever-action rifle being cocked greeted him from behind a rock outcropping, and a voice called out.

"Got no room for strangers. Keep movin'."

Lucas didn't budge. "We're here with some of your folks. And to pick up a mule."

"What do you mean, our folks?"

Lucas twisted and called to the others. "Jeb? Mary? Come on up here."

They urged their horses forward, and as they pulled even with Lucas, two men stepped from behind the rocks, rifles in hand. "Jeb? That you?"

Jeb nodded. "It is."

"Thought you was gone for good."

"We rescued my family, and now we want to see if there's anything to come back to."

"What happened with the Chinese?"

"We took it to 'em. There's a bunch still in Astoria, but we blew up their boat."

"You blew it up?"

Jeb looked to Lucas. "Well, Lucas here did."

"I had help," Lucas said.

"We've been on the trail for two days. Is there a problem with us coming into town?" Mary asked.

"Oh, um, of course not," the gunman said. "Things is different since you took off, is all. Mayor and the council are out. Hayden's still sheriff, but other than that, we're still trying to figure out how to set things up." He spit to the side. "You're the first we've seen since we settled here. Bill ever make it up your way?"

Lucas nodded. "He did. A good man."

"That he is. Well, come on, then. Don't let me stop you. Everyone's gonna have a million questions."

Lucas guided Tango down the trail to where the remains of Newport sat by the water's edge, Yaquina Bay nearly flat as huge ocean waves crashed against the protecting breakwater. Rust from the salt air bled down the steel bridge that spanned the bay. Pilings jutted from the surface where the commercial harbor had been, the docks and boats destroyed by winter storms and the effects of time. The tops of industrial fishing boat masts poked from the water as reminders of the fleet that had called the bay home only a few short years before, near where a handful of sailboats bobbed by the shore, moored to the pilings, with a half dozen skiffs beached nearby.

"Looks pretty rough," Ruby commented.

"At least it isn't radioactive," Rosemary said in a quiet voice.

A familiar figure waved at them from one of the little houses near the water. They slowed as they approached, and Lucas tipped his hat to Hayden.

"Never thought we'd see you again," Hayden said. "No hard feelings about that other stuff. I was out of line."

"Likewise," Jeb agreed. "Thought we'd check out what you have going here."

Hayden motioned to the other dwellings. "There're a lot of habitable places if a guy's handy. The weather's no worse than Astoria, and the fishing's about the same. All in all, it's a pretty decent new home. People are settling in, although it's too soon to tell how many will stay."

"Who's calling the shots now?" Lucas asked.

"Hubert got voted out. They made me the acting mayor until someone actually wants the job. Everyone else on the council got the boot, and there weren't a lot interested once Bill took off with his crew."

"Most stay with the rest of you?"

Hayden nodded. "Sure. Where else would they go? We figure if we stick together, we can make something decent here. We're in the middle of nowhere, with a water source and plenty of fish. A lot of folks have it way worse."

Jeb nodded. "True."

"You thinking about sticking around, Jeb? There're plenty of empty houses. We'd be happy to have you. All that stuff with the council…that's over. Got no problem with you personally."

"Good to hear. Yeah, we're gonna try it out, see how things work," Jeb said.

"Any idea where Ruby's mule is?" Lucas asked.

Hayden frowned. "Probably over at the stable." He indicated one of the warehouses several blocks from the water. "We keep most of the animals there." Hayden studied Lucas and Ruby for a moment. "You're welcome to stay, too."

"Thanks, but we have a home of our own," Ruby said.

Hayden eyed Lucas. "What happened with the Chinese?"

"After we've gotten some rest, we'll tell everyone what happened. Right now our horses need water and feed," Lucas said. "We're headed back tomorrow."

"Fair enough. We use the big hospital as kind of our headquarters. Can't miss it. I can let everyone know you want to talk to them later. Maybe just before sundown?"

"That'll work."

They rode along the waterfront street and turned toward the stable. Many of the homes had been gutted by fire or burned to the foundations, but there were still many that appeared viable. Lucas had warmed to Jeb and his family on the ride south from Astoria and hoped that the new spot would work out better than Astoria had.

Mary pointed at a two-story Victorian house. "Oooh. I could see us living there. Wonder if anyone's claimed it?"

Jeb looked the house over. "Only one way to find out."

They split off toward the home, and Rosemary lingered with Lucas and Ruby. She'd been asking about Shangri-La the entire trip, and it had been clear to both of them that the young woman had little interest in continuing her life with her strict parents and a dating pool of unsuitable boys.

"I don't know how I'm going to tell them I don't want to stay," she said.

"Sometimes just coming out and saying it is the best way," Ruby advised.

"It's not as easy as you think. My mom, maybe. But there's no talking to him."

"Seems a little stubborn," Lucas conceded. "But he's got a good heart."

"You think they'll accept me if I go with you? In Shangri-La?"

Ruby held her gaze. "All we can do is vouch for you, Rosemary. But I don't see why not. You're smart and able-bodied, which would be positives for the community."

"Thing is, no place is heaven, in spite of the name," Lucas warned. "Winters are brutal, and we have a lot of enemies. No guarantee you'd be safe there."

"Where is there a guarantee?" Rosemary asked. "Seems like that's just how it is now."

"True."

Mary called from the front porch of the house. "It's empty! Come see, Rosemary!"

She sighed and looked to Lucas. "I hate this. I'd already decided to leave before the Chinese took over. I feel like I can't breathe anymore. I know they mean well, but…"

"Rosemary!" Mary called again.

She slid from the saddle and walked her horse to the house with slumped shoulders. Ruby shook her head. "That's going to be a tough one."

Lucas nodded. "For all of them." He reined Tango to the left. "Come on. Let's see if we can find Jax and get the horses fed."

"I wouldn't mind eating," Ruby said.

"First things first."

The pair of men in charge of the stable were happy to help them find Jax, who was in a makeshift stall created out of pallets. His baleful gaze brightened when he spotted Ruby. She hurried to him and scratched his chin, and he rubbed his head against her like a pet dog seeking adulation.

Lucas paid the men with a few bullets and, after asking them if anyone had set up a restaurant, led the way back to the water, where a family who had taken over a café was frying fish on a grill.

They sat at one of the tables, and a boy of about twelve brought them two heaping platters of fresh cod, which they gobbled down appreciatively while cooling their throats with well water. "Caught this morning," the boy said. "It was pretty rough out on the sailboat, but we didn't have to go too far."

After their meal, Ruby and Lucas found a deserted house near the shore with serviceable beds and settled down to rest. Both were tired from the trek from Astoria and the constant tension of riding the trail in potentially hostile territory, and soon they were both asleep after having pushed a sofa across the second-floor landing stairs to prevent any intruders from catching them by surprise.

The sun was sinking into the Pacific when Lucas started awake, his M4 in hand out of habit. He listened for a moment and, hearing nothing, rose and went to Ruby's room to wake her.

They made their way to the hospital, guided by one of the newcomers whom they'd asked for directions, and when they arrived, Lucas found himself facing almost the entire population of Astoria, eager to hear his story.

Lucas gave a report in clipped sentences and finished by answering predictable questions from the townspeople – the most frequent one being whether he thought they were in danger in Newport.

"I don't know," Lucas admitted. "Probably not from the Chinese still in Astoria – they've got their hands full with the tent city, not to mention Bill and the rest out for blood. From the river radiation? Maybe. I'm no expert, but it can't be good to have all that pouring into the ocean. Then again, it's a fair ways north, and the Pacific's a big place, so could be it'll dilute it." Lucas paused. "But I have to believe the Chinese aren't just going to give up. There'll be more. Whether you'll be safe here depends on whether they see any point in taking over Newport. That I can't answer."

After a half hour of speculation, Lucas and Ruby accepted an offer for dinner extended by Jeb and Mary, and passed an enjoyable hour sharing a simple meal of fish before excusing themselves and heading back to their temporary home.

The following morning, they were up early and at the stable to claim their steeds and Jax, whose typical lack of enthusiasm was on display when one of the stable hands led him out into the morning sun. They were mounting up when Rosemary came at a run, a backpack strapped to her shoulders and a Kalashnikov in hand.

"Wait up. I'm coming with you!" she cried, out of breath.

Ruby smiled. "You told them? How'd it go?"

"They weren't very happy," she said. "Especially my dad. But my mom eventually came around. She doesn't want to see me leave, but at least she understands." Rosemary paused. "I think because I'll be traveling with you it made it a little easier than if I'd just snuck off."

"How'd you leave it?" Ruby asked.

"I told them I love them, but I need to find my future, and it isn't in Newport. My dad didn't even say goodbye, but my mom did after we both cried for a while. She said I broke my father's heart. But I can't let them guilt me into staying and being miserable."

"It's a long ride," Lucas said. "And no telling how dangerous. Sure you're up for it?"

She looked around the town and then into the stable, where her horse and kit were waiting. When she faced Lucas again, her eyes were unflinching and her jaw set.

"Try stopping me."

Chapter 5

Houston, Texas

The Crewcut bar was packed with sweating humanity as a five-piece band pounded out a passable acoustic version of a Southern rock song that served as one of the Crew's anthems. It was a popular nightspot for members of the gang, with the booze full strength and reasonably priced, and the working girls relatively healthy by post-apocalyptic Houston standards.

Larson Rawls, a lieutenant in the Crew in charge of a squad of almost a hundred men, threw back the last of his home-brewed bourbon and glared at a towering figure with bleached white dreadlocks and elaborate facial tattoos who was standing at the far end of the bar, laughing with a group of rowdy men. Rawls stiffened at the sight, and his companion, a swarthy streetfighter with a network of scars covering his nose and cheeks, signaled to the bartender and pointed to their glasses.

"Two more," he said.

The bartender approached with a bottle of local rotgut and topped them off. Rawls glowered at the dreadlocked man down the bar and reached for his drink.

"That prick makes my skin crawl, Axel. I don't see why Snake lets him get away with the shit he does," he snarled.

"Maybe we should head over to Cassidy's and see if there's any

24

new talent. I heard they was getting in some teenagers from Mexico this week," Axel said.

"Hell, by the time they make it here, they been ridden hard and put away wet more times than new meat in the prison shower," Rawls said.

"As long as they look the part, who cares?" Axel asked, and then held his glass aloft.

Rawls drained his and grimaced. "Damn if that don't burn on the way down."

Axel glanced at him uneasily. "Come on. Let's hit the trail and see what's shaking."

More laughter cut through the music, and Rawls's jaw clenched. "Bastard's laughing at us. Can't let that stand."

"Naw, he's just mouthing off to his boys. You know they're all talk."

But Rawls was already in motion before Axel's last words were out of his mouth, pushing through the crush of unwashed bodies like a pit bull after a bait dog. Axel hurried to catch up and was reaching for Rawls's arm to stop him when Rawls, sensing him, twisted and growled over his shoulder, "Don't get in the middle of this, Axel."

"I'm just saying–"

"I heard you the first time."

Rawls stopped in front of the dreadlocked man, his fists clenched. The man looked up from his friends and leveled a prison-yard stare at Rawls.

"What up, Rawls?" the man asked, his voice sandpaper on hardwood.

"Think you're pretty funny with today's supplies, don't you, Crank?" Rawls said. Crank was another Crew lieutenant whose men regularly seemed to enjoy better provisioning than Rawls's group.

"What're you smoking? We got what was coming to us. Chill out. We're here to relax."

"I could hear you across the bar."

Crank eyed Rawls and shook his head dismissively. "Stay away from the hard stuff. It ain't doin' you no favors–"

Rawls's punch pistoned into Crank's gut without warning, the blow lightning fast and with all Rawls's weight behind it. Crank's eyes widened and his mouth formed an O, and then one of his companions leapt forward, fists swinging. Rawls ducked a haymaker and booted the man in the groin, sending him sprawling. Crank gulped air and leapt at Rawls, and then the bar was engulfed in fighting as the Rawls and Crank factions brawled, following their bosses' examples. Bottles shattered as the fighting spread like oil spilled on the surface of a lake, and soon even neutral drinkers found themselves trading blows as the melee fed on itself.

By the time the bouncers restored order with several well-timed gunshots over the crowd's heads, much of the furniture had been shattered and at least half of the patrons were bleeding or unconscious. The only thing that had stopped the fight from escalating to full-scale slaughter was the bar's no-weapons policy, but even so, several dozen hardened fighters had been wounded badly enough to require a trip to the Crew's medical facility.

Snake looked up at the rapping on his door and frowned at the naked young woman lying next to him in bed.

"What?" he bellowed.

A muffled voice called through the door. "Barton wants to see you."

Snake swore under his breath. Barton was Lassiter's subordinate, whom the Illuminati boss had left to offer Snake guidance in his absence. In reality, Barton ordered Snake around like a servant, although he took care to do so in carefully guarded language. But the effect was the same – Snake had gone from being the most powerful warlord in the southwest to an errand boy for Barton's masters.

"Tell him I'm busy," Snake growled.

"I told him. He's waiting for you downstairs in the lounge."

"Damn. Fine. I'll be down in a few minutes."

Snake rose and eyed the woman, whose caramel skin and jet-black hair gleamed in the candlelight. "Wait for me to come back, but don't touch anything, understand?"

She nodded and bared a row of perfect white teeth. "Of course, Snake. Hurry back. We ain't done."

"Damn right," he said, and padded over to a table where a glass pipe and a baggie of Crew meth sat beside a bottle of tequila. Snake removed his leather pants from the back of the chair and slid them on, and then sat and pulled on his boots. He reached for the bottle and took a swallow of the harsh liquid. He grimaced and exhaled noisily.

"You can have some of this if you want. But no dope."

She pouted. "It makes me horny."

"You heard me. Maybe when I get back, I'll give you a taste." He dipped a straw into the baggie of powder and carefully scooped a pinch into the pipe bowl, and then leaned forward and held the pipe over one of the candles. In a few moments the powder liquefied, and he pulled it away from the flame and inhaled as the liquid began to smoke. Snake drew the fumes deep into his lungs and nodded rhythmically as he counted slowly to four and then exhaled a stream of smoke as his blood pressure spiked and the drug exploded through his system.

He sat back and waited for the initial rush to run its course and settle into the constant buzz he craved, and threw a glance at the girl, who was looking at him with hungry eyes. He rose and pocketed the baggie and then went for his shirt, which he'd dropped on the floor earlier as they'd made their way to the bed. "Just to keep you honest, babe," he said, ignoring her dark look.

Four heavily armed guards stood outside his suite, and he nodded to them as he brushed past, his synapses singing from the drug and his jaw clenching as he ground his teeth unconsciously. One of his underlings approached down the hall and stopped just short of him.

"Had a big brawl at the Crewcut. Lot of our guys hurt," the man reported.

Snake shrugged. "What was it about?"

"Nobody's sure, but I'm hearing Crank and Rawls got into it, and it spiraled from there."

"What the hell were they thinking? They know better," Snake snapped.

"That's just what I heard. I dunno for sure." He hesitated. "But Rawls has been bitching about not getting his fair share lately."

"Because Rawls isn't producing like Crank is." Snake sighed. "Drag their asses in here. We can't have public fights between my people."

Snake continued to the ground-floor lounge, his mind racing from the drug and the revelation that his men were at each other's throats. He couldn't afford to lose two of his top enforcers, but if he didn't do something, he'd lose even more face with his men – and he knew that since failing to provide a vaccine, his leadership was in doubt, even if nobody had been stupid enough to tell him so to his face.

It didn't help that he was having to kowtow to Barton. Snake blamed much of his misfortune on the man's interference in his affairs, even if he knew that wasn't the real cause of the unrest. The Crew under Magnus had been run by a brutal leader whom nobody dared question, and no matter how draconian Snake's proclamations, he would never measure up to that man in many of the Crew's minds. They might not say so out loud, but he sensed it with every interaction, which encouraged him to be even more unpredictable and brutal than normal. Snake had watched Magnus operate, and he understood the prison hierarchy where the most vicious sociopaths wielded the most power, so that was what he'd set out to become – but he'd still fallen short of Magnus's magnetic leadership ability and utter ruthlessness, and ever since the disaster in Louisiana, Snake had felt the need to look over his shoulder even more than usual.

He understood how leadership challenges were resolved in the prison yard. And the Crew was no different.

Barton was seated on a sofa by a granite bar, and he rose when Snake entered. Snake crossed the room in a few strides and plopped down in one of the easy chairs. Barton sat again and offered a wan smile.

"I just got word from my group about your request," Barton began. "Unfortunately there have been more setbacks on finding the parts to bring the refinery online. But we're working on it."

"That's why you pulled me out of bed?" Snake exclaimed.

"It's already eight. I figured you would be up, directing your troops," Barton answered.

Snake's eyes narrowed as he tried to figure out whether Barton was mocking him, but the man's face was as unreadable as a statue's. Snake decided to ignore the comment and sat forward. "Well, I'm here now. And I want to know what 'working on it' means. You've been promising to get us up and running for months, and we have nothing to show for it. That's causing problems for me, both internally and with other gangs. This is dog eat dog, and if they sense weakness, I'll be fighting on multiple fronts. If I have fuel, problem solved."

Barton nodded. "Yes, we've had this discussion before, and I've relayed your concerns to Lassiter and his people. But there are limits to what we can do. This is highly specialized equipment, and we can't just snap our fingers and find the engineering talent to troubleshoot it and bring it up to speed. It's an enormous undertaking, even for us."

Snake bit back the angry response that his fevered brain wanted to hurl at the pompous ass, and settled for another glare. "You've been saying that for a long time. Meanwhile, I don't have any advantage that any of the rival warlords can see, so it's just a matter of time until they make a move to test for weakness. We lost too many when Magnus fell, and we haven't been able to rebuild to full strength. So we need an edge. Which you promised…and haven't delivered."

Barton's expression didn't change. "Would you like me to tell Lassiter that you're questioning your arrangement?"

The threat was obvious, and Snake sat back and did his best to relax. "I'm not questioning anything but why *we*'ve done everything we committed to, and you haven't."

"Did I miss where you provided us with a working vaccine?"

Snake swallowed hard. "That was never guaranteed, and you know it."

"Yes, well, neither was our ability to wave a magic wand and get the refinery back into production. Not to mention that it also involves restoring the wells to life and figuring out a way to transport the raw crude from the fields to the refinery. There are a lot of moving parts." He paused and then cleared his throat. "Lassiter anticipated your frustration and has authorized another shipment of gold so you can acquire whatever you need. Mercenaries, if you can't convince qualified candidates to join your group, for example. We don't want you feeling as though we aren't supporting you. But there are practical limits."

Snake smiled at the mention of gold. "That'll come in handy, but I don't like using hired guns. They've got no loyalty, and they'll turn on you when you most need them."

"I'll leave you to figure it out. My message is that there's gold on the way, and they're doing everything they can to provide a solution to your power problem." Barton stood and graced Snake with a withering look. "Sorry I disrupted your morning routine. You said you wanted to know as soon as I had a response."

As Snake watched him walk out the door, the drug in his veins urged him to leap into action and gut the bastard with his shiv like a carp. He looked down at where his hands were gripping the arms of his chair, his fingers white, and let out a long breath.

Barton would get his. At a time and place of Snake's choosing. The smug prick obviously believed he had nothing to fear from his captive lapdog, but he'd called that one very wrong. Nobody talked to Snake like that. He ran the biggest gang in what remained of the U.S., and could have a man killed for looking at him wrong.

Which Barton would soon find out.

Once Snake had his gold, of course.

He headed back to his room, his head throbbing from tension. "Don't bother me with anything for a few hours," he ordered his guards, and then pushed through the door.

The woman was sitting up in bed, still naked. Tattoos of barbed wire encircled both arms, and an angel's wings were elaborately inked across her back. She swung her long legs off the bed and stood with an expectant look.

"That was quick."

Snake approached her with a smile and backhanded her as hard as he could. Her head snapped to the side and she cried out, and a trickle of blood oozed from the corner of her mouth.

"I've heard about enough out of you," he snarled.

Tears welled in her eyes and she stepped back. "I…I'm sorry, Snake. I didn't mean anything by it."

The rage that clouded his vision slowly eased, and he retrieved the meth baggie from his pocket and tossed it on the table.

"Do a bump and then get your ass busy. I don't have all day."

Chapter 6

Astoria, Oregon

Clouds blew across the moon, creating spectral shadows on the tent city outside the town walls. The night was quiet, the squatter camp still with four more hours to go before sunrise.

Inside the town walls, the Chinese contingent was gathering. They moved quietly, their boots wrapped in cloth to avoid any sound. Captain Liu, the surviving ranking officer in Astoria, had spent the last few days attempting to contact anyone in his chain of command, without success. When the ship had gone down, it had taken with it the long-range equipment, and his handheld radios had proved inadequate to reach his superiors in Seattle. He'd hoped to boost the transmission range with a variety of improvised antennas, but none had been successful, leaving him and the troops stranded in a town that was becoming increasingly radioactive – the water was now undrinkable due to contamination, and food stores were dwindling to emergency levels.

Liu had decided the correct strategy was to retreat to somewhere less toxic and live to fight another day. The objective of taking and holding the main water gateway to Portland had been viable before the meltdown of the reactor, but was now a slow death sentence with no point. As far as he understood, nobody would be able to use the river for the rest of eternity, so Portland and, with it, Astoria, had become liabilities rather than assets, and he needed to cut his losses before more of his men succumbed.

It rankled him to have to slink away in the darkness, but he was pragmatic; honor was for the living to debate, and he intended to remain among their number if possible. He didn't have a final destination in mind, but he would figure it out once the force was clear of Astoria – and of the fighters who'd joined the ranks of the scum outside the walls, all of them emboldened now that the ship had been destroyed and thus far more dangerous than they otherwise would have been. There appeared to be thousands of squatters, whereas he had only a hundred and seventy men. Although he despised the undisciplined American rabble that lived on the periphery of the town like vermin, he wouldn't underestimate the effect of thousands against a few hundred.

So he'd decided to make a run for it while the encampment slept rather than fight his way out, as his ego would have had him do.

His men had been given their orders and had complied, taking only what they could carry and binding their boots to muffle their footfalls. Beyond that he'd forbidden any speech, even whispered; the troops would communicate using hand signals until they were clear of the area.

Lieutenant Feng, Liu's immediate subordinate, approached in the gloom and offered a stiff salute. Liu nodded and returned the gesture, and Feng leaned into him and spoke in a soft murmur.

"The men are ready."

Captain Liu checked his watch: 2:40 a.m. If everything went as planned, they could get to the bridge south of the town in less than an hour and cross to safety, blowing it up behind them so none of the tent parasites could follow. He knew that the arms cache the advance group had told them about was on the far side of the bridge, so destroying it would cut the rabble off from arms and ammunition, increasing their vulnerability whenever more of his countrymen made their way across the ocean.

"Very well. You're to lead with Tiger Platoon. Nobody is to fire unless fired upon. All we have is the element of surprise. If we lose that, it won't go well for us."

Feng nodded. "I made sure your orders were clear. Everyone understands."

"I'll follow with Jade Platoon and the stragglers from Dragon Platoon." Liu had made the difficult decision to leave the wounded behind. There was no choice – they couldn't sneak through the tent encampment carrying litters. His compromise had been to leave those still conscious with pistols with which to defend themselves…or end their lives. It ran against everything he believed in to do so, but he could see no other way, and he'd dispatched Feng with a dozen handguns earlier that night.

The tent city had pulled back from the area around the main gate. Even the idiot Americans had apparently realized that whenever the Chinese ultimately made their play, to be squatted there would mean instant death. Liu walked with Feng to the gate and peered through a gap to confirm that all was still, and then turned and signaled to the lieutenant to move the barrier and lead his platoon to freedom.

Art stirred at the feel of fingers prodding him awake and sat up, blinking away sleep. Ray's face was a couple of feet away, his expression animated.

"Bill says they're moving the gate, General. This looks like it's it."

The general rose and adjusted the sling that supported his wounded arm. "Is everyone in position?"

"Yes. You were right they'd try it at night."

Art had told Bill's fighters, as well as the several hundred squatters who'd signed up to act as a militia, to sleep during the day in shifts and to remain awake and ready at night in anticipation of the Chinese launching an offensive. He'd sent relays to the mountain armory and secured enough rifles, grenades, and ammo to equip an army, and the men were eager to put the gear to use after the victory against the ship earlier in the week.

Now it looked as though the preparation would pay off.

"Let's get over there. Don't want our boys tipping our hand before we know what the Chinese are up to."

Ray and Art crept along the tree line to where Bill was waiting with his fighters and a score of squatters, all armed to the teeth. Bill glanced up at him and pointed to the dark mass of troops moving out of the town.

"Looks like they're making a run for it. You nailed it," Bill said.

"It's the only real option they have. Henry's group in position?"

"Yep."

Henry, an ex-marine who'd been forced onto the trail after the collapse, had organized the squatters who wanted to fight into a ragtag group and had instilled a semblance of discipline in them with the help of several other ex-military denizens of the encampment. They were massed on the far side of the entry, equipped with the twin of the radio at Bill's side, both scrounged from the dead Chinese they'd encountered along the river the day before.

"Stick to the plan," Art said. "Wait until they're all through the gate and far enough so they can't make it back, and then send twenty men behind them and cut them off. But for God's sake, no shooting until I give the word or we'll create a crossfire where we'll be mowing each other down."

"Got it," Bill said, and relayed the order to Henry in a tense whisper.

They watched as the Chinese moved stealthily along the road from town. When they were certain there were no more coming, Bill led a group of his best fighters around the edges of the tent city and to the gate, where they took up position behind the barrier in anticipation of at least some of the Chinese turning tail and trying to make it back to cover – where they'd be walking directly into Bill's guns.

Ray edged closer to Art and leaned into him. "How much longer?"

"Maybe two minutes. Once they're past the trees, it'll be a turkey shoot. There's no place to hide."

Art was interrupted when the night filled with gunfire as Henry's men opened fire. Art cursed and yelled to his men, "Make your shots count. Don't waste ammo!"

The first salvos cut down many of the Chinese, and when they returned fire, the volleys were ragged. As Art had hoped, the Chinese had been caught in a deadly pincer movement with cover limited to a few trees and the bodies of their dead. Shots echoed through the trees as Henry's men pressed their advantage, and Art swore at the sound of rifles on continuous fire targeting the column. He'd warned the men against using full auto for accuracy reasons as well as conservation of ammunition, but apparently some of the squatters had decided to 'spray and pray' versus picking their targets carefully. Undisciplined fire could result in friendly casualties from stray rounds, but it was too late now, so all he could do was hope that the culprits exhausted their magazines quickly and managed to hit at least some of the enemy force.

"They're on the run!" Ray shouted above the gunfire.

The Chinese had split in disorganized panic, and some were sprinting back toward town while the rest made for the bridge in the distance.

Bill's group held their fire until the soldiers were almost on top of them, and then cut them apart with disciplined bursts. Not a single Chinese fighter made it to the gate, and within moments the retreat was finished, leaving Bill to decide whether to give chase or stay in position.

He eyed the orange muzzle blossoms erupting from the trees and shouted to his gunmen, "Larry, Tom, Wally – stay here and cover the gate. The rest of you, follow me."

They took off at a run, firing from the hip as they made their way toward the enemy. Ray and two dozen of Art's shooters covered them as they neared, and then Bill and Ray's men converged and closed on the Chinese, who were now down to less than thirty fighters. Rounds snapped around Ray's head, and he ducked and zigzagged along the trees. When he was close enough, he freed a grenade from his tactical vest, pulled the pin, and hurled it with all his might at a clump of soldiers.

A hail of rounds slammed into the tree trunks where he'd been only moments before, and then the grenade detonated with devastating results, blowing five men to pieces and sending their limbs flying through the air like night birds. Ray dropped to his knee and picked off two more soldiers with three-round bursts, and then his men were running past him, howling like banshees as they fired into the remaining troops.

Three minutes later, the skirmish was over and Ray was standing by Art's side, studying the carnage in the moonlight. Bill joined them, and his radio crackled to life with a report from Henry.

"Henry lost six men, with two wounded," Bill said. "I've got a couple of wounded myself. How about you?"

Art frowned. "We got off light. Three dead, one winged, but he'll make it."

Bill nodded. "Doesn't look like there are any survivors, does it?"

Art's expression hardened. "Don't forget how they treated us. No quarter."

Bill and Ray exchanged a glance, and Bill grunted. "We didn't cross the ocean to take over their homes. I'll relay your order."

"Tend to our wounded and gather their weapons," Art said. "There must be over a hundred of them. Between their rifles and their ammo and any other ordnance they're carrying, we just hit another jackpot."

Ray exhaled loudly and wiped perspiration from his brow. "It all happened so fast…"

Art nodded again. "That's how it goes in a big firefight." He gazed at the dead Chinese and shook his head. "But don't get cocky. We were lucky this time. They don't all go this way."

"Let's hope our luck holds," Bill said.

"Hope's for children and fools," Art said. "Set up a triage area, and let's see how bad our guys are hurt." He eyed Ray. "You okay?"

"Sure. Why?"

He inclined his head at Ray's leg. "You're bleeding."

Chapter 7

Trading Post, Colorado

Duke was finishing up the second sandbag bunker at the entry to the truck stop that he was converting into a trading post when John called out from the roof of the main building.

"Dust cloud on the highway. From up north."

Duke scooped up his M16 and patted the spare magazines in his plate holder. "Be up in a second. You make anything out?"

"Just the dust. Looks about a mile and a half off."

Duke made his way to the building and climbed the stairs to the roof, where they'd set up another sandbagged defense position when they'd first arrived. Luis was off hunting for dinner, leaving Duke and John to hold down the fort – no problem if nobody showed, but potentially a big one if a group of raiders was working the area.

John was staring through his binoculars when Duke arrived and plopped down beside him. A tarp they'd strung from four poles for shade fluttered in the light breeze, but other than that, the area was silent.

"What have we got?"

John handed him the spyglasses. "Take a look."

Duke raised the binoculars to his eyes and scanned the highway. The asphalt was beige from years of sand and dust blowing across it and collecting in drifts, and the terrain was flat on either side for a quarter mile. The Rockies rose into the sky to the west, and Fountain Creek meandered along the railroad tracks to the east, where the taupe of the Great Plains stretched to the horizon, leaving the trading post with unobstructed visibility for miles.

He focused on the dust cloud and shifted to the highway below it. Three riders were approaching at a gallop, and he strained to make them out. After a moment, he lowered the glasses and turned to John. "Am I seeing things?"

"If you are, so am I."

"What are three women doing out in the middle of nowhere?"

"Beats me. But they're running from something – those horses look like they're ready to drop."

Duke took another look and confirmed John's impression. "Got that–"

He stopped midsentence as four more riders came into view: men, also riding hard, their clothes ratty and coated with dust, two of them with rifles in their hands, all with the unkempt long hair and beards of scavengers.

"They've got company chasing them. Doesn't look good."

"Raiders?"

"Could be. More like highway lowlifes. Bet they don't have ten good teeth between them."

"How do you want to play it?"

The smart move was not to get involved. The paint on the sign advertising the trading post was barely dry, and they didn't need to start off by making enemies of the locals, even if these looked like murderous thugs.

Duke raised the glasses again. "They'll be within range in another minute or two."

"So…take them down?"

"We don't, those women are history."

Both Duke and John knew how the story would play out if they didn't intervene. The women would be raped for days and then sold to the highest bidder, assuming the scavengers didn't just slit their throats and move on to their next victims.

Duke handed him back the glasses, and John took another look. "Nice looking, aren't they?"

"Wait until they're a couple of hundred yards off. I'll give the word."

"We both gonna shoot from here?"

"No point in splitting up. Only four of them, and line of sight's better from here than the gate."

Duke blew dust off his M16 scope and removed a spare magazine from his vest. He placed it by his side and adjusted his aim through one of the gaps between the sandbags. John did the same, and they waited as the riders neared, bouncing in their sights.

"Gonna be hard to hit anything at the rate they're moving," John said.

"No doubt. If single shots don't do the trick, switch to bursts, and I'll keep plinking."

"We don't get all of them, you know they'll be back after dark."

"Yep. Wait until they're a hundred yards off. That'll narrow the odds some. Hold your fire until I give the word."

The scavengers wouldn't stand a chance of hitting Duke and John from horseback, much less behind the sandbags, so Duke wasn't worried about a firefight. John had been right that the greater threat was any survivors returning at night to settle the score.

The women came into view, and Duke estimated the men were no more than a quarter mile behind them and closing. He waited until the women had ridden past the gate and then murmured to John, "Ten…nine…"

When Duke's count reached one, both their rifles barked, and the lead rider jerked back in the saddle before dropping his gun and clutching the spreading blossom of red on his chest. Duke fired again, and his shot missed the second rider, who was still galloping as though he hadn't registered that his companion had been hit. That changed when the lead rider tumbled from the saddle and smacked onto the road, and the three remaining horsemen reined in their steeds and paused.

John's rifle stuttered another three-round burst, and the second rider spasmed like a marionette from two of the three rounds. Duke positioned his reticule over the chest of one of the others and squeezed the trigger with gentle, even pressure, and was rewarded by the man bucking in the saddle. He fired again but missed, and the rider was able to turn his horse and tear back in the direction he'd come.

Duke sighted on the last rider and fired at him with methodical precision, even as the man spurred his horse into motion. The shots missed and Duke swore, but then John's weapon chattered four bursts and the rider toppled from his horse. His foot snagged in the stirrup, and the stallion took off in fright, dragging him through the dust and leaving a bloody trail in its wake.

Duke switched to three-round burst mode and emptied his magazine at the surviving rider. None of his shots found home, and he ground his teeth as he ejected the spent mag and slammed a full one into place. He continued firing until the rider had disappeared in the dust, and was still squeezing the trigger when John nudged him.

"It's over, Duke. We got 'em."

"The one that rode away could bring more."

"Not likely. There was blood on his jacket from the exit wound. He'll probably bleed out before long."

"Probably isn't good enough."

John glanced past Duke and pointed. "Looks like the women are coming back."

They climbed down from the roof and waited as the women approached the gate. Duke waved from the building entry. The women turned into the truck stop and rode to a halt in the shade of the overhang.

"Howdy, ladies," John said, tipping his hat.

Duke studied them. All three were in their twenties, thin but not emaciated, armed with shotguns and pistols – a poor choice on the trail against a rifle with a three- to five-hundred-yard effective range. All were wearing hats to shade their faces from the harsh sun, and from what he could tell, two had auburn hair and looked like sisters, with the third a raven-haired beauty with flashing blue eyes.

The black-haired woman removed her hat and smiled at Duke. "Looks like we owe you boys big."

Duke smiled back. "What happened?"

"We picked up a tail in Colorado Springs. We didn't see them for about an hour, and then by the time we did, they were too close for comfort."

"They part of a gang?"

"No idea. We didn't hang around. We're just passing through."

"From where?"

"Denver."

"Never been."

"Not much going on there. We thought we might as well try our luck on the road."

Duke nodded. "Your horses look blown out. You're lucky you didn't lose one."

"I know." She smiled again, and he decided he liked the way the skin at the corner of her eyes crinkled. "Would you mind if we let them graze by the river?"

"It's a free country. But it'll be dark in a few hours. Where were you planning to hole up for the night?"

"We were hoping to make Pueblo."

"Not with the horses in that condition, you won't," John said.

"There's nothing there," Duke cautioned. "Town's abandoned."

Her eyes narrowed thoughtfully. "Don't suppose you have anywhere we could put up, then?"

Duke motioned to the building. "Plenty of room, but they aren't first-class digs. More like a floor and a roof."

"Would you mind if we stayed the night?" she asked.

"Not at all. We're just setting up shop."

She swung out of the saddle and hopped to the ground. "I'm Ellen. This is Monica and Tracie."

Duke nodded to them. "Pleased to meet you. I'm Duke, and this here's John."

"Is this your place?" she asked.

"That's right. Duke's Trading Post," John answered.

"Where are you all from?" Tracie asked.

John and Duke exchanged a glance. Duke cleared his throat before answering, "Down Texas way myself. John's from New Mexico."

"You're a long way from home."

"Man's got to find opportunity where he can."

"Just you two?" Ellen asked.

"One more out hunting. Fifty-fifty he makes it back by sundown."

"I'd have thought you'd have more men out here. Three isn't a lot to hold off a gang."

"We're hiring," Duke said. "If you know how to use a gun."

She smiled again. "We sure do. We might just take you up on that. What's the pay?"

Duke held her gaze. "Negotiable." He turned to John. "Why don't you ride out and get those riders' guns and gear?" He looked to Tracie and Monica. "You think your horses have enough left in them to help?"

"Sure thing," Monica said.

John fetched his horse, and the two women rode off with him. John would drag the bodies to the railroad tracks where they wouldn't be seen and leave them for the buzzards. Their weapons and horses were now Duke's and would go into the trading post's stocks, for use by whomever he hired to act as help.

When the others had cleared the gate, Ellen walked her horse to a water trough and let him drink. Duke busied himself reloading his spent magazines from a metal ammo case of 5.56mm rounds, and snuck a glance at her when she wasn't looking.

"Were you serious about looking to hire?" she asked. "We're low on supplies and could use the work."

"Long as you can shoot straight and don't have sticky fingers, we could work something out." He paused. "You got any other skills?"

This time her smile was shy. "All the usual. We're all fair cooks, good with ponies. We could keep this place clean. Catch fish. Whatever's necessary."

"Anyone after you?"

Her expression clouded. "No. Why do you ask?"

"Three beautiful women at my trading post, you're going to get noticed. Lousy place to hide out if that's your game."

"We're on the up-and-up. But if you think it's a bad idea, we can ride out tomorrow. Your call."

"I suppose the place could probably use a woman's touch. It's a mess. Looters left it a wreck."

"And the pay?"

"Four rounds a day apiece."

"Not super generous," she countered.

"You see a line waiting to trade? It is what it is. You think you can do better farther south, don't let me stop you."

Her smile returned. "We owe you for saving our lives. Let's try it for a while and see how it goes. If business goes through the roof, maybe you'll open your wallet."

"Then it's a deal."

She walked over and shook his hand. The feel of her skin on his awakened a feeling in Duke he hadn't thought about for a long time, and color rose in his cheeks. He resisted the urge to look away and instead nodded.

"Welcome to Bartertown," he said with a chuckle.

Chapter 8

Astoria, Oregon

Lucas, Ruby, and Rosemary cantered down the road toward the final bridge before Astoria. The two-day ride from Newport had been as uneventful as they hoped their return home to Shangri-La would be. Rosemary had proven a good travel companion without her parents, and had willingly stood watch for a four-hour shift each night while Ruby and Lucas slept. She'd continued to pepper them with questions about their destination, and they'd answered as honestly as they could, trying to prepare her for the reality of living high in the mountains, where winters were brutal and hardship was a regular part of the day.

Lucas slowed as they neared the bridge and gestured at the sky, where hundreds of black birds circled over the town.

"Lot of buzzards," he said. "Maybe the Chinese made their last push."

Ruby drew closer to him and freed her gun from its scabbard. "Question is, who won?"

"We'll know soon enough."

They made their way across the bridge, Lucas in the lead, and stopped when they'd reached the Astoria side of the river. Lucas took in the road ahead, which was clogged with carrion birds feasting on the flesh of the dead.

"Those are Chinese uniforms," Rosemary said.

"Answers the question of who won."

They held their breath as their horses trotted past the corpses, the stench of decomposition thick in the morning air, and once beyond the killing field, slowed at the sight of six men with rifles blocking the road. One of them recognized Lucas and called out behind him, and then the men lowered their guns and stepped aside to allow them to pass.

They found Art with Sam and Bill outside the General's bar, where they were seated in camp chairs, deep in discussion. Lucas dismounted and lashed Tango to the hitching post, and Ruby and Rosemary did the same with their mounts. The men stood to greet them, and Lucas nodded.

"Saw the mess by the bridge," Lucas said.

"Yup," Art said. "They tried to escape night before last. Didn't take long to finish them off."

"Don't suppose there's any reason to bury 'em," Lucas said.

"Nobody wanted the duty," Bill explained. "Besides, we're fixing to leave soon, so the whole town will be their cemetery." He looked Lucas over, and his eyes flitted to Rosemary. "Did you find Newport?"

"Yes. They're getting settled. Town fired the council. Hayden's running things for now."

Lucas sat on the edge of the porch, and Ruby and Rosemary joined him. "Glad to see you make it back," Sam said. "Although you missed all the excitement."

"You get all of them?" Lucas asked.

"Yep. Lost a few men in the process, but not too many." He paused. "We were just talking about what to do next."

"We can't stay by the river," Bill said. "And I'm not sure I have much taste for heading back to Newport and waiting for more Chinese to come over the hill."

"Sam here was talking about heading to Salem," Art said. "Clearing the Portland bikers out and establishing a working system."

Sam nodded agreement. "We've got a lot of men who'll come with us – men who're pumped after taking on a whole passel of

Chinese and beating them."

"Yeah? How many?" Lucas asked.

"Counting my men and Bill's? At least six hundred. And all of them armed."

"What about their families?"

Art shrugged. "They'd all go together." He wiped a tired hand over his face. "Your timing's perfect. Just in time to join us."

Lucas shook his head. "Already said not interested."

"We beat them hands down, Lucas," Sam said. "We can do the same with the bikers. They don't stand a chance."

"Not my fight, gentlemen. We're headed home. Got a long way to ride to get there. I'm sure you'll do well."

"Kind of in the same direction, isn't it?" Art asked.

Lucas scowled. "What's that got to do with anything?"

"Wouldn't be a big deal to ride along with us, would it? Sure would be a morale booster," Sam said.

"I'm not here to cheerlead your men." Lucas hesitated. "You seen Ray around?"

"He was wounded in the fight. He's in town being tended to."

Rosemary's hand flew to her mouth. "How bad?"

"The wound is pretty clean. Through his thigh. He'll be fine. The medic cauterized it, which probably hurt more than the bullet."

"I want to see him," Rosemary said.

"Are the wounded in the same place as before?" Ruby asked.

Art nodded. "There were some Chinese in there, but they offed themselves. Just ours in there now. The Chinese supplies came in handy, though — they had antibiotics and morphine. And a ton of ordnance."

Rosemary rose. "I know where it is. Let's go."

Lucas stood and tipped his hat. "Gents."

Art smiled. "Think it over, Lucas. You got nothing to lose by tagging along."

"I'll ask the ladies. I'm just the hired help."

They found Ray in a bed beside three other wounded men, his thigh bandaged and a sour expression on his face.

"It was just a flesh wound," he complained. "Really nothing. I didn't even feel it. But they won't let me go until tomorrow. Observation, they say." He snorted. "I'm bored out of my mind here."

"You look pretty fit to me," Ruby said. "But it can't hurt to stay put another day."

"I've got things to do."

"Sure you do," Rosemary said. "Like what?"

That stopped him. "Where are your parents?" he asked.

"In Newport. I'm riding with Lucas and Ruby to Shangri-La."

His eyebrows rose. "What? And they were okay with that?"

"I wouldn't say okay, but it's done."

Lucas stood outside, watching the squatters mill around the town, carrying treasures they'd discovered in abandoned buildings back to their tents. Ruby joined him and squinted up at him. "They're right that we're headed in the same direction."

"I know. I don't want to get sucked in."

"It's not like you'd have to do much. Running a bunch of bikers out of town on a rail sounds like a slow morning for the Lucas I know."

He chuckled. "Not hardly. I'm just…I'm tired, Ruby. I want to spend my time with Sierra and the kids. I'm done fighting."

"Seems like you landed in a pretty special place in time, Lucas. It isn't everyone who could lead them, you know. Art's good, but he's long in the tooth, and he doesn't have your energy."

"I'm running on empty, Ruby."

"We'd be a lot safer riding with them at least as far as Salem. Where's the harm?"

"I don't want them to get ideas."

She shrugged. "So you help them with some strategy. It isn't like you don't have plenty to spare. Plus I've seen you in action. You enjoy it."

"That's part of the problem. What kind of man enjoys killing?"

"Not the killing part. I meant the tactics. The planning. You're a natural, and we both know it."

"I do that, it'll never end. I promised Sierra…"

"And you can keep your promise. We can ride to Salem and then part ways with them."

He studied her and sighed. "Why are you so hell-bent on me doing this?"

"I'm not. I just don't see a downside. Plus, if I were thirty years younger and you, I'd be asking myself the same questions we talked about on the trail – we both know the Chinese will be back with more men and ships. I'm not sure it'll be possible to hide in the mountains forever while they take over the country. You've got the beginning of an army here, and…I don't believe in coincidences. If you ask me, there's a reason things turned out like they did. A reason you're here."

"Doesn't seem like anyone's all that interested in what *I* want, does it?"

"You want Sierra and the kids to be safe. Ask yourself how that'll be possible if the country's invaded and run as a slave colony. Is that the future you want for them? For yourself?"

"Wouldn't be much different than how we've let it turn out, would it?"

Ruby frowned. "Don't give me that, Lucas. We both know you aren't fine with any of this. You're a good man, and you can't stand idly by while evil triumphs. It's one of the reasons I respect you, and why they want you to lead the men. You have honor. That's a rare quality in this day and age."

"Damn, woman. You do have a way with words, don't you?"

"I could write your speeches for you."

Lucas offered her a fatigued grin. "You can start on my first one. Call it 'I quit.' Doesn't have to be long."

"Does that mean we're going with them?"

"Sounds like I'll never hear the end of it if I say no. But you're going to explain to Sierra why we've been away so long."

"No problem. She knows you. I won't have to say much."

Lucas glanced at the looters and shook his head. "Some army."

"Nobody said it would be easy."

"You just did."

"Huh."

Chapter 9

When Luis arrived before sunset with a bag full of rabbits, he was surprised to find an attractive young woman manning the front gate with an AK-47, and she seemed unimpressed by his insistence that he was one of the owners. She called to Duke inside the truck stop while never taking her eyes off him, and they waited in tense silence until Duke's voice rang out that it was okay to allow Luis to pass.

"Sorry," she said. "I'm Monica. I guess we work for you now."

"We?"

"My sister Tracie and I. And Ellen."

"You work for us?"

She nodded. "Talk to Duke."

Luis scowled. "I will."

He led his stallion to the area they'd designated as a stable and eyed six new horses milling around inside the paddock fence. After removing the saddle and bags, he penned his horse and set his gear in the shed beside the rest and then walked to the main building with his dinner bag.

Another woman was sweeping the area – Tracie, he guessed from the resemblance to the one at the gate. He ignored her and made for the offices, where Duke was talking to yet another woman in a low voice. Duke looked up when Luis darkened the doorway, and grinned.

"Luis! You made it! This is Ellen. Ellen, Luis, my partner in crime."

Luis nodded to her and stared at Duke. "Can I talk to you?"

"Sure. Ellen? Maybe you can help Tracie."

"Of course, Duke," she said, and brushed by Luis, whose eyes followed her down the hall before returning to Duke.

"Of course, Duke," Luis mimicked. Duke indicated one of the chairs in front of the desk.

"Take a load off. What you got there?"

"Rabbit."

"Enough for six?"

"Want to tell me what's going on here?"

Duke gave him an abridged rundown of the day's events. When he finished, Luis just stared at him. "You can't be serious."

"I already hired them. Let's see how they work out."

"Three women at a trading post? Tell me how that won't be a magnet for trouble, Duke."

"You're looking at this the wrong way. They're attractive. We'll probably get more business once word spreads."

"Or we'll be fighting off every miscreant in the region who wants to burn the place to the ground and take them."

"We need help, Luis. Three extra pairs of hands will go a long way."

Luis's eyes narrowed. "The brunette. The one that was just here. You like her, don't you?"

"They aren't hard to look at. Tell me you don't think so too."

"Is this all about you trying to get lucky?"

Duke exhaled and sat forward. "Luis, if you have a problem with this, I'll cover them out of my cut."

"It's not a few bullets. It's…it changes everything. You'll see." He paused. "Have you told them what we're really doing here?"

Duke looked over Luis's shoulder to ensure the hall was empty. "Of course not. As far as they're concerned, we're a trading post. That's it."

"And you don't think they'll start asking questions when one of us disappears for days at a time with full saddlebags and returns loaded down with different stuff?"

"It'll be a while before we have to make a run."

"What about the transmitter? How do you explain that?"

"We have a radio. Which we charge people to use. Big deal. I'm a hobbyist. Crazy about it. Use your head, Luis. This isn't a problem. If it becomes one, we'll tell them to leave."

"All I know is that you get some good-looking women involved with a bunch of men, it leads nowhere good."

"They're not involved. They'll stand guard with us, clean the place up with us, help us get up and running. That's it."

Luis pushed back his chair and stood. "I'm going to dress these so we can eat. Rabbit stew. You have any other surprises for me?"

"There's nothing to be pissed off about, Luis."

"You did this without asking me, Duke. And now it's a done deal. How's that a partnership?"

Duke didn't respond, and Luis stormed out of the office, angrier than he'd been for a long time. He asked himself why he was so upset, but he couldn't put his finger on it. He just knew from the look in Duke's eyes and his defense of his decision that something important had changed between them, and that Duke's interest in the women's welfare wasn't entirely altruistic. Not that he entirely blamed him; the brunette was definitely a looker, especially after months without any female company.

Which was a big part of the problem. Their focus wouldn't be on survival and business any longer – they'd be sneaking looks at the women or making decisions designed to protect them.

Which meant decisions that could hurt everyone if Duke wasn't thinking clearly. And right now Luis had a good idea of what was on his mind, because in spite of his best instincts, it was on his as well.

And that could go nowhere good.

Chapter 10

A group of thirty squatters from the Astoria tent city trudged north along the coast road, carting all their worldly possessions with them. They were one of several groups who'd been offered a choice of joining the fighting force that had helped tackle the Chinese or fending for themselves. This group had chosen the latter, most of them uninterested in doing anything but surviving another year.

With the river seeping poison, they couldn't stay where they were, so they'd crossed the bridge and headed toward Canada, where they'd heard things were better than in the northwest. Nobody could put their finger on who had started the rumor of civilization flourishing north of the border, but it was a seductive idea that had taken root and had guided their actions. Now, as they came to the end of another long day with blistered feet and little in the way of provisions, the decision to take off on their own seemed far more imprudent than it had before daybreak the prior day when they'd packed up and headed north.

"This looks as good as any," Martin, one of the alpha males in the group, said at a bend in the road. "We can camp here tonight and start again tomorrow."

"How far do you figure we've come?" one of the squatters asked.

"From Astoria? Maybe forty-five miles."

"And how far to the border?"

"Reckon it's another seventy-five, at least. Like we talked about, it should take a week or so, maybe a little more. But we'll make it."

Greg, one of the other men in the group, stepped forward. "I say we keep going until it's too dark to see."

"What's the point?" Martin asked. "It's not like we'll be late for dinner or anything."

"There's a town farther up the road. We can make it if we've come as far as you figure."

"A town? I don't know this area as well as you do."

"Yeah. South Bend. It's on a river. I heard it's abandoned. We could catch fish for breakfast tomorrow and stretch what we got." He sniffed the air. "Shouldn't be too much farther."

So they continued their trek, and the sun had sunk into the west when they stopped again.

"This wind's freezing. Great idea to keep going, Greg," Martin complained.

"We got tents. And there's nothing here. We can make some fires."

"Not sure that's a great idea. They'll draw attention."

"From who? We're the only ones stupid enough to be out here."

"I say no."

Greg shook his head and motioned to his companions. "You're not the boss, Martin. We do what we want."

Martin bristled. "Not if you put us all at risk."

"Fine. We'll keep going. Have a nice life, asswipe."

"Suit yourself."

Greg and six of his friends continued up the road for another hour, until they arrived at a reasonably sheltered stretch. They pitched their tents and ate what dried food they had, and two foraged for firewood while the others made a fire pit. Some grumbled about their predicament and questioned whether they would have been better off staying with the others, but eventually the discontent faded along with the energy to complain.

The night sky was a tapestry of stars by the time the fire was blazing, and they sat around it and warmed themselves against the chill off the nearby ocean until it had burned down to embers. They tucked in to sleep while one of them stood guard, the only sounds the soft moan of the wind through the trees and the rustle of night creatures in the surrounding woods.

The moon was high overhead when the guard heard something from the road. He leaned forward from the tree he was using for a backrest and squinted to see what had made the sound, but saw nothing. After several minutes of tense silence, he relaxed, the desolate coastline devoid of any obvious threat. He was settling back against the tree when a trio of figures stepped from the shadows with their weapons pointed at his head.

"What the—"

A blow from a rifle butt silenced him. One of the men took his gun, and then five more materialized out of the darkness and headed toward the tents.

Greg poked his head from his tent and found himself staring into the barrel of an assault rifle. He looked up from the muzzle at a stern face with a Chinese army hat pulled low across the brow, and swallowed hard just before a boot knocked him senseless and the starlight faded to black.

Chapter 11

Laredo, Texas

The silhouette of the Juárez-Lincoln International Bridge that spanned the Rio Grande river was faint against the partially cloudy night sky. Clogged with the rusting hulks of long-abandoned vehicles trying to get to or from Mexico, the bridge's eight lanes were impassable and served as a natural barrier between the two countries – not that there was any recognized border anymore, nor any border patrol to police it. The Crew acted as the law in Laredo, and its grip on the town was like its other holdings: absolute and brutal.

The Crew used the old immigration checkpoint building on the Texas side of the bridge as its base in the southern end of town, with its headquarters at the airport to the north. Since the collapse, the population had thinned to a little over four thousand souls, ruled over by a tenth as many gang members who took what they wanted from the locals and taxed them ninety percent of everything they were able to produce – which wasn't much in the harsh climate. Many eked out a subsistence living trading with their counterparts in Nuevo Laredo, but the commerce was paltry, with the Mexicans even poorer than the Americans, most living hardscrabble and cannibalizing anything they could find to exchange for food or ammo.

Music from a cantina drifted across the river from the Mexican side, and the Crew members on night duty listened with frowns.

Most of their group were elsewhere in town, drinking and whoring their week's rations away, and the chore of manning the outpost was one of the least popular assignments, especially on payday.

Outside, beneath an overhang near the bridge, Kerry, a tall man with tobacco-colored skin and the arms of a boxer, cocked his head at a card table, where he was in the process of taking the other poker players for everything they had. "You hear that?"

The other players shook their heads, and one of them glanced over at the camp lantern that was providing light for their game. "Just that caterwauling from across the river."

"I thought I heard something from the bridge."

"Probably a dog. Nobody there's stupid enough to try to sneak into town after dark. They all know the rules."

The Crew's approach to border control was draconian: anyone from Mexico caught on the Texas side after dark was dragged to the river and shot. The gang had forced any Hispanics in Laredo to get the Crew's symbol tattooed on their forearm, branding them as Crew-owned, so it was easy to tell the locals from their Mexican counterparts. Once word had spread south of the border, there hadn't been any problems with looting from Nuevo Laredo – the Crew didn't take kindly to its property being stolen, and everything and everyone in Laredo was its property.

"Have someone check," Kerry ordered. He was the equivalent of a master sergeant in the gang's hierarchy, and the customs station was Kerry's for the night and the dozen gunmen there his to command.

One of the players, a barrel-chested thug with the face of a bulldog, pushed back from the table with his cards. "Not gonna leave 'em here for you thieves," he said, and made a show of counting the bullets in the pile before him.

"Hurry up, Otter. That hand's not gonna heat up by stalling," Kerry said, and the other players laughed.

Otter trudged from the card table to where the rest of the men were gathered, most swinging in hammocks strung from the steel girders that held a sweeping overhang in place. He approached five men sitting by a small fire and motioned with his cards.

"Bert, Jaime, boss says he heard something from the bridge."

"And?" Jaime asked.

"Wants us to check to make sure we don't have a runner."

Unlike the pre-collapse, where desperate Mexicans had braved the river and the border patrol in the hopes of finding opportunity north of the border, now most of what the Crew was on the watch for were Laredo residents trying to escape the hell on earth the gang had created on the U.S. side. Bad as it was in Mexico, with its own warlords and cartels running the country, the Crew's territory was worse, and Laredo had steadily lost laborers until the gang had blocked all the exit routes and issued a death penalty for anyone attempting escape.

The men tossed their cards into the pot and ambled toward the bridge with their rifles, grumbling at being asked to interrupt their much-needed downtime from long hours of rape, extortion, and mayhem.

"If it's a runner, I call dibs on popping 'em," Bert muttered.

Jaime made a face. "After what you drank, you couldn't hit the side of a bus with a shotgun."

They chuckled and reached the first of the clogged vehicles. All they heard was the wail of a horn and the thrumming of a tuba from Mexico. "Sounds like they're having a better time than we are. Don't see how, though, without two nickels to rub together."

Then the clink of metal on metal reached them from the bridge, and both stiffened. "I definitely heard that," Bert said.

They edged past a tall truck, its tires degraded to black dust, and made their way forward in the darkness, leading with their guns. Fifteen yards from the bank they stopped again to listen, but the only thing they heard besides the cantina band was the rush of the river beneath them. Bert was turning to speak to his companion when an axe blade swung from the open window of the car beside him and sliced through his sternum. Jaime raised his rifle just as a crossbow shaft sprouted from between his shoulder blades, and he coughed a stream of blood down his chin and dropped his rifle.

The axe wielder jerked the axe free as Bert struggled to swing his gun around, but the blow had sapped his strength, and he was too slow. The second blow took half his skull off in a spray of blood and brains, and he collapsed in a heap beside Jaime, who was kneeling and struggling for breath, his hands on the shaft protruding from his chest and his mouth working like a beached fish. The man with the axe leveled a blow at his shoulder and bisected him from clavicle to midchest, and then stepped back to avoid the worst of the blood that geysered from the wound.

"Grab their guns," a voice called in Spanish from behind him. Two men pushed past him and relieved the gangsters of their weapons and ammunition, working with practiced efficiency as the man with the axe wiped his blade clean on Jaime's pant leg.

When they were done, a long column of armed cartel fighters snaked its way across the bridge, taking care to move silently so as not to draw any more investigation. The gunmen stayed low, using the cars and trucks for cover, and remained in the gloom until they were near enough to the Crew outpost to hear the card players bickering.

The captain of the Laredo cartel signaled to his men, and ten broke off to the right while another dozen ran in a crouch to the left. The rest waited, motionless, weapons in hand. The lead fighters were armed with hunting crossbows in addition to sound-suppressed rifles and were under instruction not to make a sound when overrunning the outpost.

The plan was a good one, but had failed to account for Kerry and his three card sharks, who came around the corner shooting when they heard the strangled cries of their men. Otter's shotgun boomed over and over as Kerry's Kalashnikov stuttered death at the attackers, who opened up with their rifles once the shooting began. Otter took four rounds to the torso, and Kerry ducked back around the corner as a burst of slugs pocked the building behind him, his boots slamming against the cement as he made for the radio he'd left on the table. He reached it and sprinted away from the gunfight, pressing the transmit button as he ran.

"We're under attack at the bridge. Mexicans. Ton of them. I'm the only one left."

"How many?"

Kerry was cut off by an AK on full auto from behind. The rounds tore through him and knocked him off his feet. His finger squeezed the trigger of his rifle as he fell, but his bullets whizzed harmlessly into the night.

A Mexican with facial tattoos like those favored by the Crew stepped from the darkness for Kerry's rifle, his expression impassive; Kerry was just the first of many he would execute before the night was over. He shouldered the weapon and removed three spare magazines from the dead man's vest, and then returned to where the others were mopping up the last of the Crew, aware they were at a disadvantage now that their shots had telegraphed their presence.

The cartel ran into a wall halfway to the airport headquarters, where over a hundred Crew were waiting with grenades in addition to their assault rifles. The Mexicans fought ferociously but were outgunned, and after sustaining heavy losses, they retreated across the bridge, their effort to take over Laredo foiled.

Snake received word of the attack an hour after it finished, and his mood was vile after being woken in the dead of night. That the cartel had dared to make a play for Laredo was ominous – they'd have never tried such a thing under Magnus's rule, and the attempt was further confirmation that the Crew under Snake was vulnerable.

"Send another hundred men with as many weapons as they can carry. I want them there in a week," he ordered, his voice strained. "They leave at first light. I want Laredo buttoned down so tight a rat can't move without us knowing."

His underlings scurried away to carry out his instructions, but he wasn't kidding himself. He could see in their eyes the doubt about his abilities and judgment, and he knew that with the Crew seriously weakened from the loss of Magnus's force, and now the sixty men he'd lost in the Laredo episode, it was just a matter of time before he lost territory to a rival gang. Texas was too large to monitor with limited troops, much less the other states, and between upstarts to the north and east and the Mexicans to the south, he was stretched too thin, and his supply lines, such as they were, were unsustainable.

All because the Illuminati had failed to provide him with the fuel he needed to dominate the southwest. Without that juice he was a sitting duck, and he could feel the noose tightening around his neck with each passing hour.

He debated rousing Barton and delivering an ultimatum, but decided against it at the last moment. Annoying the Illuminati flunky would do no good. He'd speak with him tomorrow in reasoned tones and explain to him that if Snake's empire fell, it would be viewed as a reflection of the Illuminati's failure to fulfill their end of the deal – a failure that would make anyone else reluctant to cooperate with them.

Snake's only hope was that he could get them to see that, like a bank who'd lent their biggest customer too much money and was now watching him teeter on the edge of insolvency, it wasn't the debtor's problem now so much as it was the bank's. If the Crew's stranglehold on its holdings began to unravel, everything the Illuminati had invested in the southwest would be lost, along with the credibility they needed if they were going to act as a centralizing force.

Whether it would work or not was another story. But it was the only card Snake had to play, so he would play it for all he was worth, and bet that the Illuminati's self-interest would drive them to back him up when he most needed it.

Otherwise the Crew wasn't long for this world, and neither was he.

But there was no way he would go down quietly.

Chapter 12

Trading Post, Colorado

Ellen was humming while she cleaned outside Duke's office as he tallied his inventory. They'd spent the prior evening talking about nothing, and by the time he'd tucked in to bed, all he'd been able to think about were her flashing eyes, easy smile, and jet-black hair. She was an enigma, somewhat guarded about her past, but by the end of the night she'd told him enough to fill in most of the blanks.

She and the sisters had left Denver to get away from the church they'd been a part of, which had turned cultish over the years and no longer appealed to them. Under further probing, she'd admitted that they'd been virtual slaves and had been forced to sneak away in the dead of night with only what they could carry. Apparently the son of the church leader had been a big part of the problem, making advances to many of the single women in the congregation, and what had begun as flirtation had turned into pressure to have sex with him, which they hadn't been interested in.

Worse, the father had refused to hear any reports about his son's misbehavior, leaving them feeling like they had no alternative but to leave.

"Everyone's under his spell, and it's like neither he nor his son can do any wrong. They were like family to us, so it wasn't easy," she'd said. "But it just got to where none of us felt comfortable anymore, and we had to do something."

"So you left."

"Exactly. The whole city's under their control, so you're either with them or against them. Once our eyes were opened to what the son was after, we decided we couldn't live there anymore. It's too bad. There are so many positives to the church…"

"How many are in it?"

"Almost…five thousand? I feel sorry for some of the other girls in the same position we were. I mean, some are fine being the son's harem, but a lot of them have been pressured into it and just don't have anywhere to turn."

"It must have taken a lot of courage to walk away."

"More like run away. We weren't sure how they'd react. Some of them are real zealots."

"You thought they'd hurt you?"

"I would have said no, but now…well, we'd rather not find out."

Duke looked up from his inventory pad and offered a smile. Ellen returned it and stopped what she was doing. She'd washed her clothes in the river that morning, and her shirt was still damp, and he couldn't help but notice that she filled it out nicely.

She entered his office and sat down. "Having a productive morning?"

"Just counting beans. How 'bout you?"

"Nothing special. Although it's nice to be in the same place longer than a few hours." She sighed. "I thought it would be exciting on the road, but it's not. I mean, not in a good way."

"Most people didn't choose it. Got thrust on them by circumstance. Like with you."

"Yeah. I just wish we could find somewhere safe, you know? Everywhere we've heard about since we left sounds worse than the last."

Duke nodded. "It's definitely a dangerous world these days." He paused. "What are you looking for in a place?"

"I don't know exactly. We're all from small towns, so probably something small. Calm. Where everyone gets along and there's a sense of basic decency." She nibbled her lower lip. "Sounds like a pipe dream after weeks on the road."

Duke eyed his hands for a long moment. "What do you want out of life, Ellen? You're beautiful and intelligent. What are you after?"

She sighed. "It's going to sound stupid."

"Try me."

"I want a family with a good man who values me for who I am. I want to live somewhere safe and raise my kids to be God-fearing, with a husband I can trust, and who only has eyes for me." Her eyes misted and she sniffed. "Which is crazy in this day and age, where everyone's a thug out for whatever they can get. In most places, the men are animals."

"Not everyone."

"Okay, maybe not, but you have to admit most of them are." She managed a small smile. "Present company excepted, of course."

"Don't you think you'd get bored?"

"Not at all. Like I said, a small town's all I know. We didn't move to Denver until everything fell apart. When my parents…when they passed, the church became my family. I think that's one of the things I really liked about it – being part of it was like what I grew up with, where everyone knew each other."

"What about your friends? Monica and Tracie?"

"Believe me, we've talked about it. We all want the same thing. Struggling to survive every day's reinforced the value of a stable home." She looked directly at him and held his gaze. "I think I know a good man when I see one."

An uncomfortable pause stretched several moments.

"Why a trading post?" she asked. "And why here? It isn't exactly a high-traffic area."

"I've had a bunch of them. There's a lot to be said for being off the beaten track. Better bargaining, for starters. And you don't have to worry about a competitor trying to take you out." He hesitated. "And you meet some really interesting people."

"Don't you get…lonely out here, with just John and Luis?"

"I try not to think about it."

"I don't think Luis likes us. What's his story?"

"He's a good guy. Just a little high-strung."

"He looks like a total gangster, with the tattoos."

"Everyone's got a story. But he's always dealt squarely with me. Had to, for me to take him on as a partner."

Ellen frowned. "If you say so." She stood. "So what about you? What do you want to be when you grow up? You want a family?"

"With the right woman, I'd be the happiest man in the world. But you don't meet a lot of ladies on the trail."

Another pause.

Duke cleared his throat. "I best get back to this."

"Yeah. And the place isn't going to clean itself."

That afternoon, Duke approached Ellen as she was brushing her horse beneath the truck stop overhang. "If I knew of a place like you were describing – small, everyone honest and hardworking, family people – would you be interested in going?"

Her eyes widened. "Are you kidding?"

"No. I…there's a town you'd really like. It has all the qualities you were talking about. I mean, the winters are brutal and it's in the middle of nowhere, but they're quality people looking to create something special."

She set down the brush and adjusted her shirt, and then closed the distance between them. He drew back a step, and she took his hand and looked deep into Duke's eyes. "Would you be going with me?"

He resisted the urge to look away or squirm. "Somebody would have to introduce you."

Ellen nodded once and then leaned forward and kissed him on the lips. When he drew back and focused, her smile was dazzling.

Duke exhaled. "Ellen, you're at least fifteen years younger than–"

She stepped forward and kissed him again, this time longer, her lips warm and moist on his. When they parted, she put her finger on his mouth.

"Don't talk nonsense. I said I was looking for a good man. You think I'm going to let you go now that I found one?"

Duke swallowed hard. "I've got the trading post…"

"How far away is this town?"

"Maybe a day and a half hard ride. I'd have to radio them and let them know we're coming."

"We can't just ride there?"

"They're pretty protective about their privacy." He studied her. "Are you sure…"

"Why don't you let me take a look at it and talk about things on the way? If it's like you describe, I'm sold." She smiled again. "You're not doing this because you're having second thoughts about hiring us, are you? Trying to get rid of us because Luis doesn't like us?"

Duke laughed nervously. "I never had a doubt from the moment I laid eyes on you."

She nodded and headed back to her horse. "Good. Me neither."

Chapter 13

Aberdeen, Washington

Greg strained against the handcuffs that bound him to the steel chair he'd been sitting in for the last hour, his head pounding, his vision blurred. The forced march from where the Chinese patrol had taken them captive had lasted all night, and when he'd come to and found himself being carried by his companions like a sack of rocks, the soldiers had forced him to walk, exhausting him both physically and mentally.

Now, sitting and waiting for the hammer to drop, he was fading in and out of consciousness. His body was crying out for food and water, and his skull ached with every beat of his heart. He had no idea what they had in store for him, but he knew it couldn't be good. He'd already resolved to cooperate however he could in the hopes that he'd be spared. He'd seen what the troops in Astoria had done to the wounded, and had no doubt that whatever awaited him would be as bad or worse. His one chance was to give the Chinese whatever they wanted. His only problem was he had no idea what that was.

Two men entered, one an officer, judging by his epaulets, and the other of indeterminate rank. The officer growled a few words, and the younger man turned to Greg with hooded eyes.

"What were you doing on the road?" he asked in accented English.

Greg cleared his throat. "Heading to Canada."

68

The soldier translated for the officer, who asked something else.

"Where were you coming from?"

Greg debated lying, but chose not to. They were undoubtedly interrogating the others, so lying would do no good.

"Astoria."

The officer nodded, the name registering without translation. He snapped at the soldier, who focused again on Greg.

"What happened there?"

"The…your troops…they were massacred. To the last man. We had no part of it, which is why we're on our own," Greg said, hating the whine he heard in his tone.

"Massacred by who?"

"The townspeople. The people in the tents. There were a lot of men there, and they ganged up to fight your soldiers."

A brief conversation ensued, with the officer's words issued at machine-gun clip.

"How could they have beaten a trained force? This makes no sense."

Greg told him everything he knew about the battle, which was mostly from what he'd seen from the cover of the trees and discussion he'd heard after the fact. When he was done, the two Chinese exchanged a glance and had another exchange.

"What do you know about Portland?" the young man asked.

"It's radioactive. The river, Astoria, all of it. Toxic. The nuclear reactor upriver must be melting down. Portland's gone."

"If this is true, where are the people from Astoria? Staying by the poison river?"

"No. They moved down the coast – to Newport. Hundreds of them."

"Then who fought in Astoria?"

"They sent their best fighters."

"What were you going to do when you reached Canada?"

"Try to find a way to survive," Greg answered honestly.

The men left, and Greg nodded off, overcome by the fatigue and stress.

A slap brought him back to consciousness. He found himself looking again at the interrogator and the officer, now with another, older officer beside him.

"Tell us what you know about Newport. And about these fighters. Leave nothing out."

A half hour later, the session was over. A pair of soldiers appeared at the door, unfastened the bracket that held his cuffs to the chair, and unceremoniously lifted Greg and walked him out of the room. They led him down the hall to a courtyard, and he froze in his tracks when he saw the bodies of his companions littering the area.

The bayonet stabbed through his back with an icy lance of pain so severe it stopped his breath in his throat. His mind fought for words that would stop the unthinkable from happening, some protest that would convince them that he'd cooperated, been useful, done everything they'd asked without any coercion, and then his heart throbbed its final beat, and he realized it was too late, he was dying, and his time on earth had run out.

Chapter 14

Tango shook his head like he was disagreeing, and Lucas eyed the trail ahead of him. The ragtag army Lucas was leading had armed itself with the contents of the mountain cache, and the group was now over seven hundred strong and reasonably outfitted, if largely unskilled. Behind him the men shuffled on foot and on horseback in a column a quarter mile long, those who were walking slowing the group's progress to just over twenty miles a day.

"What is it, Tango?" he whispered.

Three men stepped onto the track in front of Lucas. He reined to a stop, and Bill and Sam, riding beside him, raised their rifles to cover the men.

"We wanna join up," one of them blurted.

Lucas studied the three – they were younger than he'd first thought, with faces coated in grime and in need of a good scrubbing. Maybe mid to late teens, but hardened by circumstance, their cheekbones jutting beneath their skin and their cheeks hollow from malnutrition, but their weapons were clean and in good shape.

"Join what?" Bill fired back.

"Whatever this is," the youth said. "We want in."

"You reckon it's smart to join something when you don't even know what it is?" Lucas asked.

"We can fight. But we're hungry. Give us some food and we'll do whatever you want."

"You family?" Sam asked.

"That's right. Brothers. I'm Reese, and this is Mark and Tim."

"How old are you?" Bill asked.

Reese straightened, and his eyes darted from Lucas to Bill and back again. "I'm seventeen. Mark's fifteen, and Tim's…fourteen."

Lucas sighed and looked to Sam. "Give 'em some provisions. Maybe they can help load magazines. But Mark and Tim are too young for anything else."

Mark bristled. "I've killed three men. I can handle myself just fine."

Lucas frowned. "I'm sorry to hear that. Heavy burden for a young man."

Mark's face registered confusion, and Bill stepped into the silence. "Go on back to the carts and tell Carl that Bill and Sam said you're part of the group. When you've eaten, find Henry or Art, and they'll tell you what to do."

"Where are we headed?" Reese asked.

"You'll find out in time."

"We went to Salem a while back. It's scary bad there. Don't go to Portland, either. Everyone's gone."

"You been there?" Lucas asked.

"Um…no. But we met some folks on the road who told us."

"How long ago?"

"Couple of weeks."

"This some kinda army or something?" Tim asked. "You got ranks and stuff?"

"Sort of," Sam answered. "It's a militia, if you want to get technical."

"That's like an army, right?"

"In a way."

"Who're we fixing to fight?"

Lucas sighed. "Anyone in our way. Now go on. Get some food and save your questions for Art. They call him the general. He's got a bum arm, and he's old enough to be your grandad. Ask him what we're doing. He'll set you straight."

Reese brightened. "Is he really a general?"

"Ask him. Now git."

The boys trotted down the column. Lucas and Sam exchanged a look, and Lucas smiled sadly. "Poor bastards."

Bill shrugged. "There's no time to be a child anymore. Got to grow up fast or you don't make it."

"Still. Sad."

"The world's full of sad. Let's hope we can make it a little better for some. If we can, that's a win."

Lucas looked away. "Still got a ways to go before we rest."

"No doubt, Lucas. No doubt."

Chapter 15

Newport, Oregon

Frantic pounding at the door of Hayden's house woke him, and he jumped out of bed and pulled on pants before hurrying down the stairs to the entry. Three men were standing on the porch with guns in their hands and frightened expressions.

"What is it?" Hayden asked.

"There's a ship at the mouth of the harbor, and a bunch of boats are making their way to shore," one of them said.

"It's the Chinese," another blurted.

"What should we do?" the third demanded.

Hayden blinked away the grogginess and glanced behind him. "Come in. Let me get dressed. You say they're on their way in?"

"That's right. They're rowing so they don't make any noise."

"How did the ship arrive without waking everyone?" Hayden asked.

"It must have cut its power a ways out. Don't ask me."

Hayden ran up the stairs, taking the steps two at a time, and donned boots, a shirt, and his flak jacket before making his way back to the living room with his M16 and pistol.

The men looked even more nervous than before. Hayden swallowed the fear rising in his throat and tried to appear confident.

"Okay, we need to decide whether we're going to fight or not," he said.

"What do you mean, *or not?* Of course we have to fight. You want to let them make us slaves again?"

"Of course not. But if everyone gets killed, does that solve anything?" He paused. "I'm just thinking out loud."

The largest of the three looked disgusted. "You're chicken."

Hayden shook his head. "There's no point in getting everyone killed for nothing. We should fight if we stand a chance of winning."

"How the hell are we supposed to win against a Chinese invasion force? They got serious weapons, training, you name it." The man walked to the door. "I'm not gonna let them take my family and make them into slaves, or worse. If you won't fight, that doesn't mean everyone's gotta lie down for them."

"We're trying to decide what to do," one of the others said. "Don't go and do anything stupid."

"We got to try to at least turn 'em back. Otherwise we're gonna be like Astoria, only worse."

The man slammed the door behind him, and the remaining men looked to Hayden. "You seriously think we shouldn't try to stop them?"

"I…look. How many do you think a ship that size holds?"

"I don't know. Maybe…a thousand? Less?"

"I remember something like six or seven hundred in Astoria."

"Yeah, that's about right. So?"

"So what chance do we have against seven hundred Chinese troops with unlimited ammo, who don't care who they kill? What do you think will happen when they open up on us with the ship guns? You want that for your families?"

"Then we have to run. But we're out of time. They'll be here in minutes."

Shooting echoed from the water, and Hayden's expression darkened. "Too late."

They ran from the house and caught the sounds of a firefight taking place by the remains of the boat docks. The men sprinted to join the fight, but Hayden held back. He'd meant it when he'd said it seemed pointless to take on an unstoppable force, and he didn't see anything to be gained by fighting it out in a guaranteed defeat situation.

More gunfire exploded from the harbor, making his decision for him. He had absolutely no doubt that the Chinese would cut down anyone stupid enough to oppose them. Hayden had signed up to be sheriff, but that didn't mean he was going to lay down his life in a futile gesture. No, it would be better to hide out and see what happened before making any moves. Dead men couldn't mount a defense, and it wouldn't be in his best interests to abdicate his position of responsibility and allow himself to be killed when he was more valuable alive.

Two men with shotguns appeared from out of the darkness. "Hayden! Come on! The Chinese are attacking!"

"I know. You go ahead. I'm going to try to flank them and coordinate a counterattack."

The men continued down to the harbor and certain death. Hayden retreated to the stable, moving through the darkness like a fish through water. When he reached the horses, nobody was there, and he entered the building as the shooting from the harbor intensified. He found his horse and fit his saddle and bags on him as quickly as he could, and then led the stallion out into the night, gunshots trailing him as he walked the horse away from town.

He wasn't sure what to do next, but he knew from Astoria that by morning the town would be under Chinese rule no matter what token resistance the misguided citizens attempted. The only thing that might change was they could decide to kill everyone as retribution for Astoria, but that wasn't logical – they'd been up front about using the locals as slave labor, and if they slaughtered the entire town, there'd be nobody to bury the bodies.

The shooting died down after another hour, and he watched through his binoculars from the trees as Chinese soldiers advanced along the streets and rousted the residents from their new homes. By daybreak, the survivors were gathered shivering in the parking lot of the hospital, guarded by twenty soldiers. Hayden could make out the panicked faces of his fellow townspeople and felt a coil of self-loathing in his gut – he'd chosen to save his own skin rather than help those who'd depended on him.

He remained through the day and watched with relief as the Chinese allowed most of those in the parking lot to return to their homes once the patrols had taken all the weapons. They directed ten of the stronger men to dispose of the dead defenders, of which there were at least forty. When they were gone, Hayden's heart sank when Hubert and Caleb were singled out and marched to the edge of the lot, where a soldier put a bullet into the back of their heads without hesitation.

Hayden had seen enough. That would have been his fate had he stayed. He'd made the only decision he could, and was alive only because of his good judgment and fast action.

Dusk streaked the sky with tangerine and violet as Hayden mounted his horse and set off along the road back to Astoria, unsure what he would do next but convinced there was nothing he could achieve by remaining in Newport. Maybe some of the fighters in Astoria would be game for returning and taking on the Chinese – assuming Bill and his group were still alive, they were the best fighters the town had.

Whatever the case, he was only one man, and it would have been unreasonable to expect him to make the ultimate sacrifice for nothing. At least that was his reasoning as the stallion settled into a comfortable pace, the only sound the clomp of its hooves on the pavement and the hoot of an owl from a treetop above.

Chapter 16

Ulysses Granger strode to the front of a large crowd, the sleeves of his white robe billowing like angel's wings as he waved to deafening applause from his thousands of followers. He approached the stage that had been erected at one end of the convention center and beamed at his flock, energized by their outpouring of devotion. He reached the stage, where his son, Elijah, was waiting along with members of his inner circle, and leapt onto it like a lion tamer into the ring.

He approached the podium and tapped the microphone. The public address system was solar powered, as were the lights, which had been dimmed to warm the cavernous space with an intimate glow. A shortwave transmitter sat nearby, ready to broadcast his sermon to the faithful all over the country – not that there were many outside Denver, where his doomsday church had sprung up after the collapse, offering a religious explanation for why the unthinkable had happened as well as a way forward and a sense of fellowship with the faithful for whom Ulysses was a holy prophet who spoke the Lord's words.

Denver had been particularly hard hit by the virus and the subsequent lawlessness until it had been cleansed of the gangs that had attempted to take it over – the local population had proven hard to bully, given it was well armed and composed of frontier types who could handle themselves as well as any marine platoon. Once order had been imposed, Ulysses's group had boasted the largest number of survivors in the area, so it was inevitable that it function as the local government for the city, with nonbelievers advised to look elsewhere for a home.

Ulysses had come out of nowhere, a gypsy preacher whose brand of fundamentalist fire and brimstone had enabled him to earn a paltry living on the road. He'd found a willing following in the shell-shocked residents of Denver, who had warmed to his new message when he'd appeared three months into the troubles with his son, a battered suitcase, and a tent. Over the ensuing years, he'd developed into a powerful phenomenon, and his fringe ideology had become the basis of his church.

"Brothers and sisters! Welcome to the house of the Lord!" he boomed, and the crowd went wild again, cheering and whooping like they were at a concert. He waited until the applause quieted, gazing out at the sea of faces before him in approval, and then shook his head like he was puzzled.

"I come here today with a message that appeared to me in a dream. It's a message that every man, woman, and child needs to hear and to take to heart."

More cheering rose from the throng. Ulysses's messages were a fixture of his church, and he regularly shared them during his larger performances.

"As you all have heard from many false prophets, we have been judged and found wanting. Many of us were punished for our sinful way of life, for our venality, our greed, our lust. For turning away from the one great truth. For allowing the blasphemers and philistines among us to pervert us with their filth. According to these false messiahs, we were unclean, we didn't believe, and for that we were smitten just as the sinners in Sodom and Gomorrah were, back in the day. It was inevitable. God is patient and merciful, but at some point He looked down at what His creations had gotten up to and said, 'Enough is enough.'"

Ulysses nodded, his expression grim. "And so He took the

majority and sent them to hell. Where they belong, for allowing immigrants and deviates and communists and porn-o-graph-y to twist our society and create a bubbling cauldron of sin!"

"Hallelujah!"

"That's what most preachers are saying, but you know what? Folks, they got it wrong. Dead wrong. Sure, some of them were sent straight to hell because of sin. But why were so many good folks also taken? And why spare some of us? That's a question I've been wondering about for years now. Why show some of us mercy when He wiped the earth of most? I've been praying on that question something fierce, and last night the answer was delivered to me in my dreams."

Ulysses paused for effect, and the convention hall was as quiet as a library, the congregation collectively holding its breath.

"The answer is that he didn't spare us anything. He called some of us to heaven with the virus, and right now those lucky ones are living forever in His presence. Not everyone who was taken was wicked – we all know that. Grandparents. Our mothers. The babies – the precious little babies. No, they were taken because He needed more good spirits in heaven with Him. They were rewarded for living righteously, not punished! That's where the charlatans, the false prophets, have it wrong. That brings me to the question that was answered in my dream. Why, oh why, are we still alive?" He looked around the room like a hawk surveying a field full of gophers. "And now I have the answer! What we think of as the world is nothing but a test. Right now we're in purgatory, between heaven and hell, where we're being judged to see if we're worthy of going up with Him or if we belong in hellfire with Satan!"

A woman near the front fainted with a loud moan, and Elijah swooped in to catch her, to cheers of encouragement. She came to after a few short seconds, hand clutched to her chest, and she glued her eyes to Ulysses.

"That's right," Ulysses continued. "We are between worlds, and this is our final test of the faithful. The Lord's a-watching, and what we do while we're here will decide where we go when we move on.

Those who continue living in sin and polluting their minds will get their reward, just as the righteous will stand at the Lord's side and live forever in eternal happiness. Everything you see around you is an illusion, folks. It's all a big show to test you so He knows who's worthy and who isn't."

More applause and shouts of adulation as Ulysses raised his arms to form a crucifix.

"He sent His son to be sacrificed for all of us, but that wasn't enough of a wake-up call. We had to keep being wicked, to keep making our hearts a home for the devil. So many were taken, but we were saved for this special purpose, and we *will* show Him that we're worthy!"

Ulysses lowered his voice from the shouted oratory to a conversational tone. "Many of you are probably wondering how this ends. I wish I could tell you. The dream didn't allow me to see it clearly. But what I can tell you, that came through loud and clear, was that He is sick and tired of false messiahs and the worship of idols and all the rest. What am I talking about? Even now, there are those who think there's salvation to be had outside of this church, who follow false prophets and believe nonsense. Folks who believe they know the answers, and that they don't need to be faithful and listen to the Word. They've moved out of our city, and I say good riddance – but there are dangers elsewhere that threaten to mess it up for us all."

A puzzled murmur washed over the attendees, and Ulysses shook his head again. "We've been given a last chance to prove we're worth saving. God hasn't decided what to do with us yet, but when He does, those who believe are gonna be saved, sure as those who fail the final test are going to burn for all eternity, and their skin will bubble off their bones, and every moment of forever will be nothing but pain and suffering and agony!"

Ulysses paused to let the mental image settle in and then nodded. "That's right. We're going to get one final stab at it, and this time we best not mess it up. That was the message in my dream. So sayeth the Lord!"

Cheers and a deafening ovation greeted his proclamation, and the faithful threw up their hands and screamed in righteous approval. Some turned to their fellows and hugged the person next to them as tears streamed down their faces, and others babbled in tongues or fell to the ground and convulsed in ecstasy. Elijah smiled at the four comely women by his side and embraced each one, his hands lingering on their form before releasing them and moving to the next.

Ulysses signaled to the choir by the side of the stage, and thirty voices rose in song as he made his way from the podium to a door at the rear of the stage. The orations exhausted him, and he was known to disappear for days to recharge his spirit, the burden of being the messenger of the word a heavy one he bore without complaint.

The crowd chanted along with the choir until the rafters were shaking from the volume of their voices, and Elijah supervised as scores of young boys circulated down the aisles with wheeled Walmart baskets to hold the donations of bullets that would rain into them like a deluge from heaven. By the time the hall emptied, they'd amassed a trove of ammo that would have been the envy of any warlord, which would join the mountain of precious stones and metals and ammo that the faithful had donated to encourage Ulysses to continue sharing the Good Word with them.

Elijah watched as the inner circle counted the rounds and took note of the contents of each basket before summing the numbers and arriving at a total that widened his eyes.

It had been an exceedingly productive sermon, which guaranteed that Ulysses's message, and by extension his influence and Elijah's, would continue to spread.

Elijah had no idea what his father's end run was going to be, and was worried over the worsening of his spells of late, but seeing the take from a single day dwarf everything they'd ever made on the road gave him confidence that even if his father faltered, he'd be able to seize the reins and guide the faithful.

"Get this locked up. I'm going to see how he's doing," Elijah ordered, and a trio of muscular bodyguards nodded and secured the baskets.

Elijah left through the same exit his father had used and walked across the enclosed street to the building that housed his inner sanctum. He took the steps to his father's suite of rooms and raised his fist to knock on the door, and then froze at the sound of his father yelling inside, his voice strident, and then angry, and then panicked.

Shouting words in a language nobody but Ulysses understood.

Elijah lowered his hand and stepped away, his face clouded. It was getting worse, not better. When they'd been traveling, Ulysses would occasionally "slip," as he called it, but lately the spells had become too regular for comfort.

Elijah retreated down the hall, lost in thought, his enthusiasm at the riches they'd collected replaced by a dread that seemed to permeate every fiber of his being.

Chapter 17

Salem, Oregon

Lucas, Sam, and Bill sat with Art and Ray by a small campfire near Clear Lake, six miles north of Salem. Sam was filling them in on the layout while the men rested, the march having been harder than many had bargained for. They'd crossed the river at Newberg and made their way south in a rain that had lasted most of the day, and now, two hours after nightfall, were debating how to proceed.

"We're going to have to do some reconnaissance," Art observed. "Chances are pretty good since we hit them and broke Sam's guys out of jail that they moved their operation. Only a moron would stay put after that."

"They aren't the sharpest," Sam said.

"Doesn't matter. I doubt they'll still be in city hall. Which means we need to find out where they are."

"So how do you want to do this?" Bill asked.

Lucas shifted and stared at the fire. "I can head in with a few faces they won't recognize. Nose around a bit."

"How many you figure we'll need?" Sam asked.

"Small group. Don't want to attract attention."

"Nobody will recognize me with this beard," Sam said. "I know my way around. I look pretty different than the last time we were here."

"Only need one more, then."

"I'll go!" Ray said. "My leg's healed."

"Sorry. You were with us when we broke Sam's group out. Can't take the chance. You got anyone, Bill?"

"Sure. Haley knows how to use a gun about as well as anyone, and he's been to Salem a bunch of times…before."

"We don't want to have to use any."

"You never know. Or if you want, I can tag along."

Lucas nodded. "That might be best. Don't know much about Haley's judgment. No offense."

"None taken."

"What are you thinking?" Art asked.

"Let's find a bar. Should be a few open, don't you think?" Lucas said, standing. He brushed off his pants and adjusted his hat. "Shouldn't need much other than our horses."

"Probably not," Sam said.

They covered the distance to Salem in half an hour and only saw a few people on the way. Once in the city center, they made their way to the area where the bars had been, and tied their horses at a watering trough at a place across the square from the one they'd frequented on their last trip. Laughter and a harmonica drifted from the front door, where a pair of bikers watched them approach.

"Gotta park your guns with us," one of them said.

Lucas nodded. "How late's it open?"

"Till the last drunk passes out."

They handed over their weapons and pushed through the door. The half-full interior reeked of stale beer and sweat. A few bikers sat at tables scattered around the room, but the patrons were mostly travelers like Lucas – not surprising, given that the locals had little to their names.

Bill ordered a round of the locally brewed beer, and a skinny woman in her forties brought them bottles. Her face was lined and hardened, as though whittled from driftwood washed up by a winter storm. Lucas paid with several bullets and gave her one as a tip, which obviously caught her by surprise.

"Thanks, handsome," she croaked in a voice scarred by time, alcohol, and more than a few hits from the meth pipe.

Lucas toasted the others and used the opportunity to look around the bar. It was too dangerous to try to strike up conversations with any of the bikers, and after finishing their beers, they decided the bartender didn't look like he would be particularly helpful.

The waitress returned and asked them if they wanted another round, and Lucas gave her a smile. "No, we're hitting the road. But I got a question for you."

One of her eyebrows twitched. "I get off at around two."

"Good to know, but we're riding out."

"Then…what?"

He indicated the bikers. "Where do they call home? We want to steer clear of them if we decide to spend the night here."

"I wouldn't ride at night if I were you. That's a good way to get bushwhacked," she warned.

"There's another round in it for you if you can tell me."

Her eyes narrowed. "Aw, hell, sweetheart, it ain't that hard. Everybody knows they took over the university after the blowup." She paused and lowered her voice. "They got beat up something fierce a few weeks back. Took the love out of them."

Lucas slid a 9mm round to her and nodded. "Then that's where we don't want to be."

"Damn straight. Meaner than snakes, every one of them," she whispered, and pocketed the bullet with a wink. "Name's Pearl. You change your mind about riding out, I'll be around later. I got nothin' special to do."

They retrieved their weapons from the bikers, who looked bored and angry, and mounted their horses.

"You know where the university is?" Lucas whispered to Sam.

He nodded. "It's about six blocks east of here, over by the capitol building."

"Lead the way."

They rode three blocks, and Sam slowed and dropped from his horse in front of a burned-out, abandoned building. Lucas and Bill did the same, and they walked their rides into the interior and lashed them to a pipe.

They made the rest of the way on foot and, when they reached the edge of the campus, stopped across the street in the gloom. Sam pointed to the barbed-wire fence encircling the grounds. "See that? Two men. Looks like a patrol." He drew a long breath. "Didn't used to have a fence around it. They must be nervous. Looks like a lot of work went into that."

Time passed, and the pair continued along the fence, walking slowly. Lucas remained motionless as he watched them disappear, and Bill started to say something when Lucas cut him off and indicated another patrol coming from the opposite direction.

When it had moved on, Lucas shook his head. "Seems like they're on alert, doesn't it?"

Sam nodded. "Probably paranoid after we stole their horses."

"Or they're afraid you'll come back and finish the job," Lucas observed. "There's got to be a way in besides the entry points."

Sam grinned in the darkness. "Funny you mention that. There's a creek that runs through the campus. Mill Stream. We might be able to use that to get on the grounds."

Lucas grunted. "Show me."

They crept along the main road's gridlocked cars and stopped at a stream that ran beneath a pedestrian walkway. Lucas eyed it. "This goes all the way through the campus?"

Sam nodded. "That's right. I remember it well from my misspent youth."

"Be hell to get a big force through that culvert," Bill observed. "Maybe if we had all night."

Laughter drifted on the breeze from the university buildings, and Lucas's nose twitched at the smell of marijuana smoke. They pulled back into the shadows, and four bikers sauntered toward the creek, passing a joint around. Lucas froze and watched them smoke, and when they left, he leaned into Sam and whispered, "You say it runs through the campus. Where's the other end of it let out?"

"East."

"Too much action around here for my liking. Let's give that a look."

Chapter 18

Rocky Mountains, Colorado

Duke rode alongside Ellen, with the sisters bringing up the rear. They'd made good time the first day, and by nightfall had found a clearing in the foothills that was perfect to make camp. Duke didn't want to risk a fire, so they'd pitched tents, and Ellen had joined him in his, snuggling with him for warmth. That had progressed to kissing, and before long Duke's interest in her had been unmistakable.

She broke off their embrace, breathing heavily. "I'm sorry, Duke. I…I want to. I do. But not like this."

"I understand," he said, his voice tight.

"It's just…I've never been with a man. I swore I wouldn't till I got married."

Duke absorbed that. "Never?"

"Remember the church? That's who ran things, so I wasn't the only one. We were all pretty strict about that. Everyone believed that the collapse was God taking vengeance on sinners, and nobody wanted to tempt fate."

"What about the son?"

She frowned. "He didn't have to follow the rules."

"How does that make any sense?"

"It doesn't. It was the hypocrisy of it, everyone pretending they didn't know what he was up to, that got to us."

"I can see why."

She stared at him in the darkness and kissed him again. "Is that a…is it a problem?"

"Not at all. I mean, I just… It's been a long time since I've been around a woman for any length of time, so I'm not great at explaining things." He paused. "But it isn't a problem. I guess I'm just surprised. I kinda figured most did whatever they felt like nowadays…"

"If they're living like animals, maybe. That's not how I want to live."

"No argument."

"Is everyone married at this town we're going to?"

"I don't know. I mean, for those it's important to, I imagine so."

"I don't want our children to grow up without morals, Duke. That isn't how I was raised. I learned right from wrong young."

"Our children?"

Ellen took a deep breath. "I'm sorry. I know that's presumptuous. Sometimes my words get ahead of me. It's just that I thought… I felt… Well, I know what I'm looking for, and it seemed over the past few days that maybe you were looking for the same thing."

Duke pulled her close. "Don't hear me arguing." He cradled her in his arms until her breathing slowed and she fell asleep, and he lay in the darkness with eyes wide, trying to make sense out of the good fortune that had dropped in his lap. A gorgeous, smart woman wanted him – no, not just wanted him, but wanted to have a family with him. His heart swelled at the thought, and as he drifted off, a smile spread across his face and stayed there most of the night.

The following day was harder than the first, all uphill, through gorges and along fire roads long fallen into disrepair. Several times the horses slipped at the edges of ravines, and Duke slowed their pace to one that would ensure they made it in one piece.

Dusk was darkening the sky by the time they made it to the valley, where a host of new log cabins had been erected and the air was sweet with the smell of pine-fueled cooking fires.

Ellen pulled her horse closer to Duke and murmured to him, "What's the name of this place? It looks like it hasn't been here long."

Duke beamed at her. "Doesn't have an official name, but the locals call it Shangri-La."

Ellen took in the sight. "Like heaven."

"Close to it as it gets around here."

Elliot and Michael, his second-in-command, greeted them as they rode toward the geothermal plant.

"Glad to see you made it, Duke," Elliot said. "And these must be the young ladies you mentioned?" he asked, smiling at the sisters and Ellen.

They dismounted, and Duke made introductions. Elliot invited them to dine with him at a rough-hewn plank table by a large fire pit. The carcass of a deer was roasting in the flames, and bowls were set out with squash and mushrooms. "Don't worry," he advised. "They aren't poisonous."

"I'm going to do the rounds, Elliot. Pleased to meet you ladies," Michael said, tipping his hat.

Residents passed by and introduced themselves as they ate, and as they were finishing up, Sierra arrived with Eve and Tim. Duke invited them to sit, and Sierra did while Eve played with Tim near the fire.

"How old are they?" Ellen asked her.

"Five and ten."

"They're adorable. You must be very proud. What are their names?"

"Tim, short for Timothy, and that's Eve."

"Eve. What a beautiful name. Is it common here?"

Sierra shrugged. "Not really. She's the only Eve I've ever met, actually. I just liked the name."

Duke regaled Elliot and Sierra with the story of the rescue from the scavengers, and then the sisters shared stories from the road. Ellen finished it off by telling Elliot about the church and all the good people who were in its thrall, and he shook his head in disapproval.

"It's sad when folks put all their faith in an authority to see them to safety. I've always said I'm eager to hire my replacement if anyone's stupid enough to want the job."

Duke laughed. "Don't let Elliot fool you. He's a tyrant."

The fire burned low, and Elliot pulled Duke aside while Sierra showed the women to a newly built cabin for the night. "They seem nice enough. Glad you were able to bring them to us. Now we just need a hundred more like them and we'll be in business."

"Well, I might be hanging around here more often, so I can help out with anything you're too shorthanded to do."

"Really! What about the trading post?"

"If Ellen and I wind up getting hitched, I'll probably split my time or something."

Elliot couldn't hide his surprise. "Hitched? Why…congratulations. But…that's rather sudden, isn't it?"

"She seems willing to have me. I figure I'd better do it before she comes to her senses."

"Hmm. Far be it for me to comment on affairs of the heart. I hope it works out for you. From what little I've seen of her, she seems absolutely lovely."

"She is. She's a keeper."

Elliot watched Duke walk toward the cabin, his bushy white eyebrows a solid line, and eventually shook his head in bemusement and looked up at the moon. "Life's constant surprises," he whispered, and then walked over to the fire to stamp out the last of the embers before doddering off to sleep.

Chapter 19

Salem, Oregon

Sam crept through the ruins of a large building on the east side of the campus a hundred yards from the university, where Mill Stream snaked its way beneath a major thoroughfare before entering the grounds. It had taken twenty minutes to make their way to the area without being seen, and the air was getting colder with each passing moment. Smoke drifted over the city from all the wood fires burning to keep the denizens warm, creating a heavy pall that irritated the men's throats and invited coughing that would give them away.

They reached the creek and paused, eyeing the opening beneath the road through which it flowed. The interior was pitch black but wide enough to simultaneously accommodate the passage of multiple gunmen, so far better than the access point on the west side of the campus. Lucas switched on his NV scope and scanned the space. The scope blinked a low-battery warning, and he cursed his failure to remember to charge the spares.

"What do you think?" Sam asked.

"Should work," Lucas said. "Assuming we can get five hundred men through downtown without being seen."

"We can come in from the east," Sam said. "That part of town's been abandoned by all but a few scavengers. It's too difficult to defend from raiders, so everybody's concentrated nearer the city center."

Lucas glanced at Bill. "What about you?"

"We should take a hard look at what's in there and how fast we can get a decent number of fighters through."

Lucas nodded. "Agreed."

They moved toward the overpass and entered the covered opening, walking largely blind, with a foot and a half of water swirling around their legs. Sam took point and inched along. The span was about twenty feet wide by ten high and stank of urine and decay. They were nearly to the campus side when his ankle snagged something, and he froze.

"Don't move," he warned.

"What is it?" Bill asked.

"Tripwire."

Lucas took a deep breath. "If it's connected to a grenade, we're history. Bill, back off," he said. "Sam, once we're clear, run after us."

Bill was already in motion when Lucas bolted back the way they'd come. He called to Sam as he neared the opening, and Sam tore after him, his boots splashing noisily through the water.

A blast tore through the tunnel, and Lucas and Sam threw themselves into the water. Flame and shrapnel blew past them, and then they were back on their feet and running hard, their ears ringing from the detonation. Voices yelled from the campus, and an assault rifle opened up from the overpass. Water fountained around them as they reached the east side, and Sam grunted and went down.

Lucas went back for him and pulled him to his feet.

"You hit?" he demanded.

"No. Slipped on a rock."

Bill was waiting on the bank as they reached the shore, Sam limping from a twisted ankle, and more gunfire erupted from the other side of the tunnel. Bill returned fire, loosing a dozen rounds at the shooter, and then spun and took off, not waiting to see whether he'd slowed their pursuers. Lucas helped Sam along and, when the shooting from the campus side resumed, released him and turned with his M4 in hand.

"Go with Bill. I'll cover you."

Sam hastened after Bill, and Lucas fired two three-round bursts down the creek, hoping it would give the bikers second thoughts about following. He wished he had a grenade to toss beneath the overpass, but it would have been hard to explain to the bouncers at the bar, so they'd stuck with the arms normal trail jockeys would carry.

More shooting answered his volleys, but the gunmen were firing blind. He spotted a few figures on the far side of the overpass in his scope and squeezed off a final burst, and then sprinted toward the ruined building. Someone yelled orders from beneath the overpass as he reached the walls.

Bill and Sam were waiting inside what was left of the structure.

"So much for surprise," Bill said.

"Either of you hurt?" Lucas asked.

"Just my ankle. But it's not broken."

"Can you run?"

"If it's a choice between that or being shot, you bet."

Several guns chattered from the creek, and bullets whined off the building's walls.

"Bill, help Sam," Lucas said. "Head into the abandoned neighborhood. I'll hold them off as long as I can."

"You sure?"

More shooting from the stream cut him off. "Move," Lucas ordered.

Sam leaned on Bill for support, and they trotted through the building to a collapsed section at the far end where the night sky was visible. Lucas studied the bikers again for a while and waited until he could make one out in the water. He switched to single fire, and the gun bucked against his shoulder. The man went down with a splash, and instantly four muzzle flashes lit his NV scope, telling him what he was up against.

The building provided good cover, but four against one was still bad odds. If Sam hadn't been injured, he would have emptied his magazine at the bikers and taken off like a scared rabbit, but he needed to buy Bill and Sam some time, which meant a gun battle where a single lucky shot or ricochet could take him down.

Lucas moved to another spot and fired twice at an approaching shooter. He didn't wait for a response and ran ten yards along the wall to a window opening and peered out, waiting. There was no more gunfire for several seconds, and then the clink of metal on cement sounded from where he'd just been.

He threw himself behind a pile of rubble, and a grenade detonated with a roar. Lucas knew that they'd rush the building immediately after the explosion, and ejected his spent magazine and slapped another in place. He wouldn't have time to find new cover before they appeared, so the rubble would have to do.

Two bikers came through the doorway at the same time with guns blazing. Lucas drilled the first one through the throat and switched to three-round burst as the second dove to the side, evading his fire. He squeezed off a burst as the man freed another grenade from his vest, and one of Lucas's rounds hit his leg. The gunman screamed in pain and dropped the grenade, and Lucas cringed as it exploded. The force of the detonation shook the rafters and sprayed his rubble pile with shrapnel and biker.

Lucas forced himself to his feet and moved back to the window just in time to see another slew of dark forms emerge from the darkness beneath the overpass. He debated picking off some of them, but decided against it – there were too many. Right now they had no way of knowing whether the grenades had finished Lucas off, and he saw nothing to be gained by offering them any information about his continued existence.

He spun and made for the collapsed area where Bill and Sam had disappeared, and had just passed through it when shots rang out behind him and rounds ricocheted off the brick by his head. Then he was around the corner and running as fast as he could, covering the ground between the building and the first of the wood-frame homes across the road in record time. He disappeared into its side yard, hopefully before the bikers would be able to make it through the building.

"Lucas!" Bill called from his right.

He veered toward another structure and spotted Bill and Sam by its side. Lucas ran to them, and they ducked around it and then hastened together through a grove of trees before emerging at a parking lot on the far side.

"We need to get the horses," Lucas said. "We can circle back. They'll assume we took off into that neighborhood. That would be the smart thing to do."

"Which is why we won't?" Sam asked.

"I'm not leaving Tango behind. And you're not walking out of here under your own steam."

"Fair point."

A long building loomed in front of them. "What's that?" Lucas asked.

"Another school," Sam said.

"What's west of it?"

"Big road, train tracks, and the hospital, far as I remember."

"Is there enough for us to get lost in?"

"Should be. As long as we stay off the streets."

"Then let's go."

Torchlight illuminated the university grounds as they circled around it. The bikers were now on full alert, and any hope of launching a surprise attack was lost. Fortunately for Lucas, they seemed reluctant to leave the campus, which made sense – they had no way of knowing whether the attack had been intended to draw them out so they could be ambushed, or even how many had been responsible for the incursion.

Lucas switched off his scope, aware that he'd need the juice if they ran into any more threats.

Forty minutes later, they reached their horses and were in the saddle.

"Now what?" Bill asked.

"We're going to need something heavier than rifles to tackle them now they're locked down in the buildings," Lucas said. "Not sure the grenades are going to be enough."

"Then…what?" Sam asked.

"Mortars, at the very least. Howitzers would be better, but…"

Sam nodded. "I know a guy who raided the national guard armory after the virus hit. He cleaned the place out with his buds and now makes a living selling ordnance."

"Where is he?"

"Over on Minto Island. He's kind of a hermit out there."

"Think you could find his place?"

"Sure."

"Then that's our next stop."

"You still thinking of doing this tonight?"

Lucas nodded. "An hour before dawn. They'll be dead tired by then from the stress of staying awake all night. If we can use their nerves against them, that'll go a long way."

"Or we could wait until tomorrow night."

Lucas shook his head. "That'll give them a chance to move or to harden the area further. Right now they don't know what's outside the walls, so they won't risk trying to put snipers in the surrounding buildings, or any of the rest of the things they should do. But by tomorrow they'll have figured it out. So it's tonight, whether we like it or not."

Bill nodded. "He's right. But if it's rifles against rifles, they'll have the advantage firing from defensive positions. They can just pick us off as we try to overwhelm them."

"Bill, ride back and tell Art what happened," Lucas said. "We'll meet up with you as soon as we've got what we need."

Bill regarded him and then jerked his horse's head to the right. "Good luck."

Sam and Lucas watched him ride away.

"How far's your buddy from here?" Lucas asked.

"Couple of miles downriver. Not much there besides his place." He hesitated. "I've got to warn you, though, he's an ornery old bastard. He's as likely to shoot us as to greet us at this hour."

"Let's go wake him up."

Chapter 20

Amber Hot Springs, Colorado

Duke slumbered in his tent outside the cabin where the women were sleeping. The moon was a golden disk in the night sky surrounded by a constellation of glimmering stars, their light bathing the hot springs in a pale glow. Predawn gusts of wind tugged at the tent's fabric, dented the treetops, and drove sprays of dust along the main path that connected the string of dwellings.

The door of the cabin opened, and Ellen's head popped out. She glanced in both directions before her gaze settled on the thermal plant seventy-five yards away. She stepped out and the sisters followed her toward the plant, leaving the cabin door open, their saddles over their shoulders.

They stopped at the fenced-in clearing that served as the town's corral, and their horses whinnied and trotted over to them. Monica unfastened the rope that bound the makeshift gate closed and let them out, and the women saddled them up with silent efficiency. Tracie ran back to the cabin and returned with the saddlebags, and then they led the horses along the central path until they were near Sierra's cabin.

Ellen tied her animal to a low branch, and the sisters did the same. The horses stood obediently, watching with silent eyes. Monica removed a length of rope from one of her saddlebags and Tracie did the same, and Ellen removed a bundle of rags from hers. She turned to Monica and nodded, and they walked resolutely together to the cabin door, where they paused and listened.

A minute went by, and Ellen nodded and pushed on the door. It opened, its rope hinges silent, and they stepped into a single darkened room. The only light came from two windows cut from the wood, empty of glass.

Sierra was lying on her side on a bedroll on the floor with Eve beside her, a heavy wool blanket over them. Tim had his own bedroll on the other side of the room. Ellen handed Tracie a rag and signaled for her to move to where the boy slept. As she did so, Monica and Ellen edged toward Sierra, who stirred when one of the floorboards creaked.

Ellen and Monica froze and waited until Sierra exhaled softly and pulled the blanket to her chin. They exchanged a glance, and then Ellen stood over her, rifle in one hand and rags in the other.

Sierra must have sensed the movement, because she half sat up and cracked her eyes open.

"Wha–"

Ellen slammed Sierra in the head with her AK, and she fell back against the bedroll, stunned.

Ellen set her gun on the floor, and she and Monica moved quickly when Eve awoke and sprang to her feet. Ellen grabbed the little girl's arms, and Monica jammed a rag into her mouth so she couldn't scream. Eve struggled against Ellen's grip, but she was no match for the woman's strength, and Monica ducked behind her and tied her wrists using a length of rope while she squirmed and sobbed into the rag.

Tim woke up and found himself staring down the muzzle of Tracie's pistol. Ellen crossed the room in a few steps and jammed a rag into his mouth.

"Tie him up," she whispered, and looked him dead in the eyes. "You make a peep and we'll kill your mommy – understand?"

Tears welled in his eyes, and he snuffled as he nodded once. Tracie holstered her gun and bound his wrists and then his ankles, using the same length of rope.

Sierra moaned, and Monica looked to Ellen, who drew her revolver and pointed it at Sierra's head.

"Don't say a word or I'll blow your brains out," she threatened in a low voice. She tossed Monica a rag, and Monica jammed it in Sierra's mouth, ignoring the blood running from her hairline.

Sierra kicked at her, but her reflexes were impaired from the blow, and she missed. Ellen booted her in the ribs, and she moaned and curled into a ball.

Monica roughly tied Sierra's hands and legs. Ellen watched, one hand on Eve's bindings to keep her from bolting for the door. When Monica was finished, she stepped back and inspected her work in the dim moonlight. Ellen nodded and looked to Tracie.

"Come on," she whispered, and the three of them dragged Eve from the cabin and out into the frigid night. She struggled and tried to kick them, but her forty pounds wasn't up to doing any damage, and they easily manhandled her to the horses.

Ellen knelt so she was at eye level and frowned at the little girl. "You keep putting up a fight and I'll go back and slit your mother's throat, understand? So if you want her to die, keep it up."

Eve's eyes widened and she shook her head. Ellen slid a wicked-looking hunting knife from a belt scabbard and held it up so the light glinted from its blade. Eve whimpered into the rag, and Ellen nodded. The little girl wouldn't pose any more problem.

Ellen swung into the saddle, and Tracie and Monica lifted Eve and draped her over the horse's shoulders, facedown in front of the saddle horn. Tracie untied the reins and handed them to Ellen, and then did the same with her horse and climbed into the saddle. Monica did as well and slid her rifle sling from her shoulder and looked to Ellen, who nodded and wheeled her mount towards the main track that led out of town.

The horses followed the dirt strip between the cabins, nothing stirring in any of the dwellings. They reached the edge of the clearing, and a voice called out from behind them.

"You! Hold it right there!"

They spurred their horses forward, and Ellen's and Tracie's took off at a gallop. Monica spun and emptied half her magazine at the approaching figures. The shots shattered the valley's calm as the burst cut both men down. One of them screamed as he dropped, and then Monica was in motion, her horse bolting after the others, its hooves thumping against the hard-packed ground.

The closest guard squeezed off a blast from his shotgun that went badly wide, and then the shotgun slipped from his grip as he bled out. Cabin doors flew open, and startled residents emerged with rifles in hand and ran barefoot to the fallen guards as others swept the surroundings with their guns in case of attack.

Arnold and Elliot approached with a lantern and a pair of assault rifles and stopped at the first of the fallen guards. Duke came at a run with his M16 at present arms, his hair askew, eyes wild.

"What the–" he started, but Arnold cut him off with a curt gesture.

"Shhh. They could still be watching us."

"Who?"

"I don't know." He turned to the throng of men that had gathered around him. "Set up a perimeter and keep your wits about you."

Duke looked down the trail. "Why would anyone shoot the guards and not keep coming?"

Arnold shrugged. "I have no idea. Maybe they were trying to sneak into town and rob some of the cabins in silence. The guards stopped them, and the shooting drove them off."

He stooped over the second guard, who was gasping for breath.

"Did you see who did this?" Arnold asked.

"I… Three…"

"Three shooters?"

A rattle from the dying man's throat answered, and then a groan. He died halfway through an exhalation and shuddered and lay still.

Arnold straightened. "Could have been scavengers. But that's not how they usually work."

Duke eyed the dead men and shook his head. "Bastards. What was the point?"

Arnold turned to face the crowd. Elliot stepped forward, knelt beside the dead man, and closed his eyes. When he stood, his expression was grim. "I don't know," Elliot said. "But whoever they were, they're going to pay for this. Two good men dead for nothing. That won't go unanswered."

Chapter 21

Salem, Oregon

A mist threaded through the reeds like ghostly fingers along the road to Minto Island. The air was heavy with the smell of the nearby water and wet grass mingled with wood smoke that seemed to permeate everything. Sam rode ahead of Lucas, guiding them down the railroad tracks, the night quiet except for the rush of the Willamette River to the west.

He slowed and Lucas caught up to him. Sam pointed at a farmhouse surrounded by a brick wall, topped by coils of barbed wire and what looked suspiciously like a machine gun nest on the roof.

"Is that what I think it is?"

Sam nodded. "Clovis kept a .50-caliber Browning for home defense. He's never had a problem with anyone trying to break in, so it was a good move. Even the bikers give him a wide berth. He let everyone know he was itching for an excuse to use it, and they believe him. If you knew the man, you'd understand why."

"Smart. Wonder if he's got any more of them?"

"If he doesn't shoot us, you can ask him."

"How well do you know him?"

"Well enough, but it's been a few years. Let's hope his memory isn't gone."

They turned off the tracks and rode toward the compound. When they reached the steel slab gate, Sam pulled on a rope hanging on one side, and a bell clanged at the house. They waited a few minutes, and when nobody answered, Sam yanked it again, this time several times.

"You got any idea what time it is?" a voice called from behind the gate. "The hell's wrong with you?"

"Clove! It's Sam. From the camp. Sorry to wake you."

"Sam? I thought you was dead."

"Only half."

A phlegmy cough answered, and then a plate in the gate slid to the side and a weathered, pockmarked face with a bulbous nose and a web of ruptured capillaries running across it stared out at them. "Who's the cowboy?"

"Friend of mine."

"Yeah? What do you boys want at this hour? I need my beauty rest. You're lucky I didn't open up on you when you rang the bell."

"Lucas here's got a need for some stuff." Sam paused. "The kind you keep in the cellar."

"You got something to trade?" Clovis asked, focusing on Lucas.

Lucas nodded. "Sure do."

"This ain't no dollar store," Clovis warned, and shut the slab. A moment later, the gate groaned to the side on a wheeled track and opened just enough for them to ride through one at a time.

Clovis shut the door behind them and slid a railroad spike into the clasp. "You can tie up your nags over there," he said, indicating a hitching post.

They dismounted and waited for him to shuffle toward the house. His bathroom slippers were filthy and worn, and his gray sweatpants and Willamette University sweatshirt stained and rumpled. "Well, come on in, then. No point in freezing out here."

He escorted them into a large living room that was surprisingly clean, its Spartan furnishings dusted and gleaming in the LED lighting. Clovis sat down in a leather reclining chair and indicated a sofa. They sat, and he gave Lucas a rheumy stare.

"So you need some gear?"

Lucas nodded. "That's right. The heavier the better."

"How heavy?"

"I'll take whatever you've got. Mortars, .50 cals, grenades, antitank rockets, you name it."

Clovis's eyebrows rose. "You fixin' to start a war?"

"You could say that."

"With who?"

Lucas matched his stare. "That got anything to do with our business?"

Sam intruded. "Clovis isn't a big fan of authority."

"I'd have never guessed."

"So who you fixin' to hit with all this?" Clovis repeated.

Lucas eyed Sam, who nodded.

"The bikers in Salem," Sam said.

Clovis cackled, and it degraded into another racking cough. When he caught his breath, he shook his head. "Just you two? Gonna need a tank at the very least."

"We've got friends," Sam said. "But the bikers have good gear, too."

"But they don't know how to use it. Buncha pussies, if you ask me." Clovis squinted at them. "How many men you need to equip?"

"A lot. But we're already fixed up with rifles and ammo and a few grenades."

"How you plan to pay for all this? It's a tall order."

"Gold," Lucas said.

"Now you're talking. How much?"

"As much as it takes."

Clovis stood with a broad grin. "Then come to my office and I'll show you what I got." He looked to Sam. "You vouching for him?"

Sam nodded. "I brought him here, didn't I?"

Clovis stared him down. "What happened to your leg?"

"Tripped."

"You look like you been dragged back of a mule train and put away wet."

"And I don't feel so great, either."

Another cackle. "Doesn't get any better from here, boys."

Clovis walked into the dining room and rolled a rug to the side, revealing a trapdoor in the floor. He grunted with effort and lifted it wide, and then reached for an LED flashlight on a side table. "Right this way, gents."

They took a flight of wooden stairs down to a large basement stacked floor to ceiling with wooden crates. Clovis tapped on a three-foot-long green steel box a few paces away from the bottom of the stairs. "60mm mortars. Six crates of high-explosive shells right over there. Perfect condition. Wrapped in oilcloth." He continued to another box. "Mk 19 Mod 3 grenade launcher. Ten cans of grenade belts, forty-eight to a belt." He paused again by still another longer one. "M30. Heavier than lead, but packs a wallop. Fires a 120mm round. Got four crates of those. Took a portable crane to get it down here through the other door." He pointed into the depths. "And I got two Brownings with a building full of .50 cal, but I'd only sell one, and it won't be cheap."

"I'll take the mortars and all six crates of shells, and if you can sell me any horses to carry them, the Mk 19 and three cans of ammo." Lucas paused. "And the Browning with ten thousand rounds. If everything works as advertised, I'll be back to buy all the rest."

Clovis eyed him skeptically. "Browning, mortars, Mk 19, projectiles and shells…that's gonna cost."

"Give me a number. We're on a tight schedule."

Clovis did a quick mental calculation and named a weight in gold. Lucas countered, and after some dickering, they had a bargain.

Lucas climbed the steps, went to his saddlebags, and returned with the gold. He counted out sixteen Maple Leafs and handed them over. Clovis inspected each with the flashlight and then balanced one on the tip of his finger and struck the edge with another. A high-pitched ringing resonated from the coin, and he repeated the process with each before he nodded in satisfaction.

"I'm too old to haul this crap upstairs," he said. "But you fellas look more than capable. I'll go get a couple of ponies fixed with a harness and cart to carry this, assuming you promise to return it when you're done."

Lucas nodded. "Deal."

Lucas began heaving crates of shells up the steps, and Sam followed him unsteadily, grimacing occasionally when he put weight on his injured ankle. They had everything piled at the back door by the time Clovis showed up again with a pair of chestnut mares and a wheeled cart with a motorcycle tire at each corner.

"Built it myself. Everything you saw came in on that thing, so it'll work for you. Pretty decent on terrain, too, if you want to stay off the roads."

"Perfect," Sam said.

Lucas opened each crate and inspected the shells, and then did the same with the three mortars and the grenade launcher. When he was finished, they piled the boxes on the cart and were breathing heavily by the time they were done.

"How long till sunup?" Sam asked.

"What do I look like, an almanac?" Clovis replied, and laughed. "I reckon maybe four, five hours."

Lucas nodded. "Then we can still make it."

"How many men you say you have?" Clovis asked. "Heard there's maybe a couple of hundred bikers."

"Enough," Lucas replied.

"Hundreds," Sam finished for him.

"Any of 'em used to be in the military? If so, they'll know how to use the mortars, although it'll take some practice to get your ranges right."

"A few."

"Then you're set. Horses are Sue and Molly."

"They look fit."

"Take good care of 'em. They're like my daughters. They're good girls."

"If you hear a bunch of explosions, stay in bed," Sam said.

Clovis eyed the cart. "Wouldn't want to be on the receiving end of that."

"That's the general idea," Sam confirmed. "Though I don't think anyone will be brokenhearted that they get what's coming to them, do you?"

"I stay out of this stuff. War's a young man's game. I just sell the miners picks and shovels and wish 'em well."

They saddled up, and Clovis handed Sam the reins to the pair of mares. "They'll follow without giving you any trouble."

Sam took the reins and grinned. "Thanks for everything, Clove."

"Hope it works out for you. I'd love to sell the rest and retire for good. Not a lot of market for heavy stuff like that, and everyone and their brother has a rifle or three." He regarded Lucas. "You think you'll need any 5.56? The basement's lousy with it."

"We might. I'll let you know later."

They left Clovis's compound and turned up the main road, and Lucas slowed. "You know the way back to the camp better than I do, Sam, and can lead the men to the university. I'll take the cart to the hospital and wait for you there. Tell Art about the stuff I got, and have his best ex-marines meet me there. The rest of the men should stage in that deserted neighborhood so we don't hit them while we're setting our range on the mortars."

"It'll take me at least an hour to get back without being spotted."

"That should work. As long as the men can be in position well before sunup, we'll be fine. I want to start lobbing shells an hour before. Once we have our range, tell Art I want the men to ring the place so anyone trying to escape gets taken out. And when everything starts, come to the hospital. I may need you to go back to Clovis's if we need more mortar rounds."

"You thinking of just bombing them out?"

Lucas nodded. "If we can avoid any of our people getting hurt, that's a win. If we turn the school into a crater, that should get the job done."

"I almost feel sorry for the bikers."

"Don't. They've ridden roughshod over Portland for years. They're predators. Anything they get, they've done worse to others."

Sam smiled. "I said almost."

"How's the ankle?"

"Throbbing, but I'll live."

"Good. Tell Art I also have the grenade launcher. Have him find someone who knows how to work it. If we can haul it up to the roof, it should do some real damage."

Sam regarded Lucas. "Remind me never to get on your bad side."

"This is strictly business. I promised I'd help, and I'm doing so. But the fewer casualties we take in the process, the happier I'll be."

"Got it. Figure we'll be back in…three hours or so, best case."

"Ride hard and see if you can cut that by a half hour."

"I will. You able to find the hospital from here?"

"North, and then to the right. Easy."

Sam nodded. "See you in a few."

"Hope so."

Sam rode off, and Lucas gave the cart horse reins a flap. "Come on, girls. Just you and me now. Let's see if we can find someplace safe you can rest while we get down to business."

The mares started forward. Lucas studied the skyline and spotted the hospital a mile away, and after wrapping the cart reins around his saddle horn, he freed his M4 and pointed Tango at the building. The cart rolled behind them on well-greased wheels, its load of death and destruction about to be put to lethal use.

Chapter 22

Lucas shifted the aim of his rifle at the sound of running boots below his perch on the second floor of the hospital. The cart was inside what had once been the main lobby, and he'd left the horses in a grove of trees far enough from the building that they wouldn't be hurt if the bikers targeted it with heavy weapons of their own.

Six men came at a run, and Lucas recognized Henry from the squatters. He lowered his rifle and hailed them.

"Up here. Stuff's through the double doors. Grab a crate and come on up."

He'd moved the mortars into the patient room he was occupying, but had left the heavier shells for the men. Henry and his group reached him a couple of minutes later, sweating in spite of the cool temperature.

Lucas showed them the three mortars and addressed Henry. "You know how to work these?"

Henry nodded. "We all do. But we'll need someone to spot for us unless we're high enough to see where the shells are landing."

"We'll shoot from the roof. That do it?"

Henry grinned. "Sure will."

"How about this thing?" Lucas asked, patting the container with the Mk 19.

"I've used one before," one of the men said.

"Good. Then you're our man. What's your name?"

"Terry."

"Okay, Terry. Last but not least, we have a new .50-cal Browning."

"Jesus. That'll annihilate anything that gets in its way."

"That's the general idea. Who's fired one?"

Four of the men, including Henry, nodded.

"Perfect. Whoever's a better shot gets first dibs. I've got four cases of ammo belts on the cart, so once we're in position, go down and bring up the rest."

"Will do."

They climbed the service stairs to the roof six stories above the street and carried their loads to the lip. The university was across the boulevard, its buildings clearly defined even in the darkness.

Sam appeared from the stairwell a minute later carrying an ammo can loaded with a .50-cal belt.

"Everyone's in position. Art had some of the men take over the state capitol building across the street from the university on the far side. It's a good position to fire from and built out of concrete, so it'll stop anything they throw at it."

"What about the perimeter?"

"We got shooters every ten yards in the surrounding buildings." Sam held up a radio. "Art's got the other one. He's sitting at the capitol with runners if you have any change of orders. They're under instructions to only fire if the bikers try to make a break for it."

"Good work," Lucas said.

"So how we gonna do this?" Henry asked.

"Set up the Browning. We'll bomb them until they start scattering, and then use the Browning to take down any that make it out of the buildings." He pointed to where torches were burning. "What's that?"

"Baxter Hall. Looks like that's what they're using as headquarters, doesn't it?"

"How many yards from here you think it is?"

Sam did a calculation. "Maybe…four hundred yards?"

Henry shook his head. "I make it more like five."

Sam shrugged. "Maybe. I'm not the best with distances."

Lucas nodded. "Set the mortar up at four-fifty. Don't want to overshoot and hit the capitol building."

Henry went to work while Lucas and one of the men set the Browning on its tripod and Terry loaded a belt. Lucas watched him work and, when he was finished, walked to the edge of the roof and peered at the campus. "Not too bright to light up their headquarters like that."

"Assuming it isn't a feint," Sam said.

"Doubt it. For all they know, it was just a couple of scavengers back at the creek."

"Maybe. But they have to be shaken."

"We'll know in a few." Lucas turned to Henry. "You ready?"

"Yup. I'll use one tube for now, and then once we have the range, we can bring the other two into play. Alan, you're the best shot of all of us. You work the Browning."

"Perfect." Lucas held out his hand to Sam for the radio, which Sam passed to him, and he depressed the transmit button. "We're going to start in a minute. Hold your fire until they try to run for it. Over."

He released the button, and Art's voice droned from the small speaker. "Roger that. Good hunting."

Lucas stepped away from the roof edge and nodded to Henry, who dropped a shell into the tube. It exploded skyward with a crack, and they held their breaths as they waited to see where it fell.

An orange fireball blasted from the roof of a building to the southwest of the hall, and Henry grunted and adjusted the mortar, sliding the base to the left and lowering it a small amount. When he was satisfied with the new positioning, one of the men handed him another projectile and he dropped it into the tube. It shot out with a whump and then a moment later detonated on the right wing of the hall.

"Bingo," Henry said, and called for another mortar. He set it up in under a minute and had one of the men fire it after he'd taken another shot with his.

More explosions rocked the building, and Terry called out, "I got men coming through the front entrance."

"Have at it," Lucas said, and Alan began firing the Browning in short bursts of twenty to thirty rounds at a time. Lucas raised his rifle and switched on the scope, and saw the brick behind the approximately twenty men on the steps disintegrate from the big slugs. He wished they had NV goggles for Alan to use, but settled for yelling guidance. "You're shooting over their heads. Drop your aim a hair."

Alan did as instructed, and the tall grass in the courtyard in front of the building sprayed dirt before several of the bikers dropped, hit by the rounds.

"Got a couple. I'd put a few hundred into the entry for good measure."

More explosions echoed across the campus as Henry's mortars continued to rain down on the building, blasting showers of brick and roof through the air and onto the surrounding grounds. Sam limped over to Lucas's side and nudged him. "Can I get a look through your scope?"

"Sure."

Lucas handed the M4 to him, and Sam raised it and surveyed the area. An instant later he lowered it and turned to Lucas with an alarmed expression.

"They've got a Browning on the roof of the—"

His warning was cut off by the stutter of the other machine gun. A moment later the glass façade on the floor beneath them shattered and sprayed into the night, and everyone threw themselves flat on the roof to avoid being hit.

Alan screamed in pain and fell backward, and the Browning's barrel rose to point at the stars. Lucas dog-crawled to him and saw instantly that the damage caused by two of the .50-caliber rounds was fatal. He hissed at Henry, who was lying with his hands over his head.

"Drop everything you can on that shooter. He's got us pinned down. Must have tracked us from the muzzle flash of our Browning."

Henry called to one of the men to slide a crate of shells to him, and once he had them, he dropped one into the first mortar and then another into the second. He continued until the entire crate was empty, nudging the base each time so it shifted the targeting minutely.

Lucas eyed the enemy nest through his scope, and the shooter was still there. The area around the building looked like the sky had rained death, but the sniper was still intact for all the damage.

Lucas made an adjustment on his scope and switched the firing selector to single fire, and then propped the barrel against the roof lip. At five hundred yards, he was near the rifle's maximum effective range, but with little wind and a ton of luck, he might manage a kill shot. He sighted the reticule squarely on the biker's torso as the man continued to blast at them, and exhaled as he squeezed the trigger.

The round sent a fountain of roof gravel into the air two feet to the shooter's left and a good ten feet short. Lucas painstakingly made more adjustments, then leveled the weapon again and fired. This time the round struck a foot to the biker's right, but at roughly the same latitude.

Another tweak, and he tried again, ignoring the high-velocity rounds snapping overhead as the biker shredded the rooftop with .50-cal rounds. Lucas settled the scope on the man's chest and squeezed off another shot. A second later, the biker jerked and grabbed at his shoulder as he ducked beneath the cinderblocks that surrounded the nest.

The low-battery warning intruded on Lucas's thoughts, blinking urgently, and then the scope went black.

"Damn," Lucas muttered, and crawled back from the roof edge over to where Alan was lying by the Browning.

Lucas pushed his corpse aside and proceeded to fire hundreds of rounds at the machine gun nest. Even if most of the shots went wide, if any found home, it was better than none, and hopefully the steady deluge would discourage any other bikers from trying to become heroes.

"Keep lobbing shells at them, Henry," he called.

"You got it," Henry answered, and ran in a crouch to get another case of projectiles as Terry set up the grenade launcher and fed a belt into it.

When he had it loaded, Terry targeted the nest and burned through twenty grenades in as many seconds. The entire roof where the Browning had been vaporized in a series of explosions that lit the night, and Henry let out a whoop at the sight.

Lucas's radio crackled and he gestured to Henry to pause the mortar and grenade assault. Art's voice came over the air.

"We have a guy with a sheet tied to a flagpole. How do you want to handle it? Over."

"Up to you," Lucas said. "Maybe see what they want."

"Roger. Stay tuned."

Lucas turned to Henry and Terry. "Great job. Got a surrender flag showing. Ease up until we find out what the deal is."

"Aw, hell. Just when this is getting good," Henry said. "How do you like that Mk 19?"

"Thing's a monster."

"Yeah. Give me a dozen of those and I could take on anything."

"Made short work of the machine gun."

"They probably figured out that it isn't a bunch of civilians coming at them. I mean, we are, but this is serious ordnance. They're used to pushing a bunch of old ladies around. Typical criminals. Face off with them with real force and they buckle."

"We'll see."

The radio squawked and Lucas raised it to his lips. "So?"

"They want a truce."

"You mean surrender, don't you?"

"They said truce."

"Hold on. I'll be there in a few minutes. Tell them anyone shoots at me, any talk's done and they'll take their medicine to the last man."

"Roger that."

Lucas looked to Henry. "I'm headed over to the capitol building. You hear shooting, throw everything you have at them and don't stop till you run out of shells."

"Will do. You think they're on the level?"

"They probably want to understand what they're up against. Sam? You think you can make it there on foot?"

"You bet."

Lucas and Sam descended the stairs and darted along the base of the hospital until they reached the street that ran along the west side of the university, figuring it would be prudent to avoid the side of the campus where the bikers were concentrated. They hurried along the wide boulevard until they were at the base of the surrounding buildings, and then slowed their pace as a concession to Sam's injury, sticking to the darkest areas of the street.

The capitol rose out of the darkness to their right, a white four-story behemoth with a massive turret to set it apart from commercial structures. They skirted around to the side, where hundreds of fighters were waiting with their weapons.

"How do we get in?" Sam asked one of the men he recognized.

"Either the front or the back. Got some men in the rear guarding it."

"Thanks."

They ran to the rear exit, where six guards bristled at their appearance until they realized who it was and relaxed. Lucas shouldered through an oversized bronze door and found himself in near total darkness.

"Art? Where you at?" he called.

"Over here. Keep walking straight down the hallway and you should see some light."

Lucas and Sam made their way along the corridor until they saw faint moonlight through the open double doors of the entrance, and approached slowly. Art and a dozen of his fighters were standing there, facing two bikers, who looked suitably cowed.

"This here's Lucas. He calls the shots," Art said.

Both bikers were large men with heavy beards and long hair. The bigger of the two, a soiled green bandana on his head and full-sleeve tattoos covering his massive crossed arms, nodded once.

"We want to parlay."

Lucas nodded. "So talk."

"We don't want to fight."

"Shame. We came a ways to do just that."

"We ain't done nothin' to you."

Sam stepped into view. "Not true. You took my friends prisoner, and you've been terrorizing Salem ever since you showed your ugly faces. That ends now, one way or another."

The biker glared at Sam and then back at Lucas. "Who's the runt?"

Lucas held his stare. "One of the guys who decides whether you die tonight."

"We keep at this, lots of people will die, and not only us."

"Got a thousand men ready to do just that. What are you proposing?"

"Leave us be and we'll let the town alone."

Sam snorted, and Lucas shook his head. "Not a chance." He sighed. "Here's your choices. Surrender and turn over all your weapons before daybreak, or we'll shoot every one of you down to the last man."

"We got civilians in with us."

"Bad luck for them. But that's still the deal."

"You think you can just show up and order us out of here?"

"Reckon not. So run back to your leader and tell him to make out a will, because you'll be dead by sunup."

The biker continued to glare at him and then finally looked away. "He'll never do it."

"Party's over. You had your run. Most of my men have had to deal with you or your kind, and they aren't as disposed to being charitable as I am. So either unconditional surrender right now, or they'll water the trees with your blood and sleep like babies after. Your choice." He paused. "I'm not bluffing. This is your only chance."

"What if we agree? What then? They'll hunt us down."

"If you give up, you'll face the town. They'll probably set up a court to charge the worst of you. Not my problem. You earned it.

Some may get to walk. Or not. But it's better than what you're facing."

"He'll never go for it."

"Then make peace with your maker, because you don't have much time left."

The bikers exchanged a troubled glance, and the big one turned back to Lucas. "You gotta give me something to work with."

"Discussion's over. Live or die – that's what you have to work with. You have five minutes to talk it over. After that, the bombing continues." Lucas spat to the side. "We see you trying to sneak out, including down the creek, the deal's off. Clear?"

The bikers left, and Art shook his head. "I never want to play poker with you."

"Meant every word."

Sam cut in. "Why let these scum off? They've been raping and pillaging like they'll never be held to account. That's done. They can face the music or the mortars. I don't really care which. Good riddance either way."

"You heard the man," Lucas said. "I'm just here for the drinks."

No more than three minutes went by before a voice called out from the second floor, "They're comin' back."

This time the two men were accompanied by a third biker clad head to toe in leather with a black leather cowboy hat pulled low on his brow. He stopped in front of Lucas, his expression neutral.

"We've got grenade launchers too," he said. "We can turn this building into rubble, and your men with it."

"Then take your best shot," Lucas said, and raised the radio to his lips. "Get the mortars ready."

"Here's the deal. You let us leave. We stay gone. You can have all our weapons except what we need to hunt."

"You must be hard of hearing. Surrender or die."

"And let the townspeople tear us apart?"

"They won't if you haven't done anything to deserve it."

"I'd rather die quick."

"Have it your way."

The biker with the green bandana stepped away from the leader. "I'll take the deal."

The other nodded. "Me too."

Lucas gave the leader a tight smile. "Wonder how many of your men are willing to die with you?"

"You traitorous scum," he snarled at his men, fists balled by his sides.

Art stepped from the shadows and faced the biker with the green bandana. "Tell you what, buddy. You go back and give your boys the same choice you just made. Anyone wants the deal can cross the street to our side. Anyone wants to go down with the ship can stay, and we'll release your man here to meet his fate."

"No!" the leader snapped.

Art nodded to his men, and two of them grabbed the leader's arms while a third cocked the hammer on his pistol and pressed it against the back of his head. Lucas motioned to the biker with the bandana, who took off at a run while the leader glowered at him.

"You're going to regret this. All of you," he hissed.

"That's a nice hat," Lucas said. "Trade you some rounds for it. Won't make it through what's coming. Hate to see a good hat ruined for nothing."

The biker returned, accompanied by at least twenty others, with more trailing from the buildings to join them. Art looked to Sam. "The jail still standing? We need someplace to hold them all."

"Let's leave that up to the locals. We can guard them in a central location and hand them over to whoever wants to run the town."

Art's men waited on the steps of the capitol while the bikers laid their weapons in a mounting pile and then stood to the side under the watchful eye of Sam and Bill's troops. When they did a count, there were a hundred and four bikers who'd surrendered.

Lucas nodded to Art, and they released the leader. "Not sure how many of your gang this is, but it doesn't matter. Mortars won't know any difference between one hundred or three."

"You're talking cold-blooded murder. You know that."

"Cry me a river. Now you going back, or you giving up?"

The leader stormed back across the street and disappeared into the building. The biker with the green bandana met Lucas's gaze. "There's only about twenty of them left."

"Their call."

Lucas retraced his steps to the hospital, and when he was almost there, his radio crackled again. Art's voice greeted him, his tone relieved.

"They came out. We'll do a sweep of the campus and find someplace to stick them. Stand down. Repeat, stand down."

Chapter 23

Amber Hot Springs, Colorado

Elliot paced in front of the morning fire, his face a study in tension. It had been a long two hours as the community had secured its borders and stood guard against an unknown threat.

Duke came in at a run, his expression bleak. Elliot looked up at him and stopped his pacing.

"What is it?"

"They're gone. Ellen and the sisters."

"What? How? Is there any sign of foul play?"

"No. The door's open and everything's cleaned out. I didn't even notice until it got light out. I was too busy doing guard duty. But they're gone, and so are their horses."

Elliot's stare darkened, and he turned to Arnold. "Search all the cabins."

Arnold took off at a run, and Duke surveyed the camp. "What the hell's going on?"

"Tell me again how you met these women."

"They were being chased by scavengers. We shot the attackers, and the women stopped at the trading post. They were looking for work as well as shelter, so it seemed a good fit. We spent some time getting to know each other, and I invited them to join Shangri-La. Just like I've invited others."

"And they're from Denver? They give you any sense that they

were being hunted by someone?"

"Not other than those marauders, no. You heard their story yourself."

Minutes ticked by, and Elliot resumed his silent pacing as the fire crackled and popped. Duke was yawning and stretching his arms over his head when Arnold's voice rang out from up the path.

"Duke! Elliot!"

Duke leapt to his feet and followed Elliot to Sierra's cabin, where Arnold was standing beside her, supporting her. Dried blood had caked in her hair and down her face, and she looked dazed.

"What happened?" Elliot demanded.

"Your lady friends knocked her out with their rifle and kidnapped Eve," Arnold said, his voice flat.

"What?" Duke exclaimed. "That's…insane!"

"They were tied up on the floor. The boy's afraid to come out, but it doesn't look like he's hurt. Just shaken." Arnold indicated Sierra. "Sierra, on the other hand, took a mean blow to her head."

"God…" Duke said, his eyes bleak. "I…I can't believe it."

Elliot stepped forward. "I have no idea what's going on here, but, Arnold, I want you to put together a tracking party and find them."

"She…" Sierra started, and broke into tears. "You have to get Eve back. Please. You have to…"

Arnold stared holes through Duke. "You have any clue where they might have taken her, or why?"

All Duke could manage was to shake his head. "I…no."

Arnold looked to Elliot. "I'll round up some men. They have a two-hour head start on us, but we might be able to make up the difference."

"I'm so sorry, Sierra. I had…I didn't…" Duke sputtered.

"She's just a baby," Sierra said, tears streaming down her face.

Duke wandered away, shaking his head. Elliot embraced Sierra and then examined her wound. "It's a bit swollen and the skin's broken, but it doesn't look like you'll need stitches. You might have a concussion, though. Come back inside and lie down. You need to rest."

She shook her head and winced at the pain. "No. I need to find Eve."

"There's nothing you can do out here, Sierra. Arnold will take care of it."

He led her back into the cabin. Tim was huddled in a corner, knees to his chest, staring at Elliot with eyes the size of golf balls. Elliot gently laid Sierra down and took a step toward the boy. Tim stiffened and began shaking.

"Tim, it's over, and your mother needs help. I know it had to be scary, but they won't be back to hurt you. You're safe."

Tim continued to stare at Elliot, but stopped shaking. "Why did they take Eve?"

Elliot frowned. "I don't know, Tim. But we'll find out."

"I don't understand."

"That makes two of us. Now come on. Stand up, and let's get your mother some water from the creek so we can clean her up. Are those your jugs over there?" Elliot asked, pointing to two scarred blue five-gallon plastic bottles.

Tim nodded.

"Can you manage one if I carry the other?"

"One of 'em's half full already. We don't need water."

"Let's go fill the other one. You can help me."

When Elliot finished calming Tim down, he left mother and son and walked to where Duke was sitting by the fire pit, staring into space. When Duke heard Elliot's boots crunching on the gravel, he looked up at him, misery radiating from his eyes.

"I can't believe how stupid I was. I mean...I...I believed her," he said in a tortured voice. "I should have known. I should have. This is all my fault."

"Don't be too hard on yourself, Duke. You couldn't have known. I thought they were fine too."

"Beautiful woman like that and an old goat like me. Stupid. I was so damned blinded by her..."

"You're not that old. Wait until you get another twenty years under the bridge. Then you can award yourself that title."

"You know what I mean."

"Duke, she obviously had an agenda, and she tricked you. All that means is you're human, and fallible." Elliot frowned. "And she was a good actress."

"Got that right." He sighed. "Poor Sierra. But…seriously. None of this makes any sense. Why kidnap Eve and shoot the guards? They just met her yesterday. It's crazy."

"Not to them. All three of them were in on it, so we must be missing something."

Arnold arrived on horseback with another man. Duke looked up at them. "I'm coming too. Give me a minute to get my horse."

Arnold shrugged. "Time's a-wasting."

Duke was back in a flash, and they took off down the trail. Arnold stopped after several minutes, hopped down from his horse, and studied some tracks in the dirt. "Three horses. They definitely came this way."

He swung back into the saddle, and they increased their pace. Half an hour later they came across fresh droppings covered by a swarm of flies. Arnold dropped from the saddle and put a finger in the feces, and then nodded. "Barely warm. They're moving fast, but not that fast. Makes sense given the condition of the trail and riding with the girl's extra weight."

Farther along the trail, a faint gunshot echoed from down the mountains, and a flock of birds took flight from the trees. They stopped as the sound reverberated, and Duke looked at Arnold. "What do you think that means?"

"Only one way to find out."

They continued along the track, pausing occasionally so Arnold could confirm they were still following the women's trail. An hour passed and they reached a treacherous area where the rocks at the side of the narrow stretch were painted with a swath of rust-colored blood. Arnold and Duke dismounted and walked to the edge of the ravine and peered over. A horse lay fifty yards down the steep face, obviously dead.

"Must have misstepped and broken its leg," Arnold said.

"Which will slow them down even more."

"First lucky break we've caught."

"Not for the horse."

Arnold walked along the trail and pointed to the tracks. "They're two on one horse now. You can see the tracks are deeper, and there aren't any footprints."

The sun blazed high overhead when the path changed from gravel and dirt to rock and they reached a fork in the trail. Arnold spent several minutes studying the trails, and when he returned to where the men were taking a break in the shade, he shook his head.

"No way to tell which fork they took," he said. "At least not here. Maybe farther down if it goes back to dirt." He eyed Duke. "You remember which one you took to get here?"

Duke exhaled in frustration. "No. I used my compass for the most part. Remember I'm as new to this as the rest of you. Only time I ever took it was to go to the highway and set up the trading post, and to come back. Sorry."

"Then it's coin-toss time. Which would you take if you were them?"

Duke frowned. "They both look like they suck."

"That's what I was thinking too. There's no obvious one, and they both go downhill."

"Well, damn."

"Yup."

"Then I'd say go with the one on the right. Most people will choose a right turn over a left."

Arnold's eyebrows rose. "Really? How do you know that?"

Duke shrugged. "That's what I'd do."

"Good an answer as any, I suppose."

They watered the horses and forked down the right trail, and had to slow further due to the conditions. It was late afternoon when Arnold held out his arm to stop the others.

"Horse. About a quarter mile away."

He raised his binoculars to his eyes and then dropped them, his mouth a thin line. "Riders. Two women on one animal."

"You see what color their hair was?" Duke asked.

"Couldn't make it out."

"Any sign of Eve?"

"No."

"Now what?"

Arnold frowned. "Now we go after them. Looks like they spotted us."

The women's horse had broken into a gallop and was tearing down the trail. The men gave chase and closed the distance. One of the women tried firing at them, but the shots didn't come close, the odds of hitting moving targets while on horseback being worse than zero for any but the luckiest or the best.

Duke and Arnold were a hundred yards from their quarry when the women's horse lost its footing and sent them both flying from its back. It quickly righted itself and continued on at a gallop, leaving women lying on the trail.

Arnold reached them first and dropped from his horse, followed by Duke. They ran to where the women lay, and Arnold took their vitals while Duke watched.

"It's the sisters," he said.

"That one's in bad shape," Arnold said, pointing to Monica and the halo of blood beneath her skull. "Landed on her head. Neck doesn't look broken, but her eyes…"

"What about this one?" Duke asked.

"She's out cold too, but she doesn't look too bad."

"Great."

Arnold looked to the other rider. "Devin, help me get this one on my horse. You take the other one."

"What about Eve?"

"They must have split up. There's no way we're going to catch up to them before dark. We'll be lucky if we can get this pair back without falling into a gulch."

"We can't just give up."

"Duke, we did everything we could. Luck's not on our side today. But maybe we can find out where the other woman's headed. That's the best we can shoot for."

"I'll keep after her while you bring them back."

"You'll get yourself killed, or pass them in the night without knowing it, or ride off a cliff. Don't be a damned fool." Arnold's voice softened. "Look. I know this is personal for you. I get that. But sacrificing yourself isn't going to solve anything."

"What if I can catch them?"

"What if there's another fork and you choose the wrong one again? What if you run into some marauders or scavengers? What if your horse slips and you go ass over appetite like they did and break your neck? All of those are more likely than you catching up to them by nightfall."

Duke fought back the anger that swelled in his chest. Arnold was right; he shouldn't be angry with him for stating the obvious. Duke wanted to catch up with Ellen for more than one reason, and it was clouding his judgment and goading him to take suicidal risks.

"You're right. I'm sorry. I…I just hate to have to go back to Sierra and tell her we failed."

"You and me both. But you left out the operating words."

Duke threw him a dirty look. "Which are?"

"For now. We failed for now. Let's mount up and get back to town so we can live to fight another day. This isn't over. Far from it. This was just the second inning."

Duke nodded and mounted his horse, wishing he felt a tenth of the confidence that Arnold's tone conveyed. "Fine. You set the pace. If your horse starts to tire, I can take her for a while."

Devin dragged Monica to his horse. "This one ain't gonna make it. Her head's split open like a melon, and you can see the bone's cracked."

"There's not a lot we can do except get her to Elliot," Arnold said.

"Ain't gonna do any good."

"Maybe so, but no harm trying."

Chapter 24

Salem, Oregon

Lucas and Ruby sat with Ray and Rosemary at a table on the sidewalk in downtown Salem, enjoying a late breakfast near the river, compliments of one of the restaurants that had been paying ninety percent of its profit to the bikers for protection. The town had been shocked that it had been liberated by complete strangers, but had quickly rallied at the news and rolled out the red carpet for its benefactors. At Art's suggestion, a town council had been convened to appoint a mayor and sheriff, and after a contentious morning of arguments and speeches, a local named Sidney had been voted in, and Lyle, one of Sam's friends, had been named sheriff by popular decree.

"I want to find a radio and call home," Lucas said between mouthfuls.

"I imagine there's gotta be one around somewhere. Didn't you find one at a trading post before?" Ruby asked.

"Everything changed after the bikers took over. Nobody with any means stuck around. I'm hoping Sam can find one."

Bill came down the street and, when he spotted them, made his way over.

"They're trying to figure out what to do with the bikers. Art's helping them through their thinking, and it looks like they'll set up a tribunal." He shook his head. "There's already a line around the block of victims they've raped, or family members and friends of people they murdered. It's gonna get ugly."

"They made their bed. Payback's a bitch," Lucas said. "You want some fish stew? Pretty good."

"Maybe later."

"Have a seat. I'll have them bring you some cider. It's fresh," Ruby said.

"Thanks. Don't mind if I do." Bill pulled a chair over from another table and sat. "So what now, Lucas?"

"We're headed home. Probably leave tomorrow after we find a radio. You heard of anyone with one?"

Bill shook his head. "Not really. But this isn't my turf. I'll ask around for you, though."

"Be much obliged." Lucas regarded Bill thoughtfully. "What about you and your men?"

"Haven't had much time to think about it. I mean, there's Newport, but a part of me wants to move my family here, farther from the coast. Seems like it'll be less isolated, and now that the bikers are done, we could make some real strides on setting up something good."

"Someone will find a way to ruin it," Ruby countered. "But you might as well try."

A horseman covered with trail dust came down the street at a fast trot and reined to a halt in front of them. Bill and Lucas looked up at him in surprise.

"That you, Hayden?" Bill asked.

"Thank God I found you. I've been looking everywhere," Hayden said, dropping to the ground and tying his horse to a light post.

"Long way from the promised land, aren't you?" Lucas remarked.

"The Chinese showed up and invaded Newport. Killed a bunch and took the rest captive. Exactly like Astoria."

"What?" Bill blurted.

"They showed up on a battleship four days ago. It was over before it started. We didn't stand a chance."

Bill's eyes narrowed. "How'd you get away?"

"I managed to escape that night. I've been riding hard ever since."

"Mighty lucky," Lucas observed flatly.

Bill nodded slowly, his eyes slits. "Anyone else get lucky with you?"

Hayden shook his head. "No."

"What about my mom and dad?" Rosemary asked, her voice strained.

"They're…they're prisoners."

"And my wife?" Bill asked.

"Same thing."

Rosemary rose. "You have to rescue them!" She looked to Ruby. "We can't leave them with the Chinese. I've seen what they do."

Bill nodded. "How many troops did you count?"

"At least a couple of hundred," Hayden answered. "Plus the ship."

"Sounds like you should talk with Art," Lucas said. "You should be able to take them if you can convince him and his boys to march on Newport."

"What do you mean, talk to Art?" Rosemary demanded. "You need to help my parents, Lucas. They're your friends. My dad risked his life to help you in Astoria."

Lucas finished his stew and dropped his spoon into the empty bowl. "I'm done with fighting, Rosemary. We're headed home. There's always going to be something I can get sucked into. Not this time." He stood and tossed two bullets on the table. "That's for the hospitality. Thank the owners again for me," he said, and stepped off the sidewalk to make his way to the park where the horses were grazing.

"You have to talk to him," Rosemary pleaded with Ruby. "Please."

Ruby sighed and nodded. "All I can do is try."

She pushed back from the table and followed Lucas, hurrying to catch up. Lucas sensed her closing on him and slowed.

"You going to try to tell me what I have to do again?" he asked.

"No. You know right from wrong."

"You don't approve?"

"I think you're acting against your nature, and I'm wondering why."

"I meant what I said, Ruby. There's always going to be another fight. Gotta draw the line somewhere."

"Tell me their chances will be the same with or without you."

"That's not the question, is it?"

"You want your friends to be slaves or live free? That's a pretty simple one, isn't it?"

"Ruby…"

"Lucas, I know you're sick of this. But I don't think you'll be able to live with yourself, much less look Rosemary in the eyes, if you don't help free Mary and Jeb."

"You seem awful sure of how my mind works."

"I know you. Behaving dishonorably isn't in your nature."

"I have a family and a life, too. What about them?"

"What would Sierra want you to do? Or what if it were them?"

"It isn't. And Sierra's never shown particularly good judgment."

"What if I'd stayed behind to help Mary? Would you be so quick to walk away?"

"Ruby, Jeb didn't come to Astoria to help me, he came to free his family. I don't owe him. If anything, he owes me."

"Not arguing with you, Lucas. But what if it were me?"

"It isn't."

"Mary nursed me back to health. She's a good woman. The world needs more like her. Seems a shame to turn your back on her."

"I have no problem with Bill and Art and whoever tackling the Chinese."

"Lucas, they're not you. We both know it. Their chances drop the minute you're gone."

"It's not my fight, Ruby."

She stopped, forcing him to stop with her. He turned, dreading what was to come.

"Then I'll go alone. I suspect Rosemary won't be riding with you after this news, either."

"Ruby…"

"Don't 'Ruby' me. I'm doing what's right even if you won't." She threw him a hard look. "Lucas, you've been running from this ever since we last talked. But I'm going to say it out loud just once. You have an army here. More men from Salem are already talking about joining. With that kind of a force, you could not only take out the Chinese, you could take out anyone you needed to – like the Crew. You could clean up the whole country, warlord by warlord, and bring a decent life to tens of thousands of survivors. I know you don't want to hear this, but it's true. You landed in this position – whether by fate or accident, who can say, but it's yours either way, and I think you need to acknowledge it and figure out whether you want to be a leader, or…or leave it to others less capable."

Lucas's face crinkled with a hint of a smile. "Isn't this kind of the same speech as before? Why do you keep giving it?"

Her jaw clenched. "I'll keep giving it till you start listening."

"I'm not George Washington, Ruby. I'm a tired man who wants to be left alone, not lead a revolution."

"I said before that you're never going to be able to live in peace. I meant that. You either solve the problem or it'll come for you every time. That should be obvious by now."

"Only thing that's obvious is you want me to talk everyone into heading to Newport."

She nodded. "For starters."

He looked longingly over at the park, where Tango was standing beside Jax, drinking from a water trough. "Don't suppose you'll leave me be until I say yes, will you?"

"Nope."

"You drive a hard bargain, Ruby."

"Own it, Lucas. Whether you like it or not, you're the man."

"Getting awful tired of hearing that."

"Destiny's a bitch."

Chapter 25

Amber Hot Springs, Colorado

Morning mist hung over the cabins of Shangri-La, cloaking the valley in white. Elliot stood with Duke and Andrew at the large barnlike structure beside the thermal plant that served as the encampment's medical clinic. Tracie lay on a cot with an IV in her arm, which Elliot adjusted periodically as he watched her regain consciousness after a long night of restive sleep.

Her eyes fluttered open, and Elliot leaned over her to assess the size of her pupils. One was still larger than the other, telling him that there had been intracranial bleeding, and that side of her face seemed lifeless and slack, indicating a stroke.

"Where…" she whispered so faintly they could barely hear her.

"You're safe," Elliot said.

She absorbed his words and closed her eyes, and then they snapped open. "My…sister…"

"She didn't make it," Arnold said. "I'm sorry."

Her eyes moistened and she drew a sharp intake of breath.

"Neither did the two guards you shot," Duke snapped, and Elliot threw him a warning glance before smiling down at her.

"Tracie, right? How do you feel?" he asked.

"Head…hurts…"

"You took quite a fall. I'm going to ask you to help me with some easy tests so I can figure out what's damaged, okay?"

"O…Okay."

He lifted her hands in his. "Press down with both as hard as you can."

She did, and he nodded encouragement as he set them back by her side. "Good. Now tell me when you start to feel this," he said, and dragged the tip of a pair of forceps along her left leg.

"Now."

"Very good." He did the same with her right, with no response. "Perfect. Now I'm going to check your vision. I'll hold a hand over one eye and ask you to follow my finger."

He covered her right eye and drew his left index finger slowly from in front of her nose toward her left ear. Her pupil shifted and followed it. He repeated the test with his right finger, and her dilated pupil barely moved.

"It's really blurry," she said when he was done.

"You landed hard. I'm not surprised." He paused. "Anything else hurt?"

"My ribs. And my lower back."

"Yes. That's to be expected." He looked at Duke and Arnold. "I'll let you rest a bit. If you need anything, just call out."

"Okay."

Elliot led them outside, his expression dour. "She's lost her entire right side. There's no way of telling whether the bleeding in her skull that caused it has stopped or is still continuing. If it is, she won't make it to nightfall."

"Who cares?" Duke snapped. "She's a murderer. Where's Ellen and Eve? Where were they taking her? That's the only thing that matters. We're losing time we don't have."

Elliot nodded. "Yes, I understand all that. But you'll get more flies with honey than vinegar, as the saying goes."

"Can't you drug her?" Arnold asked. "Give her something that will lower her guard?"

"That's what I was going to propose. But it could endanger her survival."

"So what?" Duke said. "One less predator in the world."

"Do it," Arnold said.

"A word of warning. Both of you are to stay silent. Not a word no matter what, do you understand? I've established some trust as her doctor, but you could ruin it in a heartbeat, and then she'll stop cooperating. Got it?"

They nodded.

Elliot went back inside and rummaged in a storage chest, and then injected something into Tracie's drip. "This will ease the pain and relax you."

After a five-minute wait, they turned back to her bedside, and Elliot cleared his throat.

"Tracie?"

"Yesss…" she answered, her voice dreamlike.

"I have some very important questions I need your help with, okay?"

"Okay…"

"Where were you going when we rescued you?"

"I…home."

"Home. Is that Denver?"

"Yesss."

"Was your friend Ellen going home too?"

"Yesss."

"Was she taking Eve, the little girl, home too?"

A pause. "Yesss. To the church."

"Excellent. Only a couple more questions, Tracie."

"Okay. I'm…tired…"

"That's understandable." Elliot looked to Arnold's frowning face and then to Duke before looking down at Tracie again. "Why take the little girl to the church?"

She breathed slowly and sighed. "Prophet…needs her."

"Yes," Elliot agreed. "Of course he does." Elliot hesitated. "Why does he need Eve, Tracie?"

"She…she's interfering…with the…plan…"

"Oh. Right. The plan. Tell me about the plan, Tracie."

She frowned as though trying to remember. "God's plan."

"Sure. God's plan. Which is…?"

"He wants to…take us to heaven after…we…we're tested."

"Marvelous. And Eve is interfering."

"Yesss."

"How, Tracie?"

"Her…blood. We…everyone…knows…the vaccine…"

Realization flooded Duke's face at the same time it hit Elliot. "Eve's blood was used for the vaccine…"

"Yesss. Not…the plan…she's…false…muh…muhs…"

"Messiah," Elliot finished for her.

"Right. Prophet…sent us…into the wilderness…find Eve…"

"How many, Tracie? How many did he send?"

"Lots."

"Of course. He would want many to help, wouldn't he?"

"I'm…sleepy."

"Where in Denver were you going?"

"The…church…"

"The Prophet's church," Elliot echoed.

"Yesss…God…is…love…"

"He certainly is, Tracie."

Elliot stepped away from the bedside and walked outside with the men. His face was tight and drawn in the pale sunlight. "You heard her. They're off to Denver, where some prophet thinks Eve is a false messiah. And he wants…well, I don't know. I'll ask her, but I suspect it isn't good."

"How could they have known her blood was used for the vaccine?" Arnold asked.

"Somebody talked too much when they were delivering it, is my guess."

"And how did they know to target Shangri-La?" Duke asked.

"We're rather well known since the vaccine, Duke. I mean, we saved the world. We're legendary. Which can be a bad thing, obviously."

"Ask her how they knew I could lead them to Eve," Duke demanded, his voice tight.

"I will, but my guess is one of the people you tried to recruit before talked to the wrong person. It doesn't take much, and if they were traveling along the highway from the south, they'd have at least passed through Denver."

"Who is this prophet?" Arnold asked.

"My guess is the nutcase who runs Denver. I've heard about him from other radio operators. He broadcasts incoherent sermons every few weeks. I can ask them, although I have to be careful what I say because anyone could be listening."

"If she's headed to Denver, there aren't many roads she could take," Duke said.

"Agreed. But she's got over a full day's lead on us now."

"So we'll have to go to Denver. Assuming she's still alive by the time we get there," Duke said. "We need a plan. Ellen told me there were thousands in the church. No way can we take on thousands of crazies."

"No," Elliot agreed. "Blunt force isn't the way to go, which means we'll have to use stealth instead. Just as they did with us."

"What kind of religion justifies murder and kidnapping a little girl?"

Elliot's brow creased. "There are countless examples of zealots twisting ideology to suit their aims. This is hardly the first time a religion has justified killing in the name of the Lord. One might say it's the history of the Abrahamic religions. Think about the Crusades, as an example. Or about most wars – where God is on our side, which implies he doesn't care about the enemy or their families. Whole cities have been firebombed or nuked based on that premise – that our lives are more precious than theirs. This sounds like the same moral loophole. I'd bet that's how it's framed to the true believers. For all I know, it's acceptable to kill any but the faithful. Again, it's not like that's unheard of. A variation of the rules not applying to anyone but the chosen."

"It's nuts," Duke spat.

"No disagreement. But the question is what do we do now?" Elliot said.

"See what other information you can get out of her," Arnold said.

"Anything specific?"

"How the church recruits. Who this prophet is. Where their headquarters are. Logistics we can use to find and rescue Eve."

"Very well. But I have to warn you that she could slip into a coma at any time. The intracranial pressure…"

"Then hurry," Duke said, his voice pained.

Elliot returned to the interior just as Sierra arrived with a bandage wrapped around her head.

"Should you be up?" Arnold asked.

"I want to see her."

"That's not possible," Arnold said. "Elliot's questioning her with drugs."

"I want to see her," she repeated. "What did they do with my daughter?"

"We're finding that out," Duke said.

Sierra leveled a glare at him. "You brought these people into our life."

"I know. I'm sorry. I had no way of knowing."

She waved a hand in disgust. "Words. Damage is done."

"We're going to get her back," Duke said.

"How?"

"We will. Now come on. I'll walk you home. You won't do any good here."

"One of them died?" she asked. "I saw them burying her."

"Yes."

"Good. I hope she suffered before going straight to hell."

Duke reached out to take her arm. "Let me help you…"

She jerked her arm away and pulled back. "Don't you dare touch me."

He held up his hands. "Fine. Arnold will help you back."

Sierra's demeanor cracked, and a tear rolled from her left eye down to her chin, the droplet accelerating until it stopped in defiance of gravity and trembled there. "I want my little girl back," she said in a voice filled with pain.

"We'll get her back," Arnold said, and put his arm around her. "I promise, Sierra. We'll do whatever it takes."

Chapter 26

Two hours later Elliot emerged from his cabin, where he'd spent the last forty-five minutes on the radio speaking with kindred spirits throughout the region. Arnold and Duke were sitting at the fire pit, munching on dried meat, when he neared and sat beside them.

"Well, gentlemen, I've pieced together as much of this as I'm able," he announced.

Arnold eyed him expectantly.

"The church sounds like a cult, based on what I've been able to garner. It's led by a self-proclaimed prophet named Ulysses Granger, and controls Denver, which sounds more grandiose than it actually is. Apparently that area was particularly hard hit by the virus. Anyhow, as far as we know, he has roughly five thousand followers, who are rabid and will do anything he says. They view him as being as close to a God walking the earth as is possible, and he completely controls them."

"That's just great," Duke said. "Like we don't have enough problems."

"One of my contacts told me that they're having a big carnival to attract new blood next week. Which may provide us with an opportunity."

"How so?" Arnold asked.

"If we can infiltrate them, perhaps we can learn where Eve is being kept, and free her." He frowned. "Frankly, I see no other way to go about this."

"Infiltrate them?"

"Yes. If some of us were to pose as travelers, with a few of the young women from our group, we would fit their target for recruitment. The idea would be to join the cult, mingle, and learn all we can about them."

"We'd be recognized," Duke said. "We have to assume Ellen will see us."

"I never saw her," Arnold said. "And they weren't here long enough to meet most of the town."

"That's correct," Elliot said to Arnold. "What I would propose is that you and Devin select two of the sharpest and most capable women between the ages of eighteen and twenty-five, and pose as couples from New Mexico who are tired of the road and are seeking lasting peace."

"What about me?" Duke demanded. "I got us involved in this nightmare."

"You could act as support, hanging back outside Denver."

"Support?"

"With whomever you need to help. But you couldn't go into the city – it would blow the entire plan."

"What if they don't take us?" Arnold asked.

"Seems unlikely. These types of groups need to proselytize to grow. That's the constant in all cults – they require fresh blood to increase their reach and their influence. They're constantly recruiting."

"So we pretend that we've lost our minds and want to follow some prophet?"

"That's the essence of it. Once a part of the cult, you can then nose around until you find Eve, and then come up with a plan to free her."

"Just like that."

"I'm not saying it'll be easy. But without more information on how they're structured and what their security and defenses are like, we can't formulate a strategy." He wiped his brow. "I'm sorry. That's the best I can come up with."

"Any suggestions on who we should ask to go on this suicide mission?" Arnold asked.

"I've heard that Anne is more than competent. And perhaps...Julie? They would both be welcome additions to any group, I should think."

"What if they say no?"

"Tell them to speak with me. But do what you can to make it clear what's at stake. We don't have weeks to put this into action."

"Denver's a four-day ride if all goes well," Duke said. "Three and a half if you really push and are lucky. If it rains, all bets are off."

"Any idea what this carnival is all about?" Arnold asked.

"It's a gimmick to attract any travelers down on their luck or any dissatisfied residents in the nearby communities. Greeley has a decent population that's being protected by a militia, and Littleton and Aurora are run by criminal strongmen. The cult's only real hope to grow is to lure some of their neighbors into the fold, or attract travelers opportunistically. It's the perfect cover for us, really."

"Let me go find the women and Devin," Arnold said. "We still have most of today to ride if we're quick about it."

"I'll pack," Duke said. "Can't see what dragging a battalion along with me will do but put them on alert, though. Better just me and Luis. I can swing by the trading post on the way to Denver."

"You'll need to agree on a preexisting spot to meet on the outskirts of Denver," Elliot said. "I have a map of the city somewhere. Tracie indicated that the cult's taken over the downtown area and the suburbs around it. They use the convention center as their headquarters. I'll dig out the map, and we can decide on a good spot."

"I'll bring enough gold and ammo to trade for extra horses and weapons," Duke said. "Other than that, can't think of much else we can do but sit and wait."

"All right," Arnold said. "It's not much of a plan, but it'll have to do. We'll make it up as we go along."

"There's no chance of Tracie staging a miracle recovery and escaping, is there?" Duke asked.

"Hardly," Elliot replied. "The pressure is increasing, albeit slowly. If she makes it to nightfall, that will be miracle enough." He rose. "Let me go find that map. I rather miss the old days when I could pull up satellite imagery to study an area."

"I miss electricity," Duke said. "And cars. And not having to sleep with one eye open and a gun in my hand."

"Yes, well, let's meet back here in half an hour. Hopefully the ladies will agree to help, and we'll get this show on the road."

Chapter 27

Western Oregon

Lucas and Art rode abreast of Sam and Bill, at the head of a long procession of men on horseback, possible now that the bikers' animals were theirs. A head count put the fledgling army at over a thousand strong after a decent number of Salem's young men had taken up arms and joined, and spirits were high after the easy victories in Astoria and Salem.

The mounted troops now accounted for well over half their force, and in the interest of travel time, Art and Lucas had decided to leave those without horses in Salem while they rode to Newport. If en route they couldn't concoct a strategy to defeat two hundred Chinese with over six hundred men, they figured that four hundred more on foot, tired after marching hundreds of miles, wouldn't tip the balance.

Lucas and Sam had gone to Clovis's in the late morning to return the cart and buy his entire inventory, which had overjoyed the old man as much as the news that the assault on the bikers had been successful. He'd sold them everything except his beloved rooftop Browning and five thousand rounds in green ammo cans, which he'd reasoned would be sufficient to keep any threat at bay – and if not, insufficient ammunition likely wasn't the problem.

They'd loaded ten carts with his arsenal and trundled it to the camp, and then selected what they could comfortably carry in saddlebags and on two carts. Because of the terrain, the roughly sixty-mile trek would take at a minimum three days on horseback, and they would have to slow as they approached the town for fear of inevitable patrols.

Lucas had begged Ruby to remain in Salem with Rosemary to avoid any more drama than was already baked into the situation, but his pleadings had fallen on deaf ears, and the two women were part of the medical triage team that would care for any wounded.

Art had handled the logistics of supporting such a large group. Unlike the trek from Astoria to Salem, where they'd had to forage whatever they could, the residents of Salem had bent over backward to show their appreciation for the group's actions on their behalf, and had loaded them down with fruit, vegetables, and meat, ensuring they would arrive in Newport well fed and with no delays, other than to refill their containers with potable water.

Hayden trailed behind Lucas, and Lucas's dislike of the man hadn't abated with time. Lucas didn't for a minute believe he'd lifted a finger to help his fellow townspeople, and figured that he'd turned tail at the first sighting of the ship. It wasn't his problem, but he had no interest in spending a moment more than necessary around him and had deliberately made himself unavailable, too busy with planning and organizing to dither.

The afternoon sky darkened as they crossed the river and headed west, and they'd barely made it an hour before the heavens opened up and rain transformed the highway into a muddy slurry, slowing their progress to the point where they only made fifteen miles before calling it a day and making camp.

The storm continued through the night, explosions of thunder making it impossible to sleep, and by daybreak when they were on the move again, Lucas was having serious second thoughts about having allowed Ruby to talk him into heading up the army. As if reading his mind, she appeared by his side and threw him a sad smile. He shifted in the saddle, his eyes bloodshot and his clothes soaked, and gave her a dark look.

"Head up the army, she said. It's for the good of the world, she said. But she didn't say anything about saddle sores and pneumonia, did she?" he muttered.

"Good morning to you, too, handsome. I was going to ask whether you slept well, but I see you didn't."

"Did you?"

"Like a baby."

"Figures."

"Clean conscience and an innocent mind."

That drew a smile. "Nice someone has either."

"One of the benefits of age is you forget most everything."

"Can't wait."

Ruby grew serious. "Sorry, Lucas. This is pretty miserable."

"Next time you try to talk me into something, don't."

She nodded. "Unless it's important."

"That's what I was afraid you'd say."

Chapter 28

Denver, Colorado

Colorful streamers hung from lampposts along the largest thoroughfare in the city, and the aroma of grilling meats and baking confections wafted along the boulevard from sidewalk stalls. Groups of white-clad pedestrians ambled along the street, beaming smiles at other passersby, while children squealed and ran between them, laughing as they raced after each other in a never-ending game of tag.

A mime on stilts worked his way along the street, periodically blowing fire into the sky to the cheers of spectators. Teenage girls in white tunics followed, distributing daisies from overflowing baskets, with smiles as beatific as their eyes were vacant.

Music from the plaza in front of the convention center echoed off the empty towers of downtown, where a bluegrass band was strumming for all it was worth while a singer with a hillbilly drawl crooned a standard for the audience that watched from the expansive lawn. A boy maneuvered a kite high in the cobalt sky while three admiring girls watched, and a litter of Labrador puppies frolicked on the grass under the watchful gaze of their mother.

Arnold and Julie rode toward the gilt-edged arch that formed the official gateway to the carnival, and a pair of young men in ivory smocks and permanent smiles greeted them and told them that their horses would be attended to while they enjoyed themselves at the festivities. Devin and Anne dismounted behind them and handed the men their reins, and Arnold checked his padlocked saddlebags before turning to the closest of the greeters.

"What about our rifles and ammo?" he asked.

"You won't need those. This is a weapons-free zone. No guns allowed. But if you like, you can lock your pistols and ammo belts and magazines in your bags – not that anyone would steal them. That kind of thing doesn't happen here," the man assured him.

They did as suggested. When they were done, the young man stuck his fingers in his mouth and issued a shrill whistle, and a boy came running and led the horses away.

"How do we get them back when we're through?" Arnold asked.

"We'll be here for the duration. Just give us these markers and we'll bring them from the stable," the man said, handing him four numbered poker chips.

"Can we get some feed and water?"

"Don't worry. They'll be attended to. On the house!"

Arnold and Julie strolled through the arch with Devin and Anne, and Julie leaned into him and whispered, "Tell me this isn't *Stepford Wives* creepy."

Arnold grinned and whispered back, "Definitely feels culty, but no surprise."

"What now?" she asked.

"Enjoy the food and drink, and wait for someone to pitch us on making this our life's work."

"You think they will?"

"Guaranteed."

They walked to a cart where a portly woman was grilling chicken kebabs. The smell was mouthwatering, the onions and slices of apple on the skewers bubbling as the chicken cooked. "How much?" Devin asked.

"Oh, everything's free during carnival! Eat as much as you want. There's more where that came from."

"No shortage of food here, huh?"

"Oh, no. Never. The Lord's blessed us with plenty," the woman said, her porcine face beaming with a sheen of moisture. "These will be done in a few minutes. You can get some cider or ale over there while you wait."

They made their way to another cart, where a girl was pouring lemonade from a pitcher into plastic cups. Arnold took one, and Devin smiled at her. "Got anything stronger? Lady over there mentioned ale?"

"Yes, sir! We make it ourselves! Best ever, it's said."

"I'll try one."

The girl extracted a cold bottle from an iced compartment and handed it to him. "Enjoy, and God bless!"

Devin took a pull on the ale and nodded his approval. "That's really good."

"Told you!"

When they'd all gotten drinks, they went back for their chicken, and each took two skewers. They wolfed the delicacies down in no time and stopped at another cart with strips of deer grilling over a mesquite fire.

An hour later they were stuffed, finishing off their feast with sugarcoated rice cakes and dried berries over homemade ice cream.

"Where do you get the ice?" Arnold asked the man as he scooped a generous second portion for him.

"Oh, we have refrigeration from the church's solar bank. Most of our homes have solar. After the reckoning, we were able to salvage huge amounts of it — there was a company that had solar plants in mobile trailers. Hundreds of them. Prophet Granger says we have enough to support a hundred thousand people!"

"That's amazing. And nobody's tried to take over the city?"

"Back in the beginning a few tried. But with God's help we were able to deal with them, and we've lived in peace ever since." He handed Arnold his ice cream. "Are you staying for the big celebration? It's in three days. It's supposed to be the biggest ever! And the Prophet's going to speak!"

"Haven't decided. But we'll think about it."

"You should. It'll be amazing."

"I'm sure."

They strolled over to where another band was now playing on a raised stage in front of the convention center, near a two-story bronze statue of a bear peering into the hall. A pair of smiling men with perfectly groomed hair and plastic smiles approached them, trailed by two beautiful young women, all wearing white.

"Enjoying yourselves?" one of the men asked.

Arnold nodded. "This is incredible. Like nothing we've seen."

"Where you from?"

"Down Albuquerque way."

"Ah. I've heard the roads south are dangerous. You're lucky you made it."

"That they are," Julie said. "Lot of highwaymen and marauders working the outskirts of the cities. It's bad news."

"You have any problems like that here?" Devin asked.

"Oh, no. They know better than to mess with us. No, here there's no crime at all. There hasn't been for years. Ever since the church took over."

"That's amazing."

"We don't tolerate that sort of thing. And it's unnecessary. Everyone has access to all the same resources. We work as a collective, so there's plenty of food and drink, not to mention power and medical care. We all work hard, and we live according to the Good Book and the words of Prophet Granger. Nobody wants for anything, and our children are raised to be honest and productive."

"Sounds like…paradise," Julie said.

"It is for those who are part of our group."

"Will you stay for the celebration?" one of the women asked.

"We're…we don't have any place to stay," Devin answered.

"Oh, don't worry about that! We take care of all newcomers like they're family. We have a hotel set up just for you. With power and water. Free!" She paused. "All you have to do is go to services with us every evening. There's a big buffet after. It's my favorite time of the year!"

Arnold and Julie exchanged a glance. "Sounds great."

"Are you two…married?" the man asked.

"We haven't had anyone formalize it, but we live like we are," Arnold answered.

"Then you're in luck. If you like, we'll be doing a big wedding after the celebration for everyone who wants to make it official. It's really popular."

"Really?" Julie gushed. "Oh, Arnold!"

"How about you?" the woman asked Anne and Devin.

"We're married. We got hitched last year before we left Albuquerque," Devin lied.

"Perfect."

The other woman regarded Arnold and Julie. "Hope you'll be okay with separate rooms until the ceremony. We frown on relations before you're married by the church. It's just a formality, but we have to set a standard for the children."

"Oh, sure," Arnold agreed. "For the children."

"Then it's decided," the man said, flashing a gleaming white smile. "You'll be our guests for the week."

The woman winked at Arnold. "And if you like, you can talk to us about making it permanent. We're always looking for God-fearing people to add to the church. There are a ton of benefits, as you can see. Everyone's happy and safe and well fed, and we live righteously."

"After what we've been through, that sounds great," Julie said. "What's involved?"

"We'll have a big baptism after the celebration and before the marriage ceremony, and we ask that you read a booklet of the Prophet's writings. Other than that, you just have to take a vow to behave according to the church's rules, and that's it. The church does everything else for you."

"What are the rules?"

"It's all in the Prophet's booklet. Mostly the commandments, with some additional guidelines to help everything work smoothly."

"I can't wait to read it," Julie said.

"Me too," Arnold managed, without a trace of sarcasm.

"That's great. Whenever you're ready, we can show you where the hotel is and get you registered," the man said. "Save room for dinner.

The buffet is incredible," he added, eyeing Arnold's ice cream.

"Perfect," Arnold said. He exchanged a glance with Devin, who was smiling as though he'd just found a solid gold coin. So far everything had happened as hoped, and the church's recruiters seemed anxious to add them to the roster by making the offer so good they couldn't refuse. It was a compelling approach. If they'd really been travelers, the sight of so much plenty would have seemed miraculous, and only a fool would have declined the chance to make it their daily reality. That there was a dark side to the offer wouldn't become apparent until later, he was sure. If the cult worked like most, only the top cadre would know the truth, like its use of murder and kidnapping to achieve its ends.

No, if they'd been travelers, it would have seemed like the opportunity of a lifetime, and the carnival a spectacle of idyllic harmony and abundance.

That some of the flock had been sent out to locate and grab an innocent child and kill anyone who got in their way seemed as distant as the North Pole from the peaceful gathering of white-clad, smiling faithful.

Which made them that much more dangerous.

Chapter 29

Houston, Texas

Snake was marching down the hall of the Crew building headquarters with his bodyguards when he heard voices from one of the meeting rooms off a side hall. He signaled for his men to stop and walked to the room, where three of his subordinates were sitting with Barton. They all looked up when Snake entered, and Barton nodded a greeting.

"Snake, good to see you. We were just discussing some of the problems you've been having with the border cities."

Snake eyed his men. "And why wasn't I notified that you wanted to have this discussion?"

"I'm to blame," Barton said. "I didn't want to waste your time with all the questions I had."

"What's the purpose of asking them?" Snake asked.

"I want to better understand the situation on the ground." Barton looked to the men. "Thanks for coming. I'll touch base if I need anything else."

They stood and filed past Snake, who glowered at them as they brushed by. When Barton and Snake were alone, Barton indicated a chair. "I wanted to hear an accurate report without anyone pulling punches because you were in the room. When the boss is there, you might sugarcoat things or omit ugly facts. I was encouraging them to bitch about what the problems are so I could tell you and we could figure out solutions."

"You should have told me."

"Perhaps. But what I've learned is that the Mexicans appear to be probing your forces for weakness. And frankly, I wouldn't put it past someone in your circle to be passing info to your enemies."

"A traitor," Snake said flatly, still standing.

Barton nodded. "Correct. Or more of an opportunist who's hedging his bets. Maybe more than one. Any time there's a change in leadership, there are going to be those who are dissatisfied with the situation and will try to curry favor with rivals. It's to be expected."

"Which is treason. I'll kill anyone who's doing that."

"Of course you will. But everyone knows that, so they'll keep their actions well hidden. I'm nosing around the edges to see if I can spot any patterns that would tell us where to look."

Snake sat heavily and stared at Barton. "When is the gold supposed to arrive?"

"They said soon. They didn't give a date."

"Soon doesn't do me any good in acquiring quality fighters to reinforce the trouble spots."

"Surely you can trade ammunition or something else you already have."

"You mean deplete my stores instead of using your promised payment?"

Barton sighed. "I mean doing what you have to in order to hold onto your territory regardless of the timing of the gold shipment."

"Is it coming over land or by ship?"

"They didn't say."

Snake's frown deepened. "And you didn't ask."

"It changes nothing in terms of its arrival, does it?"

"There's a big difference in the way my men view me between a warship showing up as a sign of support versus a couple of guys with a mule."

"When I next speak to them, I'll make a point of asking."

"I don't suppose there's been any movement on the refinery?"

"Our people are working on it. But frankly, Snake, the Crew is only one group out of many we're dealing with, so there's a limit to how many resources I can get my people to throw at it."

Snake sat forward. "Which is different from how it was pitched when I agreed to play ball. Nobody said we might be able to help, or might not, depending on how we felt."

"You were offered the same deal Magnus was more than happy to take."

"And now he's dead, and that deal did him no good. Didn't save him and didn't help him, as far as I can see."

Barton's eyes narrowed. "I'm here to support you, Snake. But that doesn't mean I can pull a rabbit out of my hat whenever you need one. You have to lead your men, not me. We chose to back you because you seemed like you could make this work. I hope we didn't make a bad decision."

Snake waved the comment away with a dismissive gesture. "Every time, it's the same thing. You give me nothing but promises, and end with a threat. Meanwhile I've got enemies trying to slit my throat every time I turn around. Remind me again what I'm getting out of cooperating with you? Not what I'm supposed to get, or may get – what I'm actually getting."

"You're being supported by the country's owners, Snake. If you aren't happy with that, all I can do is relay your sentiments."

They stared at each other for several uncomfortable moments, and then Snake shook his head and stood. "I've got to take care of other things. No more meetings with my men without me being there. I might get the wrong idea, and you don't want that."

Barton didn't answer, and Snake stalked out, his face twisted with anger. Things with the Illuminati man were going from bad to worse, and now he might be organizing a coup with Snake's subordinates. There was no way of knowing whether Barton was telling the truth, but Snake had to assume the worst.

Which meant that the three men with whom Barton had met would need to be watched very carefully, because they could all represent a mortal threat to Snake.

And if nothing else, Snake was a survivor, with a survivor's instinct for self-preservation. He couldn't take the chance that they were hatching a plot to supplant him.

He nodded to himself, his decision made. All three would have to die before nightfall – there would be no hesitation on Snake's part, or he could find himself dead instead.

The three were important lieutenants with loyal followings, though, so he'd have to be careful how he went about the executions. If he simply took them into custody, their men might revolt. He'd have to make their deaths appear to be the acts of outsiders – enemies seeking to weaken the Crew.

How he went about it would be the hard part, but Snake was infinitely resourceful when it came to protecting his own skin, and had any number of assassins who could carry out the job without batting an eye. He would assign one to each lieutenant and then arrange to have the assassins killed immediately after they'd done their jobs, eliminating the chance that one of them might talk.

Now he just needed to think up a plausible story to sell to his troops.

Snake smiled as he neared his bodyguards. Barton would know exactly what had happened, and it would send an unmistakable message to him that he couldn't ignore: mess with Snake and the world would collapse around you.

Even if you were the Illuminati's golden boy and thought you were invulnerable.

Because in Snake's world, nobody was – except him.

Something even the Illuminati would do well to remember.

Chapter 30

Arnold and his companions approached the convention center, merging with the large crowd. Most were wearing white, which was obviously the official church color of the Denver carnival. They entered the massive hall and were directed to an area reserved for newcomers up by a podium at the front, where a choir was standing by a group of musicians who were plucking out a soothing melody.

Arnold counted several hundred other people in trail clothes, most of them emaciated from years of hardship. The women seated in front of them were little more than skin and bones inside smocks that looked like potato sacks, with hair the straw-like consistency of the chronically vitamin deprived. Sallow skin hung from their faces and arms like tallow.

Julie took the seat beside him and offered a fake smile, which he returned. She'd proved an ideal choice for the mission, and he'd grown fond of her over their days together. He hadn't really taken the time to get to know her in his role as the Shangri-La head of security, but now that he'd had the opportunity, he wondered at the fact that she was still single – most of the eligible females had paired off long ago. But when he'd probed her about it the night before, she'd shrugged his questions off by saying she hadn't met anyone she wanted to spend serious time with, and he'd left it at that.

Devin and Anne were also getting along well. Anne's husband had died the year before, leaving her with an eight-year-old son who was being cared for by her sister while she risked her life to rescue Eve. She could have said no to the request, but she knew and liked Eve and was friends with Sierra, and she'd decided to take the plunge after considering how she would have felt if it had been her son who'd been snatched.

The volume from the band increased as the hall filled, and Arnold wondered at the amount of power necessary to operate the lights that illuminated the interior and drove the ventilation system. The church obviously had access to not only solar panels but banks of batteries that could still hold a charge in numbers that boggled the mind.

At the end of the song, a hush settled over the room, and a murmur rippled through the crowd when a man in his early thirties with a full head of brown curly hair hopped onto the stage, his white robe and red sash bright under the LEDs, and took the podium. He adjusted the mic and stared out at the throng before speaking, and when he did, his voice was evenly modulated with the practiced tone of an experienced speaker.

"Ladies, gentlemen, members of the church, and especially our guests here for the carnival, welcome to the Church of the Ever-Present Lord. We're delighted each and every one of you could make it, and hope you'll join us in offering thanks for the bounty we've shared today and will continue to share until this spectacular week ends!"

The hall shook with a hail of *amen*s that rose from thousands of mouths, and Arnold exchanged a glance with Julie – there was no denying the energy in the room.

"For those who don't know me, I'm Minister Elijah Granger, son of Prophet Ulysses, who will be giving the celebration sermon in three days' time. I'm joined by Minister Carvin there by the choir and Minister Fogarty by the piano. Gentlemen, take a bow, please."

The other ministers did, and the crowd applauded politely, as did Arnold and his group. When the clapping faded, Elijah paced behind the podium like a caged animal before stopping abruptly as though seized by a sudden thought.

"These are dangerous times. Troubled times. I don't need to tell anyone that. The world's filled with evil, and Satan is everywhere we turn. It's a blessing that we've been able to carve out an oasis of peace here and keep the demons at bay!"

More *amen*s, and Arnold shifted in his seat.

"All this week we're gathered to give thanks – thanks for our prosperity and the abundance of blessings we've received, thanks for the leadership and vision of my father, and thanks for the faith of the righteous who were led here by divine guidance. But most of all we're here to give thanks to God for giving us another chance to redeem ourselves for the wickedness of our kind, to live pure lives of goodness and prove that His faith in us was deserved."

The sermon lasted another half hour, building in intensity as Elijah warned of eternal damnation for those who strayed from the path or turned their hearts against the church's message – which was really his father's interpretation of the visions that came to him during his spells. The last five minutes of the sermon warned of a second apocalypse that would sort the faithful from the sinners, with promises of eternal life for the good and the ravages of hell for the bad. He ended with an allusion to a ritual of cleansing for the newcomers, and then the choir's voices rose in song and the congregation sang along for five traditional hymns that even Arnold knew.

Tithing baskets were passed around, but not to the guest section, which surprised him until he figured that it would further create a sense of obligation to the church for its generosity. Once the baskets were back at the stage, Minister Carvin took the microphone and gazed at the guests with a welcoming smile.

"I'd like to invite newcomers to form two lines, one of men and the other of women, for the first cleansing ritual. Don't be shy, and don't worry, it won't hurt to have all your prior sins banished and forgiven, no matter what they were."

Everyone did as asked, and filed forward to where Carvin and Fogarty pressed metal crucifixes against their heads and uttered phrases in some language Arnold didn't recognize, although he thought it sounded a little like the Latin he'd heard in church growing up. When it was his turn, he submitted with a meek expression, and Carvin held the cross against his temple and muttered his magic words. When Arnold looked up at where Elijah was standing, he saw that the minister was staring past Arnold, his eyes glued on Julie.

A shiver ran up Arnold's spine, and then as though reading Arnold's thoughts, Elijah's stare shifted and bored into him with the intensity of a laser. Arnold looked away immediately, but not before a sense of dread chilled his blood.

Then it was over, and the next person in line was stepping forward. A cherubic girl with flowers in her golden hair took Arnold's hand and led him back to the guest area, Elijah's eyes following him every step of the way, he was sure.

Once outside, Julie whispered to him as they strolled to an oversized tent where the buffet was being served. "Tell me that wasn't seriously creepy – the son. The perv vibe radiates off him big time. Or was that just me?"

"No. I caught it too. I just hope he doesn't suspect anything."

"Why would he?"

"I don't know. But he was giving me the death stare."

"Really? You weren't imagining it?"

"No."

"You do look healthier than most of these skeletons. Maybe that's why. Or maybe he has a thing for guys."

"Not the way he was looking at you, he doesn't. Maybe he saw me with you earlier or something. I just hope he doesn't have me killed in the middle of the night so you're suddenly available."

She slowed and turned to him. "Why, Arnold, if I didn't know better, I'd say you were jealous."

"Not jealous. Worried."

"Getting last-minute jitters about the wedding? Don't leave me at the altar," she joked.

"No sign of Eve, though."

"No. Didn't see her with any of the kids."

"That's not good."

"No, it isn't," she agreed. "Do you think she'll be the main attraction of this celebration the son kept going on about?"

"I'm afraid we're going to have to stick around to find out. In the meantime, we can dig around and see if we can find anything that would lead us to her."

She sniffed the air and smiled. "Everyone's super friendly, and the food's phenomenal. It could be worse."

"I suppose so. But not for Eve."

Her smile faded and she nodded grimly. "No, not for Eve. Or Sierra, either."

Chapter 31

Newport, Oregon

Lucas studied the Chinese warship through his binoculars from his position in the hills to the east of town. The big vessel was docked at the concrete pier in front of what had been the NOAA Marine Operations Center. Its gray bulk was easily seven hundred feet long, with a ninety-foot beam – designed like a ferry, from what he could see, which made sense given its mission to transport troops and equipment across the ocean. Lights glowed in its superstructure, and the sound of a generator carried across the water, the ship's self-contained power system providing the crew with round-the-clock comfort while aboard.

He lowered the glasses and looked at Art.

"Bigger than the one they sent to Astoria," he said.

"Yep. The question is how many are on board."

They'd been watching the ship since arriving that afternoon. Their main force was four miles inland, with Art and Lucas serving as advance scouts and chartered with scoping out the situation in town.

From what they'd seen over the last four hours, there was only a skeleton crew on the ship, with the lion's share of the Chinese bivouacked at a pair of hotels on the beach, across the bridge that spanned the mouth of the bay. Regular patrols of four soldiers each made their way through Newport's streets on a seemingly random schedule while the residents worked in forced labor crews watched over by gunmen. If the Chinese ventured past the town perimeter, neither Lucas nor Art had seen any patrols leave, and it appeared that they weren't bothering with defensive sorties in a rural, isolated area on the Oregon coast.

Which made sense, given Lucas's experience with them in Astoria. Nothing in the wilds could pose a threat to a massive warship or a well-armed force two hundred strong, so there was no point to burning energy and time patrolling the roads that led into town.

A small advantage, but one that Lucas and Art were grateful for.

"What do you think?" Art asked.

"I want to see what they do tonight. If it's like Astoria, they'll keep the patrols to a minimum. I'd say we hit them like we did in Salem – before dawn."

"With the boat docked that way, it would be easy for it to use its guns on the town."

"Right. We'll have to take out the ship before we hit the troops."

"That's not going to be easy. They've set up a roadblock on the only entry point to that dock."

"I saw that."

"What are you thinking?"

Lucas raised the binoculars again. "I'm thinking the ship is probably pretty confident it's invulnerable the way it's positioned, and with a guard detail blocking the approach."

Art nodded. "I would be."

"Me too."

Lucas outlined his idea. When he finished, Art stared at him in silence for several beats.

"That's genius."

"Not really. Path of least resistance."

They continued monitoring the area for another three hours, and when they were confident they understood the Chinese night routine, retraced their steps to their horses and rode back to the main camp, where the men were resting in anticipation of the battle to come. After eating, Art and Lucas held a war council that included Henry, Sam, Bill, and two ex-navy veterans named Gary and Kirk. Lucas went over his proposed plan with them and fine-tuned it based on their input, and by the time he settled onto his bedroll to snatch a few hours of sleep, he felt they had a good chance of pulling it off.

When he awoke, the camp was bustling as the men readied themselves for the march to Newport. Lucas had considered, and then discarded, the possibility of traveling there on horseback, but it made more sense to leave Ruby and some of the younger members of the ragtag brigade with the animals and make their way on foot. Even with the best of intentions, a large force on horseback would create noise, and they didn't need a whinny or snort to alert the Chinese when they were within striking distance.

They'd agreed that Lucas would lead the assault on the ship while Art directed the attack on the town, using the mortars and grenade launchers they'd brought. Since the Chinese had made the mistake of holing up at the beach motels, Art's militia would be able to block them from three sides with the sea at their backs while Henry and his mortar crew went to work on them.

The countryside was dark as they worked their way to the coast by moonlight, and when they arrived at the town perimeter, Lucas shook hands with Art and whispered to him, "Don't start until I radio you or you hear shooting."

"You got it. Best of luck."

"Thanks."

Lucas led Gary, Kirk, and fifteen handpicked fighters from Sam's and Bill's groups through the deserted streets and to the waterfront far from the Chinese presence. When they arrived at the marina, they ran to the shore, where four fiberglass dinghies were beached. Three had oars, and they pushed them into the water and climbed aboard in silence, taking care not to splash or bang their guns against the hulls. Once everyone was loaded, they began rowing to the far shore, where the ship loomed over the harbor, its lights burning bright in the superstructure.

Lucas had concluded that the guards would be watching the road, not the water, because there was no practical way to scale the hull on the side of the ship facing the bay. That presented them with the opportunity to make their approach by water and, once landed, to board the ship while the guards focused on threats from a direction that would never materialize.

They were three-quarters of the way across the harbor when Lucas motioned for the oarsmen to stop rowing. A lone soldier was walking along the quay, a rifle hanging from his shoulder, plodding along the shore with the slow determination of the chronically bored. He stopped and peered out at the water. Lucas held his breath and slowly brought his M4 to bear, the battery for the NV scope freshly charged.

The guard's head was the size of a melon in the scope's high magnification, and Lucas could make out eyeglasses and wisps of a mustache on a thin, youthful face. Time seemed to slow, and then the soldier spit and continued walking toward the ship, his pace the same as before.

Lucas exhaled in relief and lowered the rifle, and after the skiffs drifted for a few minutes, he nodded to the oarsman, who began rowing again. The breeze had blown them farther from the pier at which the ship was docked, and it took several more minutes than he'd hoped to make it to shore, where they jumped from the tenders onto the rocky beach, weapons in hand.

The group stayed motionless until Lucas made it to the top of the slope and scanned the area with his M4. The man they'd seen had disappeared back to the guard post at the rotunda on the access road, where Lucas had earlier counted a six-soldier detail. He assumed that the detail was stationed on the ship, not with the troops in town due to the distance, and expected there were at least twelve more guards on the vessel at any given time.

Lucas signaled the men to follow him, and ran in a crouch toward the gangplank that led to the main deck six stories above the pier. The heavy lines tethering the ship to the landing creaked as they neared the base of the gangplank, and then they were clambering up the steep ramp, taking care to do so as soundlessly as possible.

Lucas reached the deck and swept the area with his rifle before moving aside and signaling for the others to board. When they were all on deck, he pointed with two fingers at the entry to the superstructure. Kirk nodded and went first – he would take most of the men and go belowdecks where the bunk areas would be, and Lucas would take a contingent of five men and work up. There would likely be at least one watch officer on the bridge at all times, even in port, and any other officers, as well as crew, were likely to have quarters in the structure, where the canteen and break areas would also be.

Lucas waited until they disappeared down the superstructure's metal stairs, and then crept up a flight to the first-level landing, which a quick inspection revealed was empty. The second level wasn't, and they surprised eighteen crewmen, all asleep in their bunks. A quick search told them none had any weapons, so Lucas left a pair of gunmen to watch over them and led Gary and two others up toward the bridge.

The galley and officer quarters were on the next level, and Gary dispatched three officers with a sound-suppressed .32-caliber pistol as they slept – allowing them to live wasn't an option given the limited number of men in the boarding party. The sounds of the shots were muffled by the silencer as well as pillows held over the officers' heads, and in under a minute Lucas and the men were climbing the steps to the level just below the bridge.

A shot echoed through the hull from below, and Lucas swore as he reached the upper level at the sound. The watertight steel doors lining the hall looked the same as the ones below, and Lucas motioned for Gary to throw open the first door while Lucas covered him. Gary was almost to the opening when another door farther down the hallway swung wide and a sleepy-looking man wearing an undershirt appeared.

With a rifle in his hands.

Gunfire erupted in the corridor, and ricochets whined off the steel walls as the man fired wildly. Lucas threw himself to the floor and squeezed off three shots as he dropped, but none of his rounds hit the shooter. He rolled and fired two more times, and one struck the man's midsection, knocking him backward.

A head poked from the doorway, and pistol shots barked at them.

One of Gary's men cried out in pain, and the other loosed a three-round burst that drove the shooter back into the room. Lucas was on his feet and running before the echo of the shots had died, and tossed a grenade through the doorway as he blurred past.

The explosion was deafening in the confined space, and when Lucas returned to survey the damage, his ears were ringing like his head was inside a church bell. Six Chinese crew lay dead and dismembered from the blast, and part of the far wall was destroyed, the pipes and electrical runs mangled by the detonation.

Another door sprang open and a crewman emptied a submachine gun into the hall before Lucas could react. Gary's companion's head spackled the wall behind him with blood and brains, and then Lucas's M4 barked once and a hole appeared in the center of the crewman's back – he'd failed to check the other end of the hall.

Lucas lowered his rifle, pulled another grenade from his vest, lobbed it into the room from which the dead crewman had appeared, and then stepped back with his hands over his ears. The blast shook the superstructure. A quick look into the room told the same story as before – bodies were strewn around, and the bulkhead walls were destroyed.

The rest of the quarters proved empty, and after checking the wounded gunman, who'd died during the fighting, Gary and Lucas mounted the steps to the bridge, Lucas leading the way.

The bridge was empty except for a single crewman in white who had ducked behind a cabinet that managed to hide all but his shoes. Lucas inclined his head at Gary and indicated the other side of the bridge, and Gary nodded and moved around the wide pilot's console, rifle at the ready.

The man was unarmed, and Lucas did a quick frisk before pushing him to where Gary stood.

"Watch him. I want to check out what happened below."

Explosions in the distance reached Lucas as he headed down the steps to the main deck, and he peered through one of the portholes at Newport. The hotels on the beach were lit up with fires, and every few seconds another mortar detonated, sending plumes of flame into the air.

He stopped at the crew quarters, where his two gunmen were guarding everyone. After verifying they had the situation under control, he moved down to the deck level, felt for the Chinese radio Art had given him, and transmitted.

"Art," he said.

The older man's voice answered. "We heard the shooting, so we're shelling the bastards. Going to hold off on the grenades until we see what the mortars do. What's up on your end?"

"We've got the—"

Boots running up the gangplank outside stopped him, and he twisted the volume off and replaced the radio in his vest. He crossed to the open door that fed onto the deck and peeked around it to the top of the gangplank. He didn't see anyone, but the sound of footsteps on the ramp told him that the guards had also heard the commotion. He ducked through the door and switched his firing selector to three-round burst just as the first guard's head appeared.

The M4 stuttered and the guard tumbled backward, and then Lucas was at the rail, leaning over and spraying the remaining five guards with rounds. The soldiers stood no chance, exposed on a steep incline, and he cut them down without mercy.

When they were all dead, Lucas returned to the superstructure and descended the steps, ejecting his spent magazine as he went and inserting a new one. When he arrived at the first lower level, the corridors were empty, and the watertight doors all open.

He continued down another level. Same story on that floor, but when he arrived at the third, two of Kirk's men lay in crimson pools, obviously dead. Lucas cocked his head and listened, but heard nothing. He was about to step from the stairwell when shooting echoed from below, and he turned and raced down two more levels to find himself in the middle of hell.

Chapter 32

Lucas peered around the corner of the doorway into a corridor awash in blood, the bodies of four of Kirk's fighters splayed on the floor and six Chinese guards dead at the far end. Kirk and his remaining gunmen were firing at the soldiers using the fallen and the doors for protection, and the Chinese were returning fire from behind the cover of two steel doors.

Lucas tugged a grenade from his flak jacket, pulled the pin, and tossed it underhand down the hall.

"Fire in the hole!" he yelled over the gunfire, and Kirk and his men steeled themselves for the blast.

The steel orb rolled the length of the corridor and exploded at the Chinese end. Lucas tore in the direction of the blast, M4 in hand, fighting not to slip on the slick blood that coated every surface. Kirk emerged from behind his cover and joined him while his men hung back.

Lucas made it to the first door in seconds, and Kirk continued past him to the second. Three Chinese were writhing on the floor with blood streaming from their ears, and Lucas finished them with three shots from his rifle. Kirk's rattled from the second doorway, and then he turned to Lucas, his expression drawn.

"Thanks."

"No problem. Any more of them?"

Kirk shook his head. "That was it for soldiers. There could be more crew below, but it's clear from here to the deck." He frowned. "We used all our grenades on the other decks."

Lucas felt in his vest and extracted a grenade. "Last one. You can have it. Check the rest of the boat and then meet back up on the bridge."

"Will do."

Lucas returned to the level where the crewmen were being held by his men. He studied the wheel handle on the watertight door and nodded.

"Step outside," he said. "We can lock them in by jamming the wheel."

The men did as instructed, and Lucas closed the door and turned the wheel until the heavy bolts had locked in place. He held out his hand for the closest man's AR-15. "You can get another one upstairs. We lost a few men, but their rifles are fine."

The gunman handed him the weapon, and after ejecting the magazine and slipping it into his vest, Lucas jammed it between the spokes of the wheel lock so the steel barrel blocked it from turning.

"All right," he said. "Let's head up to the bridge. Kirk's mopping up below."

They followed him up the steps and retrieved the downed men's weapons, and then climbed the last flight to the bridge, where Gary was sitting with his rifle pointed at his captive.

"He speaks a little English," Gary said. "That could come in handy."

Lucas nodded and peered out the windows to take in the scene from Newport. Explosions lit the predawn sky as Henry's team continued to pummel the Chinese troops. Lucas pulled the radio from his pocket and turned the volume back up.

"Status?" he asked.

"We're throwing everything we have at them, but they're not giving up. They have grenade launchers too, and they're using them."

"Casualties?"

"A few, but the mortars are fine. That's what will win this for us. No way they can survive hours of this. How about you?"

"I'm securing the ship. Should be done in a few minutes, and then I'll head over there."

"Keep your eyes open. Couple of the men got hit by a patrol we missed."

"The hostiles still out there?"

"Negative. We took care of it. But there could be more."

"Roger that. I'll let you know when I'm on my way."

"Good news on the ship."

"Yes. Now let's finish this."

Lucas switched the radio off and moved to Gary's side. "The others will be up here shortly. We locked the crew in their quarters. We can deal with them later."

Gary nodded. "What do you want me to do once we've secured the boat?"

"Mount a watch at the top of the gangplank and shoot anything that tries to come aboard unless it's me."

"I can do that."

"And see what your friend there knows about operating the boat. Seems a shame to let a warship fall into our laps and not use it."

"What are you thinking?"

"Depends on how much damage we did with the grenades. Some of the wire runs and hydraulics are pretty badly damaged."

Lucas turned and made his way back down the stairs, and stopped when he heard footsteps rising from below. He waited with his M4 trained on the stairwell and then relaxed when he saw it was Kirk and his surviving fighters.

"That was it. I mean, there might still be the odd crewman hiding somewhere below – it's a big vessel – but we can do a more thorough search once the fighting's done."

"Gary's up top. Send the men down to collect all the stray weapons, so if someone slipped past you, they can't ambush us later."

Kirk nodded. "Will do."

"I'm going into town. Sounds like that's not going easy."

"I'd fight to the finish if it were me."

"Seems they have the same idea."

Lucas emerged from the superstructure and stood on the deck for a moment, eyeing the empty guard post near the road below, the boom of mortars rhythmic background music for his thoughts. He made his way down the gangplank, stepping over the dead, and hit the ground running, speeding to the highway, a dark blur in the gloom.

He slowed when he arrived at the bridge and swept the span with his scope. Seeing nothing but abandoned vehicles, he picked his way through them until a half dozen shots dimpled the truck beside him and he dropped to the asphalt for cover.

The gunfire sounded like it had emanated from the far side of the bridge, and Lucas crawled to another vehicle and raised his M4 to search for the source of the shooting. After scanning the shore, he spotted a pair of men hiding behind a rusting pickup truck at the Newport side of the bridge.

Who weren't Chinese.

He lowered his rifle and radioed Art. "Got a pair of our cowboys by the bridge taking potshots at me. Can you call them off?"

"Sorry. Got hectic over here. Sounds like word didn't spread fast enough. I'll take care of it."

Lucas waited, and five minutes later a runner reached the men, who waved at Lucas after talking to the newcomer.

Lucas exhaled and resumed his trek, a half smile on his face at the thought that, after all the close calls he'd had with enemies, he could have been gunned down by his own men. He would have laughed out loud at the irony if it hadn't been so immediate and real, and settled for a shake of his head as he wended between the vehicles, his boots crunching on broken glass underfoot.

He found Art at the hospital, which they'd taken with only a short fight with a few guards, and was inside while Henry and his mortar crew worked from the roof. Art was speaking with Sam when Lucas entered, and they both looked up at the sound of his footsteps.

"What's the situation?" Lucas asked.

"The hotels are almost completely destroyed, but the Chinese have spread out and are picking at our boys. I held off doing a final push until you secured the ship. Figured you'd want to direct it."

"Nah. You're doing a fine job. I'll sit this one out. What's the plan?"

"To lead with about a hundred grenades from the Mk 19s, and then close the circle and hit them with everything we've got."

"You're sure all of them are on that stretch of beach?"

"Yes."

Lucas thought for a moment. "I have an idea."

Ten minutes later, Lucas and two men were on one of the sailboats with a Browning .50 caliber and several thousand rounds of ammo. The men, both of whom had sailing experience, raised the main sail. The wind filled it with a flap of fabric, and when it was taut against the breeze, the boat cut across the small waves toward the breakwater.

It took half an hour to reach the open ocean, which was thankfully calm ahead of an inbound storm from the north, and another ten minutes to arrive five hundred yards off the beach. Fireballs continued to punch from the ruins of what had been the hotels only hours earlier as the eastern horizon glowed pink from the first rays of the rising sun.

The boat bobbed in the swell, and Lucas sat cross-legged on the bow with the Browning pointed at the shore. The men lowered the sails, and the craft rose and fell in the gentle rollers.

"Can you keep the bow pointed at the shore?" Lucas asked.

"Without power, not really. Sorry."

Lucas raised the radio to his mouth. "I'm in position. Whenever you're ready. Shift the mortar fire forty feet more toward the ocean – they're on the beach, on the other side of the berm they're using for cover."

Lucas waited for the shells to begin dropping on the Chinese, and when they did, he opened fire with the Browning. His aim was less than perfect because of the boat's movement, but he adjusted to the swaying and in about ten seconds had found his range and was raining .50-caliber slugs onto the sand.

Some of the soldiers figured out what was happening and fired at the boat, but it was beyond the accurate range of their rifles, and none of their rounds struck it. Lucas returned the favor and blew the shooters apart, the Browning having quadruple the range of the assault rifles on a bad day.

Between the mortars and the big machine gun, the battle was over in minutes, with the Chinese force cut to pieces to the last man.

Lucas hailed Art on the radio again. "Okay, you can stop. It's over. None left."

"We got them all?" Art asked.

Lucas eyed the bodies littering the beach and sighed heavily. "Yes. Put together some search parties to hunt for any stragglers, and go door-to-door to let the people know they're safe and the Chinese have been taken care of."

Chapter 33

Denver, Colorado

It was the evening before the closing celebration, and the conference center was packed even tighter than the previous nights, filled with the entire population of Denver, by the look of it. Arnold and Julie took their seats in the now-familiar guest seating area, Devin and Anne in front of them, and waited as the choir serenaded the crowd with the usual collection of hymns and spirituals.

When the music died down, Elijah approached the podium with more reverence than for the other sermons and tapped on the microphone before clearing his throat and giving the sound man a thumbs-up.

"Welcome, welcome, everyone. Tonight is a special night. As everyone knows, after a week of fellowship and reconnecting with one another, tomorrow is the closing celebration. My father will conduct tomorrow's ceremony, but he's so excited about something he can't wait until tomorrow to share, so he wanted to address you tonight as well."

A collective gasp sounded from the throng. Arnold had to fight the urge to smirk.

"Without further ado, I present to you the one true Prophet of the church, Ulysses Granger!"

The choir broke into song as the gathering rose to its feet. Ulysses strode to the podium from the side of the stage, hands held high as the applause and cheers reached a fever pitch, his eyes glowing with dark intensity beneath a high brow, his white suit nearly blinding in its brightness.

"Thank you, thank you," he said, waving. "Now take your seats. We have business to attend to. Serious business. The Lord's business!"

The congregation sat, and Ulysses waited until the room quieted before continuing.

"It's been a miraculous week. Truly so. We've got a host of new folks who have decided to join the church, and more are on their way – our radio transmissions have reached those seeking the light in the far corners of the earth, and they're coming, I have it on good authority," he said, and pointed a finger at the sky. "The highest authority!"

More clapping and foot stomping and cheers.

"But if that's not reason enough to celebrate, I bring you important news! The Lord has delivered unto us one of the false messiahs I've warned about – led her to us like a moth to flame. I'm referring to the girl known as Eve – whose blood is the blood of the serpent, and which has been used to interfere with His plan to eradicate the sinful and the unworthy from the earth!"

A curtain stage right opened, and Ellen stepped from the shadows wearing a white tunic. Julie elbowed Arnold; and then Eve, similarly attired, emerged from backstage and blinked in the glare of the lights.

The crowd gasped at her appearance and a moan filled the air. Ulysses shook his head and pointed at Eve.

"Don't be afraid. We're in the Lord's house, and nothing can harm us when we're enjoying his protection. It's He who delivered her to us for tomorrow's celebration, which will be the most important event in our church's history."

He paused, and the crowd went silent, hanging on his every word.

"Tomorrow this…creature…will be the centerpiece of our festivities, as a symbol of our faith. She's worked in union with dark forces that seek to corrupt our world, but we will have none of it. The snake shall not be victorious in this struggle, and our Father delivered her to us as a sign that the time of ascension will be upon us soon. All scores will be settled, all debts paid, and the deserving shall take their rightful position by His side while the sinful shall descend into the fiery pits of eternal hell, where they'll pay for their worship of false prophets and occult messiahs and graven images."

Eve blinked at the audience, tiny on the large stage, her expression slack, her eyes drugged. Ellen reached out and pulled her back to the curtain, which they both ducked behind.

Ulysses finished up his announcement with another declaration that tomorrow night's celebration would be the most important and pivotal point in the church's history, and then vanished behind the curtain as well.

Julie leaned into Arnold to whisper something, but he shushed her and shot her a warning glance. They sat through a half hour of Elijah railing against the wickedness of mankind and the justification for eradicating most of the planet's population because of the species' sinfulness and the lust that presumably resided in everyone's hearts, and then dutifully filed to the front, where they were blessed and reminded about the mass baptism the following night, before the choir resumed its singing.

Outside, once well away from eavesdropping ears, Arnold motioned for Devin and Anne to join him and Julie beneath a tree.

"So we know they've got her," Julie said. "She looked pretty out of it."

"They probably drugged her," Devin said.

"What do we do now? Sounds ominous that she's going to be the showpiece of tomorrow's thing," Anne said.

Arnold frowned and looked to the convention center. "We need to find out where they're holding her, and rescue her before these psychos can do anything really evil."

"How do we do that?" Julie asked.

"I'm working on it."

"What does that mean?"

"They must be keeping her with Ulysses and his inner circle. Find him, and we find her."

"Sure, okay. But how?"

"That's the part I'm working on."

Chapter 34

Denver, Colorado

Arnold sat in one of the few bars in the downtown area, where fellow travelers as well as members of the congregation were nursing beers. Arnold recognized one of the food vendors and carried his beer to the man's table and smiled at him. "Tough one, huh?"

The man smiled in return and raised his glass. "Yeah. These things take it out of you." He pointed at a chair. "Take a load off."

"Thanks," Arnold said, and sat.

"Where you from?"

"Down Albuquerque way."

The man frowned. "Heard it's rough farther south."

"Yeah, it is. Texas is supposed to be a nightmare," Arnold said.

"Shame. But not surprising."

"Why's that?"

"We had the same thing happen here after the virus. A ton of scumbags tried to take over the city. We had to fight 'em tooth and nail, but eventually they turned and ran, of course. Criminals don't like a fair fight."

"Glad you won. This place seems like one of a kind."

"Yup. We're all lucky. Praise God."

"Amen."

Arnold took a long pull on his beer. "So whereabouts do you live?"

"Over on the other side of the church. There's no shortage of apartments and houses. Bunch of big hotels, too. I got one of the rooms in the Four Seasons."

"Got to say it seems a little weird with all the empty high-rises. Kinda like living in a ghost town, isn't it?"

The vendor laughed. "That's sort of how I felt at first. But you get used to it. And there's safety in numbers."

"Where do the muckety-mucks live? Like Granger's group? They have someplace special they staked out?"

The man nodded. "They call it the compound. It's the old performing arts complex. There's, like, ten theaters. Right next door to the convention center."

"Why do they live in theaters?"

The vendor shrugged. "I don't know. But they do. Father and son got their own deals going. Dad's a loner, lives with a bunch of guards and clergy in the big building – the inner circle of the church, like that place in Italy, you know? Son took over one of the others and has his crowd over there."

"Right. The Vatican. Sounds like quite a production. Lot of people involved?"

"At least a couple of hundred. They're also the city government. I've never been in there, but I got a buddy who's a carpenter, and he said they built it out like nobody's business. Rooms for everyone, power, water, the whole deal."

"Why does the father have so many guards?"

"Dunno. That's just the way it is. Nowadays you need firepower to keep the bad guys at bay. The place is locked down tight, and they patrol it twenty-four seven – and everyone knows it. It'd be suicide to attack the Prophet; not that anyone would."

"He's quite a speaker, isn't he?"

"The man's the voice of the Lord," the vendor intoned, and finished his beer. "So you planning on joining us?"

"Looking that way. My wife is sold."

He smiled knowingly. "Then you are. You won't regret it. We're like one big family."

"That's how it seems. You want another one?" Arnold offered.

"Nah. I got to be up early again tomorrow for the big show. We're expecting the whole congregation for the last day. Almost six thousand strong. Going to be hectic."

Arnold watched the man leave. Of course the Prophet would live in a compound guarded like an army base. That would also be the logical place to keep Eve – right next to the convention center, so convenient, and no chance of a five-year-old escaping; not that they were known for that.

He swallowed the last of his ale and rose. It was a nice night out, if a little chilly. Perfect for a walk.

The bar was three blocks from the hotel, and he continued past it to the darkened convention center. On the far side, the performing arts center was brightly lit, power obviously being no problem for the church. He strolled along the boulevard on the other side of the street and spotted guards at each corner, along with a group of three men patrolling the grounds. They spied him and stopped to watch him continue along his way, and didn't resume their patrol until he'd rounded the corner.

Chapter 35

The sun rose over Newport, revealing a killing field on the beach. The bloated corpses of some of the Chinese were floating on the incoming tide, pulled into the water by the ocean's surge.

Art surveyed the ruined hotels with Lucas, Sam, and Bill, and then turned to the ship.

"We might have an opportunity here," he said. "That vessel came from Seattle, and China before that. And it's ours now."

"Opportunity?" Bill asked.

"It could get us to Seattle in a day instead of weeks."

"Who said anything about going to Seattle?" Sam asked.

Lucas shook his head. "It took some hits during the fight. Grenades tore it up pretty bad."

"Assuming we could repair it sufficiently to take it to Seattle, we could be there before the Chinese smelled a rat, and could surprise them on their own turf."

Lucas sighed. "We have no idea how many men they have there, or what their defenses are like. Or even the layout of the city. There's a hell of a difference between rousting some bikers or taking on a couple of hundred newly arrived infantry versus facing a dug-in army."

Art nodded. "Lucas is right. But the men are flying high after three victories, and morale is a big part of any fight. That ship could easily haul us all north, and we could land wherever we decided. Think about it. Instead of wearing ourselves out traveling all the way across the state by horse or on foot, we could be in Seattle tomorrow."

"No rush getting us all killed," Lucas grumbled.

"We wouldn't have to attack. We could reconnoiter, like we did here. If it doesn't look good, we could always retreat."

"They're going to know something went wrong here soon enough," Sam said.

"How would they?" Bill asked.

"Nobody answers the radio, that would be one tip-off," Lucas said.

"Ah."

"How's your wife?" Sam asked Bill.

"Fine. A little shaken up, but the Chinese didn't…they didn't mistreat her."

"We don't know if we could even get the engines to start," Lucas said.

"That's a yes or no, right?" Art asked. "Let's assume it's a yes. Seems to me the choices are either wait here for the Chinese to send another boatload of soldiers from China, or take the fight to them and make it so expensive to try to take over the country they decide they'd rather not."

"Assumes they don't have another boat in Seattle," Lucas said.

"You mentioned one of the prisoners speaks some English? We should interrogate him."

"Do whatever you like," Lucas said. "But a whole lot of things would have to go right for us to make it to Seattle and crush the Chinese. Only reason we succeeded in Astoria was because the radiation got most of them first."

"True," Art agreed. "Not saying it would be easy. But if we could pull it off…we'd have saved the country."

"For now. There'll always be someone. If it isn't the Chinese, it's the Illuminati. Not them, the Mexicans. Or the Russians."

"We got to start somewhere," Art said. "It's worth taking a hard look at the ship and figuring out what we would need to do to cruise it to Seattle."

"How many miles is that?" Sam asked.

"Maybe…four hundred or so by water," Art answered. He looked at the boat again. "That thing should do an easy twenty knots if it's like the ships I've been on. We could be there in a day."

"Assuming it still runs," Lucas corrected. "And that we could find someone to operate it."

"Kirk and Gary were in the navy. I'm sure we have others. After all, Astoria was a fishing port."

"It's the size of a skyscraper," Lucas said. "Different scale."

"A boat's a boat. Let's head over there and check it out."

Lucas looked to Sam. "You okay with this?"

Sam shrugged. "Always loved a boat ride."

"You?" he asked Bill. "Your wife okay with you taking off again…possibly forever?"

Bill grinned. "Don't get her hopes up."

"Lucas, it can't hurt to look," Art said.

"Ruby and Rosemary are still up with the horses," Lucas said.

"I'll go bring everyone into town. Don't let that keep you," Sam assured him.

Lucas threw up his hands. "Fine. Let's go see what the story is. Need to bring some men to spell the others anyway. And we need to figure out what to do with the prisoners."

"They're navy, right?" Art asked.

"That's right. Crew."

"They could be helpful with the ship."

"Don't bet on it. Likely to sabotage it as anything."

"Not if they have a man shadowing them at all times."

Lucas frowned again. "Every plan sounds easy till it all goes to hell."

Art patted his shoulder. "Come on. Ease up. You have to admit we're on a roll."

"A smart man knows when to walk away from the table."

"No question. But…do the math. This looks like the same kind of ship they sent to Astoria, doesn't it?"

"Roughly. That one had more guns."

"But the point is they're roughly the same size."

"Sure."

"Which means they probably sent around the same number of men, right?"

"This one's got more space than that one did."

"Humor me, Lucas."

He shrugged. "It's your story."

"We just took out a couple of hundred here. If they sent about the same number of troops in both ships, that would leave them with maybe…five or six hundred, tops, assuming they didn't lose any taking Seattle."

"Sounds about right."

"We have over six hundred men."

"They'd be defending fortified positions they picked. That's a bad scenario."

"Agreed. But we wouldn't necessarily have to go at them hard. We could do it differently than we have so far."

Lucas's right eyebrow rose. "How's that?"

"We can talk on the way. I'll round up some men. How many you figure we'll need to relieve the others?"

"Maybe…a dozen or so."

"I'll bring twenty."

When they arrived at the ship, Kirk had the Chinese crew washing the blood off the gangplank at gunpoint. When Kirk saw the reinforcements arrive, he signaled the Chinese back onto the deck and pointed them to a spot in front of the superstructure, where the rest of the militia sat with their weapons in their laps.

"We brought company to spell you," Art said, once on deck.

"Great."

"Where's Gary?" Lucas asked.

"On the bridge, trying to figure out how bad the damage is."

"Where's the prisoner who speaks English?" Art asked.

Kirk laughed. "I wouldn't say that. He knows a few words, but he can't carry on a conversation or anything."

"He might be playing dumb. It would make sense anyone they sent would have at least a decent grasp of the language."

"Maybe not the crew. They wouldn't interact with the locals," Kirk said.

"Fair point."

Art motioned to the gunmen he'd brought. "Tell the men what you want them to do," he said. "Consider yourself in command of them until further notice."

Kirk brightened. "Mostly guard duty."

"Tell them," Art said.

Lucas showed Art the way to the bridge, where Gary was studying the instruments with a sour expression. The Chinese crewman was seated at the end of the console, watching Gary.

Gary looked up at them when they entered, and shook his head. "The explosions messed up some wire runs and steering stuff. A shame."

"Do the engines work?" Lucas asked.

"Haven't tried them yet."

"Try them."

Gary scanned the console and zeroed in on a section with a pair of throttles and transmissions. He regarded the controls and tried a toggle. Lights blinked to life, and he turned to the crewman.

"Engine," he said, pointing at the array of buttons and switches.

The crewman gave him a puzzled look, and then understanding registered in his eyes. He stood, walked to the console, and pointed at an array of switches. Gary nodded and flipped them on.

"I think those are the blowers. I'm not entirely sure, but if it's like an American ship, it would make sense," he said.

"What if they're not?"

Gary shrugged. "Then we're all going to die." He flashed a grin. "Kidding."

Lucas's expression didn't change.

Gary pointed to the back of the boat and made an engine

vrooming sound. The crewman pointed at two buttons with plastic covers over them to prevent them from being inadvertently pushed. He raised the covers and depressed one. A vibration shivered beneath their feet, and a cloud of black smoke rose into the air from the stern. Gary tapped a large dial and smiled. "It runs."

"Try the other one."

He repeated the process, and the other motor started. The crewman stepped forward and adjusted the throttles, and the revs settled at eight hundred rpm.

Gary turned to Art and Lucas. "The engines may run, but most of the electrical equipment doesn't. The GPS is dead, which doesn't surprise me, but so's the radar, the depth finder, sonar, you name it. The grenades must have shredded the wiring. And I have no idea whether the steering works. You saw the pipes that were destroyed. If one of those is a hydraulic line for the rudders…" He stopped. "I'm guessing you're interested because you want to know if the ship's seaworthy, right?"

Art nodded. "Good guess. How long would it take you to check all the emergency systems? Bilge pumps, fire, fuel, steering?"

"I…I don't know. Couple of hours, at least."

"Then get started. Pull anyone you need from the men."

"Repairs could take ten times longer," he warned. "Depending on what they are."

"I'm guessing they have a machine shop on a boat this size," Art said. "And I'll bet they have machinists on the crew. Make them an offer they can't refuse."

Gary swallowed hard. "Tall order."

"I want to know if we can be steaming for Seattle by this afternoon with our entire force on board," Art said.

Gary stared at him like he was nuts. "You're kidding."

"Not at all. If this thing can run up the coast, we're going along for the ride and taking the fight to Seattle."

Lucas didn't say anything as Gary watched Art leave the bridge. Instead, he followed him out and stopped him at the landing. "What about the horses?"

"There's plenty of room on board, isn't there?"

"Not for six hundred men and animals there isn't. And there are logistics. Feed. Water. Waste. Big undertaking. I wouldn't rush into it."

"Then we only bring half the horses. Whatever. If we can take back Seattle, we can accomplish anything, Lucas. We'll be unstoppable. We'll have thousands of fighters begging to join us."

"And?" Lucas asked.

"And then we finish what we started."

"What's that?"

"Ridding the country of the cancer that's rotting it from within."

"*We* didn't start anything, Art. I went along for the ride and did what was necessary to save my friends. This is your crusade, not mine."

"You keep saying that, but you're still here."

"I keep getting sucked into situations I want no part of."

"You saying you don't want to free Seattle from Chinese invaders?"

"I want to go home, Art."

The older man nodded sympathetically. "I hear you. Maybe after a detour, huh?"

"This was the detour."

"Then what's another four hundred miles between friends?"

That caused Lucas to smile. "You and Ruby should hook up. You're made for each other."

Art frowned in puzzlement.

"She keeps pushing me to do the same thing," Lucas explained.

"Smart lady. I knew I liked her for a reason."

"What if they can't get the ship seaworthy?"

It was Art's turn to smile. "Then you get your wish and can go home and chop wood or make babies or whatever, and the rest of us will stay here and do what's right."

Lucas shook his head and made a face. "You know this isn't going to be easy."

Art gave a humorless laugh. "Nothing worth doing ever is."

Lucas stared out at the water and sighed. "Well, hell. I suppose a boat ride isn't such a big deal."

"Now you're talking." He paused. "By the way, nice shooting out there today."

"They never stood a chance. Not proud of anything I did this morning."

"Which is why you need to be part of this, Lucas. Anyone else would be taking laps. Not you. That's the difference between you and just about everyone here, and it's an important one. I've seen a lot of leaders. You're a natural commander because you don't care about the glory and you'd rather not have to do any of it. Those are always the best kind. They value their men's lives and never underestimate their enemies. It's a rare quality, Lucas. You can't teach it or fake it."

Lucas started down the stairs, his steps heavy. "If you say so."

Art watched him go and, when his footsteps had faded, nodded slowly to himself. "I do."

Chapter 36

Laredo, Texas

Dawn was breaking when one of the Crew doing guard duty on the Rio Grande bridge spotted movement by the river below and walked over to check on it. He leaned over the railing to get a better look. A lasso snaked from the underside, encircled his neck, and dragged him halfway over the railing, strangling him with the rough rope. His rifle dropped to the pavement as he fought for breath, and he grabbed the cord with both hands.

Powerful arms jerked him the rest of the way, and he tumbled toward the water. His neck snapped like a dry branch when the rope stopped his fall halfway down, and there he hung, limbs twitching, the other end of the rope cinched to a pipe beneath the bridge.

A line of cartel fighters continued crossing from the Mexican side, the men suspended upside down. They pulled themselves along the pipe that ran the length of the bridge, arms bulging from exertion. When the first reached the U.S. side, he swung his legs down, dropped onto the ground beneath the bridge, and freed his assault rifle.

Ten minutes later, sixty gunmen stood on the Texas bank, all heavily armed, waiting for the signal from their leader – a stocky man with tobacco-colored skin and long black hair cinched back in a ponytail. He signaled to the men to follow him along the bank, and a hundred and fifty yards from the crossing, they filed up the slope to the riverfront road, where they wouldn't be seen by the Crew outpost at the bridge.

More fighters crossed in the same manner, and soon two hundred Mexicans, armed with Kalashnikovs and several dozen LAW antitank rocket tubes, were gathered in the abandoned buildings that lined the Rio Grande. Nobody spoke, and when the leader motioned to them, they split off in groups headed by cartel lieutenants who were responsible for neutralizing specific targets.

The Nuevo Laredo Cartel had learned from its prior attempt to displace the Crew, and had tracked the arrival of reinforcements through a network of informants on the Texas side. They knew the Crew's current strength, their patrol and meal hours, and the various buildings they'd taken over. The old immigration checkpoint had been beefed up to forty men, and the afternoon following the attack, they'd dynamited the smaller bridge to the west of the one the cartel had just used to cross over.

They also knew from an informant that the two hundred and seventy-six gang members in town constituted the entire Crew force within a four-day ride, and if the cartel could take Laredo and move a thousand fighters into place within that time, the Crew would never be able to displace them and would give up trying when their losses mounted.

The cartel had raided a Mexican armory and decided to come at the Crew with everything it had rather than hoping for an easy victory using stealth. It had transported rockets and rifles and grenades to the Mexican side, equipped its ex-military armed wing, and was ready to seize control of the vital trading city and increase its presence on land that had once belonged to Mexico.

The three groups took off in different directions, with the leader taking his men toward the strategic bridge outpost. Once that fell, there would be nothing to stop the four hundred additional fighters waiting on the Nuevo Laredo side from spilling across, guaranteeing a swift victory.

The leader didn't waste time with attempts at secrecy and instead ordered his six LAW rockets to target the outpost. The projectiles streaked toward the structure and exploded with devastating force, blasting concrete and rebar in deadly showers that killed half the Crew fighters outside before they knew what had hit them. The Mexicans ran toward the outpost as the dust cleared. The fighting lasted less than a minute, the Crew gunmen disoriented from the blasts and unable to mount any sort of defense.

Once the immigration station was theirs, the leader radioed the waiting cartel fighters on the Mexican side, and the bridge filled with gunmen making their way across. He didn't wait for the force to arrive, and left one of his subordinates to lead them toward the Crew headquarters, where explosions were already shattering the silence in the center of town.

He arrived there in the middle of a firefight, with Crew shooters sniping at the Mexicans who'd surrounded the building and were returning fire with mixed results. He watched the volleys from behind a partially collapsed wall, and radioed his lieutenant to bring the bridge force to the headquarters for a final push. He radioed the other group, which had been chartered with taking out the hotel the Crew had commandeered for sleeping quarters, and was told that they were mopping up pockets of resistance – the lion's share of the sleeping men had been killed before they'd had a chance to wake.

Loud pounding at his chamber door woke Snake from a dead sleep, and he staggered through the half-darkness to the doorway, a submachine gun in hand.

"What?" he snarled.

"Distress call from Laredo. They're under attack."

Snake swung the door open and glared at the messenger. "What?"

"The Mexicans again. But this time they've already taken out two-thirds of our men." He took a breath. "They're saying they need to evacuate."

"Let's go," Snake said, and stormed to the radio room at the end of the hall as his bodyguards rushed to catch up.

The operator looked up in surprise from where he was listening through headphones and, when he saw Snake closing on him, pointed to another set hanging on a hook. Snake pulled them over his head and turned to the operator. "I want to talk to them."

"Last transmission was a minute ago. It sounds bad."

"Get someone in charge on the horn."

The operator toggled the transmit button and spoke into the microphone. Nobody responded. Snake elbowed him out of the way and growled into the mic, "This is Snake. Answer, dammit."

A voice responded ten seconds later. "We're taking heavy fire. Hundreds of men attacking. We're going to have to pull back or—"

Snake cut him off with the transmit button. "Listen to me, you shitgrub. You'll fight them off or you'll die trying, do you understand? The Crew doesn't retreat or surrender. If you can't beat them back, you're as good as dead when reinforcements arrive. Do you read me?"

Snake and the operator listened for a response, but none came. A minute went by, and then another, and the only sound was the hum of dead air with occasional static from interference.

Snake jerked the headset from his ears and tossed it on the table. "Call me if you get anything more. I'm going back to bed."

The operator watched Snake, wearing only his underwear, march to the door and exit, the tattooed serpents on his back writhing as he moved.

There were no further transmissions, and by the time the sun was high in the Texas sky, Laredo was no longer held by the Crew. The Nuevo Laredo Cartel was the city's new governor, with a fighting force of well over a thousand men ready to defend the new territory to the last man.

Chapter 37

Denver, Colorado

Julie and Anne strolled past the vendors lining the approach to the convention center. They were wearing the white tunics they'd been given for that night's celebration; the hems were decidedly short, and the homespun fabric clung to their curves. Julie's long legs were tanned bronze, and she wore sandals she'd bought at one of the street stalls – relics from before the collapse, made from synthetics that would outlast the buildings around her. Anne wore her combat boots, and the pair turned heads as they laughed together, to anyone watching them two young women without a care in the world.

They passed the conference center entry with its massive bear sculpture and continued to the performing arts center, where an unsmiling guard with a rifle stopped them.

"Sorry. This area's off-limits."

"Really? Why? I thought the whole town was open for the festival."

"It is. All except this area. Church property."

"Oh, um, okay. We saw all the buildings and were wondering what it was."

"Now you know."

Julie flashed a smile. "Okay. We didn't mean any harm." She pointed to a green area across the street. "Is it okay if we hang out under those trees and eat?"

The guard looked her up and down. "I don't suppose there'd be anything wrong with that."

"Perfect. Thanks."

"No problem."

They went and got freshly baked breakfast rolls and apple cider from one of the carts and walked over to the small park across from the compound. They had no real plan other than to watch the comings and goings and try to learn anything they could. A perimeter wall built from a hodgepodge of brick, cinderblock, and stone encircled the grounds, its construction obviously post-collapse. It stretched all the way from the edge of a park to one side of the convention center, blocking the access road. People came and went through an ornate gate at the front of the compound, and Julie stiffened when she saw Ellen stroll through.

"That confirms she's one of the church bigwigs," Anne whispered.

"Yeah. God-fearing murderer and kidnapper," Julie said under her breath.

Others trickled through the gate to enjoy the final day of the festival, and Julie spotted a familiar face among a group of men and women. "There's the creepy son," she said, and stood, stretching so the tunic rose high on her thighs, displaying a tanned expanse of muscular leg.

Elijah looked over at the pair of women. He stopped what he was doing when Anne rose as well. Both women laughed, flashing white teeth in the sunlight, and he broke away from his entourage and crossed the street.

"Good morning, ladies," he said, his voice a purr.

"Morning," Anne said.

Julie smiled and looked down demurely. "Good morning."

"Beautiful day, isn't it?"

"Oh, it's perfect," Julie said. "I love it here. It's like…like heaven."

They chatted about nothing much, and Anne excused herself, holding up her empty cider cup. "You want some more?" she asked Julie.

"Sure. Thanks," Julie said, and handed Anne hers.

Anne strutted away, and Elijah's eyes followed her before settling back on Julie. "The dress means you're joining us permanently, I take it?"

"Yes. It's so…impressive. I've never seen anything like it."

"And your…I believe you came with a young man, didn't you?"

Her expression clouded. "Yes, but he's not going to stay. He said this wasn't for him. We got into a huge fight about it."

"Oh, dear. I'm sorry to hear that."

Julie shrugged, looked away, and then brightened. "It's probably for the best. He was kind of a jerk."

"Yes, well, still. It can't be easy."

"I'll get over it."

"Do you have any other…friends here?"

"Just Anne. We met on the trail coming to Denver. She's really sweet and a lot of fun. Not like the jerk. He was a total sourpuss."

"A shame. You seem like you can do better than that."

"Well, I hope so. Though I suppose it will take some time."

Elijah snapped his fingers. "I have an idea! Why don't you have lunch with me today, and I'll see if I can think of anyone suitable? You can tell me all about yourself, and I'll see what I can do. I know everyone. And you're far too beautiful to be alone. It's a crime against nature."

Julie blushed and looked away, allowing Elijah time to fully appreciate her considerable charms. When she looked back at him, she did her best to appear both shy and interested. "Lunch with you? I'm…it would be an honor!"

"Wonderful. Then it's settled. Come to the gate at noon and tell the guard you're my lunch guest. What was your name again?"

"Julie."

"Julie," he said, savoring the syllables like a fine wine. "Excellent. I can't wait. Is there anything special you'd like? There's no limit."

"Oh, um, no. Whatever you'd normally eat. Don't go to any trouble."

He returned to his group, and Anne arrived with the cider. "What did Creepo want?"

"I have a lunch date with him today."

"Ew."

"I know. But it's the only way any of us are going to get in there. You saw the guards."

"How far do you think he's going to try to take it?"

"I played young and dumb, so he's got a good chance. Besides, you can tell he's used to getting anything he wants. He's got that spoiled thing going on. He probably thinks I'll show up and spread for him before appetizers arrive."

"So what are you going to do?"

"Whatever I have to in order to find Eve."

Noon arrived quickly, and after telling Arnold what she'd managed, Julie was at the gate early, with some vanilla extract she'd bought from a vendor dabbed on her neck and arms, and wildflowers woven through her hair by Anne, who'd felt the innocence they lent her would be a further aphrodisiac for the lecherous son.

A woman in her late thirties greeted Julie at the gate and escorted her to Elijah's suite of rooms in one of the smaller theaters. Julie admired the towering glass and steel arches over the walkway, and pretended awe at the extent of the facility as well as the condition, which was immaculate by post-apocalyptic standards.

"In here," the humorless woman said, holding open a glass door. Julie entered, and the woman closed it behind her and indicated a hall to the right. "He's waiting for you in the last room on the left."

"Thanks," Julie said, and headed down the corridor.

Elijah was seated at a dining table laden with a feast large enough to feed a party of twenty. He stood when she came in, and she beamed a ten-thousand-kilowatt smile at him. He motioned to the food. "I wasn't sure what you might want, so I told the staff to just make some of everything."

"That's…amazing. You shouldn't have."

"Nonsense. A young woman who's been through hardship should be denied nothing." He indicated a seat. "Please. Sit."

Julie did so and smiled again. "This is a gorgeous building. Do you live here all by yourself?"

"Running the church with my father is demanding work. I need space where I can retire and think."

"You have to give me a tour."

"Of course. After lunch." Elijah reached for a pitcher. "You should try this. It's excellent. It's a fortified fruit punch one of the deacons makes. Absolutely delicious."

"Fortified?"

"With neutral spirits," he said, as though that was an answer. Julie knew he was describing alcohol, probably white lightning, and couching it in double-speak so she wouldn't object. She'd expected as much, if not outright drugging of her food.

"Oh, um, sure. Do you like it?"

"I love it," he said, and poured her goblet full and his half full. "You must be parched from walking in the sun all morning."

She took a sip and smiled. "Hmm, this really is good." She thought it tasted like at least fifty proof, the flavor of the moonshine masked by cherries and apples and berries.

"I find it just the thing after a hard day."

Julie eyed the platters of food. "What is all this?"

"We have a little of everything. This is rabbit stew, and this is venison, and this is ham, and pork belly. Chicken curry, poached trout, steamed and grilled vegetables, ten kinds of fruit in a fruit salad. Fresh baked bread, and soup to start."

"I…I can't remember when I saw this much food…"

"Fate has been kind to us."

Julie picked at the samplings he ladled onto her plate, watching him to confirm he was eating the same dishes as she in case he'd drugged them. They made small talk about the burdens and responsibilities of tending the church's flock, and she felt the alcohol as the level of her cup dropped. When she'd eaten all she could, Elijah invited her to sit with him in his living area.

"More fruit punch? I think it's the best I've ever tasted," he asked.

"Maybe later. After the tour. I can't wait to see everything. It's like some kind of wonderland."

"Oh, sure. Perhaps we can do that later…"

She pouted and then smiled. "I don't know. More punch will make me woozy. I'll be too tired later. Can't we go now?"

Elijah leaned forward and brushed a lock of her hair from her brow. "Of course we can. It's just…I don't often have company, so I've forgotten my manners. All I seem to do is work these days. It's been forever since I got to spend time with someone as…breathtaking as you, Julie."

Another smile. "Show me around, and then I'll have that second drink, Elijah. And thank you for taking time out from your day to have lunch with me. You really didn't have to."

"I wanted to. I…I sense there's something different about you, Julie. Something…unique."

I'll bet, she thought, but didn't say it. Instead, she took his hand and stood. "Come on. Let's see what you've built here."

He rose, a disappointed smile in place, and smiled back at her. "Sure. Anything in particular you're interested in?"

"Anything you're proud of. I think what you've done here is incredible. It's like the collapse never happened."

"We've worked hard to restore civilization. With God's help."

They walked through the complex, and he pointed out the various buildings. "This is where the church elders meet to deal with matters of government. And that serves as our courthouse, where we hear accusations and dispense justice." He paused in front of another. "This is my father's retreat. And this is where the inner circle of the church live."

"Inner circle?"

"Those who've devoted their lives to the church. Like nuns and priests in other religions."

"Ah. Can they have…can they marry?"

"Oh, certainly. Our view on relations is more progressive than some. My father was told in one of his visions that we're perfect creations, and if we allow ourselves to be purified, our actions are also pure. As long as we don't have sin in our hearts – greed, sloth, envy, jealousy, and so on – then our actions are all part of a larger plan."

Julie noticed he didn't mention lust, and her smile was genuine. "Oh. Then why the separate rooms for men and women at the hotel?"

"Because you haven't been baptized yet, so you aren't pure in God's eyes."

Her lower lip extruded in another pout. "I want to be pure, too."

It was Elijah's turn to smile, a predatory grin. "I can baptize you after the tour if you like."

"You can?"

"Of course. I'm the number two man in the church. I'll be doing the mass baptism tonight as well."

"Would you?"

"Absolutely."

Julie leaned into him and kissed him on the cheek, and then put her hand over her mouth. "Oh. I'm sorry. I…"

"Don't be. You're one of God's children, and I'm one of his messengers. There can be no sin between us."

"Really?"

"I have it on the highest authority."

They continued walking the grounds, and Julie stopped where workers were affixing a large ventilation shaft to the side of the convention center.

"What's that?"

Elijah frowned. "I…I'm not sure. Repairing something, probably." Elijah approached the workers, who stopped when they saw him. "What are you doing?"

"A project for your father."

Elijah appeared confused. The worker indicated one of the buildings they'd walked by. "Direct orders from him."

"He didn't say why?"

The worker shook his head. "The Prophet says jump, we jump. That's how it works."

"Very well. Carry on."

Elijah edged closer to Julie and took her hand. "Come. I'm getting thirsty. Let's get something cool to drink, and then I'll baptize you."

They retraced their steps to Elijah's suite, and when they were inside, he poured two more goblets full from the iced pitcher and handed her one. "To purity!" he said, and watched as she gulped down several large swallows while he sipped his.

She put the cup down and smiled. "That's really so good."

"It is, isn't it?" He took her hand again. "Let's go to my bathroom, and we'll wash away the sins of the past."

Julie followed him to the adjoining bathroom, and he pointed to a tub that was built to accommodate two people. He turned on the water and eyed her as it began to fill. "We have water tanks on the roof. Gravity fed. And solar heaters. That way we don't need pumps, but we have running water."

"Ingenious." She eyed the tub. "So…what do I have to do?"

"Once it's half full, I'll bless the water and immerse you in it, and you'll be purified."

"Just like that?"

"Not everything in life has to be difficult. You've already done the hard work by coming to us and deciding to join the church. This part is easy."

The tub filled, and he shut off the stream, murmured a few words, and then stepped back. "Take off your shoes and get in the tub. Don't be afraid when I lower your head below the surface for a few seconds, and don't splash. When I pull you from the water, it will be done."

Julie climbed into the tub with Elijah's help, which consisted of his hands around her waist. When she was in, she looked up at him.

He said something in a language she didn't understand, and then gently pushed her head beneath the water and held it there for a count of three. Then he pulled her from the tub with both hands and handed her a towel.

She dried off as best she could, noting that her soaked tunic was nearly translucent and left nothing to the imagination about her body. Elijah eyed her the way a wolf eyes a bunny and took her hand.

"Now for that drink," he said, and led her back to the living area. They got their cups, and he invited her to sit with him on a large sectional sofa with a big-screen television and a computer in front of it.

"Now that you've been purified, I can give you some idea of the work we're forced to do to protect the congregation. You have no idea the wickedness that we have to be on guard against," he said. "Just this week I found someone selling perverted filth outside town. We seized his entire stock and banished him from the city limits, but still. It's a danger to our children."

He switched on the computer and the screen blinked to life. A young woman in a skimpy Greek smock approached a handsome gladiator whose hands were bound behind him. She said something unintelligible and then pulled the smock over her head, revealing her naked form. Julie didn't need to see the rest to grasp the plot as the woman removed the gladiator's loincloth and went to work.

"Shocking," Elijah said in a husky voice, his hand on Julie's thigh.

"I don't know. It looks…interesting." Julie paused. "Do you wish you were the gladiator?"

"I…"

"I mean, tied up and helpless as a woman does whatever she wants to you?"

He nodded, his face flushed, and Julie leaned into him and whispered in his ear, "Do you have any rope?"

He nodded again.

"Show me."

He led her into the bedroom, to a closet, where he had a rack with ties and silk sashes hanging from it. She took a handful and walked to the four-poster bed.

"Lie down," she said, and he dutifully obliged. She tied his right wrist to the bedpost, and then his left, and then cinched his legs. When he was spread-eagle, she stood and walked to the dining room again.

"Where are you going?" he asked.

"You'll see," she called over her shoulder.

She reappeared a moment later with his goblet and the pitcher. "Drink this," she said, and held it to his lips. He did and, when he was done, sighed. She smiled and returned to the dining room. This time when she came back, she was holding a serrated steak knife.

Elijah's eyes widened at the sight, and he began to protest, but she cut him off with a finger to his lips.

"No. Not a word. We're going to have a discussion, and you're going to tell me what I want to know, or you're going to be missing one part of your body you seem to use as your brain. Do you understand? You scream, I'll stuff a sock in your mouth, and then I'll start cutting. Do you want to be fileted like a trout, or will you cooperate?"

His eyes narrowed. "Who are you?"

"Your worst nightmare. Now the first question. Where are you keeping Eve?"

Chapter 38

Pacific Ocean, Washington coast

The bow of the Chinese vessel pounded through increasingly rough waves as it battered its way north. The sky had darkened as the afternoon wore on, and was now an endless gray with flashes of lightning in the distance.

The ship had been declared seaworthy by Kirk and Gary, but barely – the electronics were nonfunctional and the steering iffy, even with the emergency repairs to the hydraulics. In spite of the problems, Art had met with the heads of the various factions under his command, and the decision to head to Seattle had been unanimous, if uneasy for some.

Lucas had sat out the discussion, having made his reticence clear to Art and seeing nothing to be gained by belaboring his misgivings. Ruby had, unsurprisingly, felt that finishing off the Chinese in Seattle was the right call, and had recommended guerilla warfare rather than a frontal assault. She'd agreed to stay behind with Rosemary and her family and make her way to Salem with the group that would return with the horses while Lucas and the militia steamed north.

In the end, they'd loaded two hundred animals on the ship and nearly six hundred fighters, who'd augmented their armaments by raiding the mini-arsenal they'd found on the ship. The men were in high spirits at the thought of ridding the country of the invaders once and for all. Henry's squatters, especially, had been excited at the idea, and even Lucas had caught some of their enthusiasm as the ship had cruised from the harbor and accelerated to twenty-two knots on the open sea.

A search of the superstructure had revealed planning documents for Seattle used by the Chinese command, and a map with areas circled in yellow gave Lucas and Art a good idea of where the enemy troops would be concentrated. Harbor Island appeared on a number of smaller maps, and the downtown and the waterfront had been recurring areas of interest.

Attempts to question the crewmen had proved largely futile; the only one who admitted to speaking some English was the one who'd been manning the bridge when they'd captured the ship. Lucas had instructed him as well as he could to tell the crew that they were to help operate the vessel, and that if any of them tried anything, they'd be summarily executed. Art had put two of his troops over each crewman with orders to shoot if they didn't cooperate. The Chinese had seemed to understand the threat and, so far, had proved helpful in getting the ship up to speed.

Lucas snatched a catnap for several hours as the big boat motored north, but adrenaline roused him, and he was now on the bridge with Gary, Kirk, and Art's circle of advisors, who included Sam, Bill, and Henry. Gary was acting as captain, steering using the compass, and watching the temperature, oil, and fuel indicators with a wary eye. Because the autopilot wasn't working, he was constantly making adjustments – the fifteen-foot rollers from the port side continuously knocked the ship off course, and the wind, gusting to thirty knots, made matters worse.

"How long until we get there?" Henry asked.

"We should be able to make the Salish Sea by eleven or so tonight if our speed stays steady," Kirk answered, "though sea conditions will play a big part. It looks like we're headed straight into a squall."

"How much worse than this can it get?"

"I've heard of twenty- to thirty-foot seas farther north. If we get into thirty or bigger, we'll have to cut power. Even a ship of this size will have a hard time. And with the steering…"

"Let's hope it doesn't get worse, then. Seattle's, what, about a hundred and twenty miles from the mouth of the Salish?"

"More like a hundred and fifty."

"Then we can get there before dawn?"

"That's…it depends on visibility. We don't have radar or GPS, so we're going to be doing this blind."

"You have the charts. Can't you plot a course using those?"

"That's what we are doing. But it gets hairier in a strait than the open ocean. All we have to do here is avoid running into Washington, so we leave a nice margin from land and we're fine. If we only have a few miles between two land masses in complete darkness, it's a lot trickier, so we have to slow down. A ship this size doesn't just stop on a dime. It could take over half a mile at speed. That's not a lot of leeway."

"If we arrive after daybreak, we'll have to stay out of sight somewhere in Puget Sound until tomorrow night."

"That might be tough – these engines aren't exactly quiet. They'll hear us from many miles off."

"Is this as fast as it will go?" Lucas asked.

"We're at eighty percent," Gary said. "I can probably get us another five without blowing her up, but we can't run wide open for four hundred miles."

Art frowned. "Do the best you can. Another couple of knots might make the difference."

Gary inched the throttles forward and eyed the oil pressure. "That's about max."

The sea grew more confused as they proceeded, until they were slamming through twenty-foot waves with breaking whitewater on top. The massive ship shuddered each time it struck one; even its tremendous bulk struggled against Mother Nature's fury. Rain lashed the decks, and visibility dropped as silver curtains blew nearly horizontal, and the wipers on the glass barely made a dent. The lightning intensified until it seemed they were sailing through a maelstrom, the waves chaotic and coming from every direction, and the steering groaning at the strain of controlling the ship's course.

"We have to slow down," Gary said. "We can't maintain this speed in these conditions."

"It's a rough ride," Art agreed. "But what's the worst that could happen?"

"We get thrown off course so much we lose time getting back on track. Or the steering breaks and we're rudderless and can't control the ship."

"Okay. We'll make it up later."

Gary eased back on the throttles and the vessel slowed, and the banging each time the bow hit a wave became a low-pitched pounding.

When darkness fell, the sea became an oil slick. The clouds blocked any star or moonlight, and it seemed they were moving through ink.

"All right. This is weird," Sam said.

"Yeah," Henry agreed. "I can't see anything."

"Seems like the seas are settling down some," Kirk said from where he was plotting their location. "Maybe the cloud cover will thin as we get closer to where we need to make the turn."

"How accurate you reckon that is?" Lucas asked, indicating the chart.

"More or less. Problem is there's no way of getting the speed absolutely accurate in seas like this, so I'm sort of guessing."

"Guessing?" Lucas echoed.

"I learned this in the navy, but haven't used it in forever. All the modern boats had GPS."

"So we're not completely sure where we are," Sam said.

"Nothing's perfect," Kirk agreed.

"What if you get it wrong?"

Kirk frowned. "Let's hope I don't."

Chapter 39

Denver, Colorado

Julie crept along a girder high above the walkway that connected Elijah's building to the one where Eve was being kept, her tunic dry after five minutes in the mountain sun. The steak knife was snug against her side, held by the sash she'd improvised from one of Elijah's, and a Glock 9mm pistol she'd found in his bedside table was clutched in her right hand.

Once he'd told her everything she wanted to know, she'd debated slitting his throat and leaving him for the ants, but she couldn't bring herself to do it. Instead, she'd forced him to drink the contents of the pitcher, and he'd passed out cold – a state he'd be in for many hours, she was sure.

Her gambit of playing honey trap had worked, and she now knew that Eve was being held in a locked room in Ulysses's converted theater, with only one guard watching over her. Julie was confident that she'd be able to overcome a guard, who was always a woman, per Elijah, but not so sure she'd be able to escape with Eve without being noticed. Before she'd met him for lunch, she'd told Arnold what she intended to do, and he'd agreed to stand by with their horses a block from the hotel. It had seemed close enough when she'd left, but now, painfully aware of the number of guards and the distance she'd have to cover, it didn't look so easy, and she'd reconciled herself to the idea that she might have to shoot her way out of the compound.

Julie reached Ulysses's building and approached a rooftop door at the top of the elevator shaft. She tried the handle and was relieved when it opened. She took the steps cautiously, her sandals silent on the concrete, and paused when she reached the ground-floor landing. Julie pressed her head against the steel fire door and listened and, when she heard nothing, eased it open and peeked through the gap.

According to Elijah, the little girl was being held in what had at one time been a dressing room in the backstage area, which was now the residential wing for the inner circle, with the green room serving as a break area, the dressing rooms converted to bedrooms, and the sundry makeup and wardrobe spaces converted to supply rooms that housed weapons, garments, and the icons, vessels, and Bibles used in the sermons.

The area sounded empty, which was to be expected only a few hours before the big celebration was to take place. Everyone would be at the adjacent convention center, helping with the preparations, hopefully leaving Eve and her guard alone.

Julie had no issue with taking life if she had to. Before she'd joined Shangri-La, she'd been part of a group of travelers who'd had to fight off marauders multiple times, and she'd taken her share of scalps. But it was never easy, and she hoped that she could knock the woman out rather than having to dispatch her, although she wouldn't hesitate to do what she needed to in order to free Eve.

She inched along the hallway, stopping every so often to listen for signs of life, and reached the turn where Elijah had indicated Eve was imprisoned. Julie peered around the corner and her breath caught in her throat when she saw who was on guard duty. Ellen was sitting on a folding metal chair, a book in her lap, an AK-47 leaning against the wall beside her.

Julie moved so fast that Ellen barely registered her sprinting down the hall, and was grabbing for the AK when Julie collided with her, knocking her from the chair. Julie clubbed her in the head with the butt of the Glock, but it was a glancing blow, and Ellen landed a punch to Julie's midsection that knocked the wind out of her. Julie rolled off her after Ellen followed up the punch with another to Julie's chest, and Ellen was reaching for the rifle when the blade of the steak knife plunged into her back.

Ellen screamed in agony and continued to try for the AK, but Julie twisted the knife handle, stopping her. She tried to turn to punch Julie again, but Julie yanked the knife free with a spray of blood and stabbed it through Ellen's neck, instantly severing her spine.

Ellen collapsed against the floor, her chest working but her mouth slack, and Julie pushed herself away. She looked down at her tunic, which had speckles of crimson dotting the front, and shook her head. Any ideas she'd had about slipping away unnoticed were now impossible unless anyone she encountered was blind.

Julie watched Ellen expire without emotion, and when she was sure the woman was dead, untied the sash and slipped the tunic over her head. She turned it inside out, inspected it, and donned it again. The red stippling was now on the inside, but the fabric was mottled pink on what was now the exterior.

It would have to do.

She crouched by the dead woman and felt for a key, and then exhaled forcefully – the door had a sliding bolt on the outside, not a deadbolt. Julie slid the bolt and opened the door, and looked inside.

Eve was sitting on the floor in the corner in nearly complete darkness, as far away as she could sit from a half-full bucket in the opposite corner in which to relieve herself. Julie's nose crinkled at the stench, and she knelt down and whispered to the little girl.

"Eve, I'm here to rescue you. Stand up. Are you okay?"

Eve blinked at the unexpected light seeping through the doorway and struggled to her feet. She took several tentative steps and looked up at Julie, relieved.

"Is this real?" she asked in a tiny voice.

"Yes. But we're going to have to be super quiet so nobody hears us, okay?"

Eve nodded and then looked past Julie to where Ellen's corpse lay splayed on the floor. Her eyes widened, but she didn't say anything for a moment. When she did, her voice was shaky.

"You're…Julie. From home."

Julie managed a smile in spite of the gory circumstances. "That's right."

"You have blood on your face."

Julie wiped at it with the back of her arm, and Eve tilted her head, still watching her. "There's water down the hall. They let me drink three times a day."

"Great. Show me," Julie said, holding out her hand.

Eve took it, and they walked together below what had been the stage. They stopped at a mop sink, and Julie twisted the faucet handle, and a murky stream splashed against the basin. Julie did a hasty cleanup, and then removed her tunic and scrubbed at the blood until it was so faint she could barely see it. She pulled it back on, and Eve stared at her with huge blue eyes.

"You're all wet and wrinkled."

"But clean. Now come with me. Remember what I said about staying quiet."

Eve's whisper was soft but firm. "Okay."

Julie snagged the AK as they passed Ellen on the way back, and guided Eve up the stairs to the roof. Once outside, they walked to the edge, and Julie studied the surroundings. The conference center was to the left, and she could see the shaft that had been installed, the workers now nowhere to be seen. Just beyond it was a pedestrian walkway that connected the theater complex with the center.

"Eve, you need to be really brave, okay? It's safer to use the rooftops to get over to that walkway. Once we're there, we can run across to the big building and see about getting inside the convention center."

"I'm not scared. But you don't want to go in there."

"Why not?"

"The crazy man said everyone's going to die tonight."

"What?"

"He said it's all part of God's plan."

"How?"

"Gas or something."

Julie's eyes strayed to the ductwork that the workers had erected, and a chill ran through her. "Why?"

"I don't know. He just told me that he was doing God's work and everyone needs to die."

Julie scowled at Eve. "Can you wrap your arms around my neck and hold on while I crawl across that glass area?"

Eve looked determined. "I'm not a baby. I can do it."

"Okay, then let's give it a try." Julie slipped the AK strap over her head and adjusted the rifle so it was lying flat against her back, and motioned to Eve. "Climb on."

Eve did, and Julie began the long crawl along the girders that would take them close enough to the walkway to run for it. She was halfway across the expanse when she froze — two guards were walking toward her four stories below, unaware of the drama playing out above them. They took their time, deep in conversation, and Julie held her breath until they'd progressed beyond where she and Eve were staring down at them.

"That was close," Eve whispered in Julie's ear, and it was all Julie could do to keep from laughing out loud at the little girl's calm.

They made it to the building next to the walkway, and Julie studied the side for obvious handholds she could trust. She found a promising area with steel support beams over the theater entry, and after testing her weight, whispered to Eve, "I'm going to lower myself down those and then jump to the walkway. Whatever you do, don't let go when I land."

"Okay."

Julie completed the maneuver in under a minute and dropped onto the walkway. Eve grunted from the force of the fall, but held on for dear life. Julie smiled at her tenacity. "You can let go now. We're going to run over there, up those stairs, and across to the convention center."

Eve slid down, and Julie freed the AK from her back, chambered a round, and looked to the girl. "Ready?"

"Yes."

They sprinted to the steps and tore up one level to the walkway that crossed the street below. Julie checked to make sure there were no guards in sight, and then they raced across and stopped at the glass doors of the hall. Julie tried one, but it was locked.

"Damn."

Eve pointed to the chains holding the doors in place, and Julie looked through the glass at an interior promenade with steps leading down to the main floor. There was nobody around in the upstairs area, so she gripped the AK by the stock and slammed the steel barrel against the glass panel like a battering ram. The tempered glass shattered but held together, and she drove the barrel through multiple times until the glass fell out in a sheet of fragments.

A cry rang out from below, but they were already through and running the width of the convention center, staying low. When they reached the other side, there were two stairways that led down, and Julie opted for the one on the right since the alarmed voices were coming from the left.

They made it to the lobby area, and a woman screamed, "Stop! What are you doing?"

Julie didn't slow, Eve's hand in hers and the AK in the other. She shouldered through the doors, and then they were outside the center, bolting toward the buildings across the boulevard, where Arnold, Devin, and Anne were waiting – assuming nothing had gone wrong.

Shouts followed them as they ran but no shooting, and when they turned the corner, they nearly slammed headlong into Arnold.

"Get on," he hissed to them, holding the reins to his and Julie's horses. Julie shouldered the AK sling and swung up into the saddle, and Arnold did the same before pulling Eve up behind him. "Hang on," he ordered, and when he felt her small arms encircle his waist, he spurred his steed forward and took off at a gallop, Julie following close behind.

Chapter 40

The hours crawled by, the seas flattened to five-foot rolling swells, and the moon eventually peeked through the clouds enough to silver the surface in the distance. When the ship had reached the latitude where they were to make the turn into the Salish Sea, they could barely make out the northernmost tip of Washington's Pacific coast to starboard.

Kirk gave everyone a tired smile. "So far, so good," he said as the big vessel leaned into the turn.

"Now it gets tricky," Gary reminded them, and any relief on the bridge evaporated.

"Pick up the speed," Art ordered, and Gary goosed the throttles again. Soon they were flying over the surface with the wind at their back, making twenty-four knots according to the gauges.

"At this rate we'll get there before dawn," Kirk pronounced from the chart table. "We're only twenty minutes behind schedule, and this should make it up. We have about…ninety miles of relatively open channel here before it gets dicey near the Strait of Juan de Fuca."

"Dicey?" Lucas asked.

Kirk indicated the chart. "See for yourself. Lot of direction changes, and the channel narrows a lot. If there's anything off on our reckoning or course, we're screwed."

Lucas approached the chart table and studied the chart. He looked

215

around the bridge and yawned. "Sounds like we have four hours to get some rest. I'm going below."

He slept surprisingly soundly and only woke when the vibration from the engines changed. Lucas returned to the bridge to find the ship enshrouded in fog so thick he could barely make out the bow. He exchanged a glance with Art, who looked beat, and moved to the windshield before turning to Gary and Kirk.

"Would it do any good to put someone on the bow?" he asked.

Gary shook his head. "Not really. By the time they saw anything, it would be too late."

"Turn forty degrees and maintain course for…thirty minutes at eighteen knots," Kirk called out.

Gary made the adjustment and eyed Kirk. "Then?"

"Another thirty degrees for thirty-six minutes."

"How accurate you figure that speedometer is?" Lucas asked.

"It's pretty on, based on what we saw on the ocean. But here we have no way of knowing whether the tide's going in or out. If it's going out, it'll show us making eighteen knots, but we might only be doing sixteen or seventeen against a one- or two-knot current. Same if the tide's coming in. Might add a knot or two."

Lucas squinted at the wall of white. "Not pumping me full of confidence."

Kirk shrugged. "You asked."

They made the next turn, and the knot of tension in Lucas's gut eased slightly.

"How much farther?" Bill asked, his voice hoarse from fatigue.

"About…forty-seven miles."

Lucas checked the time on his mechanical watch. "That'll put us there around six. Sunup's about six thirty. Doesn't give us much time to unload."

"Get the men ready," Art said. "I want everyone off the boat in fifteen minutes once we land."

"We've still got about three hours," Kirk pointed out.

"No harm in being prepared."

Henry, Sam, and Bill went to rouse the troops and relay the order, and Lucas walked over to Gary. "How's your Chinese buddy done so far?" he asked, looking at where the man was slumbering in a chair in the corner.

"He was good when we were repairing things. There's not much for him to do now."

"Lock him below."

"What are we going to do with the crew once we land?"

Lucas frowned. "I'll leave that up to Art."

Kirk stood and woke the crewman, who looked around the bridge in confusion before his eyes settled on Lucas. Kirk led him away, pistol in hand, and Lucas stared again into the wall of fog. "I'm going to get some fresh air."

"Suit yourself. Just don't fall in. The decks will be slicker than snot."

Lucas descended to the deck level and let himself out. He walked to the bow and stood in front of the gun turret, listening. All he could hear was the rush of water against the bow and the drone of the engines, and within minutes his face and hat were damp from the fog.

He headed back to the bridge and waited until everyone had returned. Art had the maps in hand, and they went back and forth about the best places to dock the vessel and how to disperse from there.

The next turn happened in the middle of a heated discussion, and Kirk gave them a heads-up. "Only an hour to go. Where do you want to berth the ship?"

Lucas rose and walked with Art to the chart table, and Art put a beefy finger on a spot. "There's a big pier right here. I was there years ago. It's far enough away from the city that they won't see us put in, and we'll be off the boat before they can make it there. Probably an hour from Harbor Island? And there are enough homes in West Seattle so we can disappear. It's a big area, especially if you don't know what you're looking for."

Lucas thought for a moment. "What do you want to do with the crew once we're off the boat?"

Art's expression hardened. "We can't let them tell the others who came off the ship." He turned to Henry. "You have any problem tossing a grenade in with the crew?"

Henry swallowed before answering, and his Adam's apple bobbed up and down. "Pretty cold-blooded, ain't it?"

"We're not the ones who crossed an ocean to invade Seattle and enslave the population. You tell me."

"They were just doing their job."

"And I need you to do yours. You want me to find someone else? Not a problem, if so."

"Nah. If it's got to be done, I'll handle it."

"It does. I'd let them live if I thought it wouldn't endanger us. But we're at war here. These guys didn't surrender — we got the jump on them. They're enemy combatants, and as such they get the same treatment as the soldiers at Newport did — and as the soldiers in Seattle will."

A scraping sounded from the bow, and they all tumbled forward as the ship abruptly slowed from eighteen knots. Cups and trays flew from the tables and smashed against the windshield, and the lights on the instrument panel went dark. Gary cursed and threw the engines into reverse, but the ship kept grinding against the bottom, the bow groaning in protest as momentum carried it forward, and the steel hull plates twisted beyond recognition until a spit of land in front of them darkened the haze.

Chapter 41

Denver, Colorado

Ulysses stormed into Elijah's quarters with six of his bodyguards and stood openmouthed at the sight of his naked son, snoring, bound to the bed like a slaughtered hog.

"Elijah! What the hell is going on here? Wake up!"

When Elijah didn't move, he gestured to his bodyguards. "Untie him."

They rushed to obey and had him free within seconds. One of them looked up at Ulysses, his jaw set. "He smells like a brewery."

Ulysses strode to where the pitcher was sitting beside the bed, sniffed it, and then hurled it across the room. "Drunk! The greatest disaster to befall us, and my son's drunk!"

He spit on the floor in disgust and turned from the spectacle of his son. "Sound the alarm. They're not going to get away with this. We'll catch them. They can't make it far."

"Sir, we'll take care of—"

Ulysses cut the man off. "I'm perfectly capable of riding a horse, you dolt. Now move. We're losing time."

They hurried down to the ground level and out of the buildings and made for the church stable. Ulysses barked orders at the men, and ten of his best were in the saddle and ready to ride a few minutes later.

"Follow me!" he commanded, and rode away at a gallop in the

219

direction of the railway tracks. The report he'd gotten had been that two riders had been seen tearing through town, and an enterprising guard had followed them to the tracks, which led south out of the city. They had at most a twenty-minute lead, which Ulysses could narrow given that he didn't care whether he blew out his horse – his party only needed to catch up to the fugitives, not carry them all the way back to their cursed Shangri-La.

He had no doubt that was who'd engineered the escape and murdered one of his faithful in such a grisly manner. But they wouldn't get away with it. Tonight was to be the pinnacle of his ambition, when he would take his entire congregation with him to heaven as the voices in his head had commanded. At first he'd been hesitant, but as they'd become more insistent, he'd seen the logic – by choosing to go home with him at the height of the celebration, they would be welcomed as having passed the ultimate test, and would be worthy of eternal life in the loving arms of the Lord.

These interlopers would not be allowed to ruin his moment of triumph. The brat would be dragged back, and the celebration would go on as planned. Anything else would be failure, and he'd come too far to consider it.

He would not be denied. Not now. Not with everything – not with heaven – so close.

His men rode as hard as he did, and as dusk painted the sky with ribbons of ochre and crimson, he cried out in victory. "There! See? The Lord has led us to them, and they are ours!" He spurred his horse harder and ducked low in the saddle to gain even greater speed, and his men struggled to keep up.

"Arnold!"

Julie's voice was barely audible over the clatter of the horses' hooves, but he slowed and waited for her to catch up to him.

"Behind us. Big party of riders."

"Damn. Well, we knew they'd give chase."

"How much farther?"

"I can't tell. Maybe a mile or two."

"They'll be on top of us by then."

"Not if we push harder," he said through gritted teeth, and goaded his horse back to a full gallop. Julie did the same, and they practically flew along the tracks, loose gravel spraying behind them.

Five minutes later, Arnold called to Julie, "There it is!"

The distinctive outline of a big-box store materialized on their right, and Arnold veered toward it. The light was almost out of the sky as they reached the parking lot and continued past a row of metal dumpsters filled with soil and construction rubble.

"We got company," Arnold yelled as he passed the dumpsters, and Devin's voice answered from behind the nearest one.

"I see 'em."

"You take the ones on the left; Luis and I will take the right," Duke hollered from behind another dumpster, his rifle steadied against the lip, Luis by the side with his weapon steadied on a pile of cinderblocks.

Devin waited until he couldn't miss, and signaled to Anne. They both opened up on the riders at the same time, their rifles chattering as Duke's and Luis's did the same.

Six of the riders jerked in the saddle and fell to the ground. The other five split off and made for the corner of the building for cover, but Duke's rifle on full auto took two of them down before they made it.

"Circle around and make sure they don't flank us," he said to Luis, who nodded understanding and leapt to his feet.

"You want some of this?" he called to Devin, who joined him as he ran toward the far side of the structure.

They were nearly to the corner when the sound of hooves on pavement forewarned them, and they ducked beneath the overhang and waited for the riders to show themselves.

Two appeared, and Devin's and Luis's rifles barked in unison at the riders' white uniforms standing out in the faint light. Both tumbled backward and dropped to the asphalt, their rifles clattering away as the horses raced off without their riders.

"One to go," Devin said, and then a three-round burst from the tracks shattered the silence.

Arnold came riding around the corner a few seconds later, and Julie appeared out of the darkness.

"That's all of them," he said, returning his rifle to its saddle scabbard.

"There'll be more behind them," Devin warned.

"Sure. But they won't be able to find us in the dark, and by daybreak we'll have too much of a lead."

Duke and the rest ran to their horses and swung into the saddle, and they rode away. Duke checked behind them every few minutes with his NV scope. He called out when they were a quarter mile away. "More riders approaching the Costco."

"Then let's veer off the tracks," Arnold said. "There are fifty roads leading south from here. There's no way they'll catch up to us now."

Another group of church guards led by Minister Fogarty slowed as they neared the store. Fogarty motioned to the men to dismount, and they crept forward in the darkness, staying low, leading with their rifles.

Fogarty almost tripped over the first corpse and grimaced when he saw two more, all unmoving, the stink of death in the air. The men fanned out, and then a moan of horror sounded from the corner of the building.

Fogarty ran over to where one of the guards was doubled over, retching. The distressed man pointed at a fallen form on the ground, and Fogarty walked over to the corpse and gasped.

Even in death, three red blossoms stitched across his chest, Ulysses was instantly recognizable. His mouth was frozen open in a silent scream, his eyes wide in shock, and his white pants had been soiled as he died.

Ten minutes later, Fogarty pointed his horse north toward the church as the others continued the hunt. The Prophet's stiffening form was slung facedown across the back of his horse, and tears of anguish streamed down his face in the moonlight.

Chapter 42

Seattle, Washington

Lucas was on his feet in a flash and rushed to the windshield to look out. The bow was crumpled like a soda can and buried up to the railing in dirt. Just beyond it, buildings loomed in the fog. Alarms clamored from the console, and steam hissed from a broken pipe on the far side of the bridge.

"Damn," Kirk said, fighting to stand.

"Where are we?" Lucas snapped.

Kirk felt on the floor for the charts and found the one he'd been working on. Lucas flicked his disposable lighter to life, and Kirk traced their route until his finger was resting on land.

"Looks like West Point. North of Seattle, maybe…five miles. Nowhere near West Seattle."

"Five miles," Lucas repeated. "Art? You okay?"

"Yeah. Just bruised."

"We need to get the men and horses off as quick as we can."

"He's right," Art said. "Men, go downstairs, assess the damage, and let's figure out how to make this happen." He stood. "Shut off the engines so we don't blow up."

Gary felt along the console until he found the kill switches and obliged. The hull stopped shivering, and the alarms quieted.

"Is the generator still working?" Art asked.

"Looks like it."

"Why aren't there any lights?"

"Beats me." He pointed at a glow from the stairs. "Looks like it's just up here."

"Okay. Let's evacuate," Lucas said. "Seems like the men can get off the bow, doesn't it?"

"Yeah."

"Then that's what they should do, assuming the stairways are still passable. The horses can swim to shore from the stern."

"Where are you going?" Art asked.

"No way I'm leaving my horse down in the hold. If he's going to swim for it, I'll be on his back."

Lucas took off down the stairs, leaving Art and the others to figure out the situation on the bridge. He was at the cargo deck in two minutes, where the men were carrying weapons and ammo in the opposite direction, making for the deck. Emergency lighting in the floor and ceiling illuminated the cavernous holds, and he dodged past departing fighters to make it to the rear chamber.

He reached the animals, who were panicking and a danger to their handlers as they stomped their hooves and thrashed about. Lucas barked instructions to the men and worked through the throng until he found Tango, who looked frightened but manageable. Lucas murmured words of comfort to the big stallion and stroked his neck, and the terror slowly seeped from his eyes, and his rapid breathing quieted.

"How do we get this hatch open and the ramp lowered?" Lucas called.

"We're working on it," a voice replied from the rear.

"Work harder," Lucas said. "We need out of here."

Cold water lapped at his boots, and he looked down. The entire surface had an inch of water sloshing around, and the level seemed to be rising – there hadn't been any when he'd found Tango.

"Got water coming in, boys. Going to get serious pretty soon. What's the holdup?"

"The damned gizmo's jammed. We've got the bolts open, but it won't lower."

Lucas patted Tango again and led him to the stern, where three men were huddled around an instrument panel with glowing red and green lights. One of them looked up at him and shook his head. "It's no good, boss."

"There has to be a manual release," Lucas said, and scanned the huge ramp.

"I don't see one."

Lucas twisted and looked in the other direction. Another ramp led to a higher level, for vehicles to drive up to where smaller boats and other equipment were stored. "We need to get these animals out of here before this thing sinks."

"I hear you. If you got any ideas, we're all ears."

Lucas led Tango up the ramp at the far end and arrived at a series of hatches in the side of the hull with large cranes beside them. He tried one, and it creaked open a foot, and he found himself looking down at the water from three stories above.

"Fellas! Get up here," he called. The men came at a run, and Lucas indicated the hatches. "If you can get those open, we can lead the horses up here, and as the stern floods, it'll get closer to the water. Once we're a story up, the horses can jump without getting hurt and swim to shore."

Lucas tied Tango to a brace and joined the men in sliding the covers away. After considerable effort, they had cleared an opening approximately twenty-five feet wide, intended for loading equipment and provisions, judging by the cranes.

"Let's bring the horses up on this level. Water's rising, so be quick about it."

They went to the lower hold and passed the word among the handlers. The water was now calf deep, so Lucas didn't have to press the sense of urgency. It took twenty minutes to get all two hundred and something animals to the second-level hold, but they managed, and watched as the water rose to cover the level below.

A faint light was beginning to glow through the fog by the time the water had risen enough for the horses to safely disembark, and Lucas astride Tango was the first to dive in with a loud splash. The water was freezing and shocked the breath from him, but Tango's desire to survive kicked in, and the horse swam for the shore only a hundred yards away. The bottom rose gradually and Tango found his footing, and then they were shedding water as they emerged onto dry land.

Scores of other horses followed their lead. The animals were met by the men, who were waiting on the shore for them. Dawn had broken by the time all the animals were safely out of the water, and once they were, Lucas rode to where Art and Sam were watching.

"We need to get clear of the ship. Only a matter of time till someone sees it."

"We were just saying the same thing. We've got all the gear. Looks like we lost two men in the crash – broken necks. The rest are in good shape."

"Then let's get out of here." Lucas looked to his left. "What's that?"

"Looks like a water treatment plant or something."

"The fog's a godsend, but it'll burn off soon enough," Sam said.

"You okay?" Art asked. "Your lips are blue."

Lucas managed a smile. "I'll live. Let's make tracks."

"Will do. Henry, Sam, you're in charge of the men on foot. We'll ride ahead and scout out someplace we can put up for the day."

"How many radios do we have?" Lucas asked.

"Eight."

"Give them four, and keep four for the cavalry. Probably best if we split up. Safer. Might be smartest to find some empty houses and hide in those until nightfall. Smaller groups are less likely to attract attention."

Art nodded. "So much for all the planning, huh?"

"Like I said before, everybody's got a plan till it all goes tits up." Lucas paused. "Once we find someplace safe, I want to head into town and see if we can get any intel on where the Chinese brass are concentrated. We cut the head off the hydra, we should be able to mop up the rest easier. We saw that in Astoria. No reason it shouldn't play the same here."

"I'll go with you."

"Me too," said Sam. "No way I'm going to be able to sleep with this much adrenaline in my system."

"Then it's settled. Let's find some defendable places in case we're attacked, and then we'll scope out the main Chinese base."

Chapter 43

‘

Denver, Colorado

Elijah glowered at the members of the church's inner circle. His head was throbbing with the worst hangover of his life, and even after several morning shots of his miracle potion to stave off the worst of it, he felt like he'd been mauled by a bear.

News of his father's death had shocked him to his core when he'd been told, but worse, he was humiliated at having been discovered with porn playing on his television, tied to the bed, naked, and wasted out of his mind. Even though nobody had dared to ask what had happened, he could see the mistrust and condemnation in the eyes of everyone at the gathering, and could practically hear the sniggering as the story circulated of his debauched interlude while his father was being murdered.

To make matters worse, he'd been briefed about his father's insane intent to poison the entire church, which had been discovered after the celebration had been canceled. One of the ministers had had the presence of mind to ask what the new shaft was hooked up to, and had found the nerve gas canister placed directly in front of a huge fan. It didn't take a rocket scientist to figure out what had been planned, and Elijah had hurriedly silenced the worker who'd led the minister to the fan by sending him on a pilgrimage from which he'd be lucky to return in a year.

Now Elijah was the putative leader of a church in disarray, with the inner circle arguing over how to proceed.

Elijah cleared his throat, and the room fell silent. "I've heard everyone's recommendations, and I can assure you that I knew nothing of any plot to poison our fellowship. That's nuts. I suspect some trick by those who broke the girl out – that makes the most sense. Not only were they determined to rescue their demon child, they intended to murder all those who threatened the reign of their dark master." He hesitated and looked each member in the eye before continuing. "Any suggestion that my father, who was a victim of these animals, had anything to do with this scheme is a slur on his good name, and helps them achieve their goal of destroying the church from within. I knew him better than any of you, and there was no way he would have carried out this…unspeakable horror."

"But the worker–" one of them started.

"The worker who was all too willing to leave on a moment's notice after telling this preposterous story? Probably working in league with them. How else do you think they were able to breach our security and break the girl out? It would be impossible without inside help. For all we know, their accomplices are still among us. Even in this room."

That silenced any dissent. The allusion that any of them might be suspect chilled any arguments, which was what Elijah had intended. Elijah had no problem believing his insane father might have gone down the road of other cult leaders who'd lost their minds and decided to kill their flocks by mass suicide or fights to the death against unbeatable odds or outright murder, as had been the case with the gas.

But one of the things Elijah had learned from his father was to never allow a good crisis to go to waste, and the current one created a tremendous opportunity for him: to take over the church, purge his enemies, and consolidate his power, while rewriting bits of history that weren't flattering of him.

"The question," Elijah intoned, "is where do we go from here? The church is growing. As saddened and shocked by my father's death as we all are, we have to put aside our mourning and do what's right for the church. We've built something truly amazing here, and I for one am not going to allow it to crumble. It was my father's life's work, and I intend to make it mine as well." He stopped and fixed Minister Fogarty with a hard stare. "I'm not blaming anyone for allowing my father to put himself in harm's way. I know how headstrong he could be. But I'm not going to allow his murder to go unavenged. Those responsible for it must pay, as will their henchmen among our ranks."

"How do you intend to do that? We can't even be sure who took her, much less where they went. And Ellen is…no longer with us."

"She gave us an idea of where it is. That should be enough."

"Then what now?"

"I think we have to speak to the congregation and paint a path forward; show solidarity and a vision for our future. Only once we've reassured everyone of our resolve should we share our plan to go after this so-called Shangri-La and burn it to the ground with everyone in it."

"We're hardly an army, Elijah," Minister Carvin admonished.

"We're almost six thousand strong."

"More than half are women and children."

"Look, Ellen said there were no more than a couple of hundred at their camp, many of whom were also women and children. We outnumber them thirty to one. Surely we can figure out a way to avenge my father's death, not to mention the brutal murder of the guards and Ellen, who sacrificed everything to bring the false messiah to us."

Minister Fogarty spoke up. "I think you're right about needing to reassure the flock. We have several hundred guests who might be having second thoughts as well. We've gone to considerable trouble and expense to lure them here. We need to take action before this year's carnival is a total waste."

"This evening, we'll have the funeral and memorial for my father. I want everyone to outdo themselves at organizing a tribute that will awe everyone – a tribute deserving of a great man, a visionary, and the messenger of God. I'll deliver the eulogy, as well as a sermon that'll reassure everyone that we're on track and will continue to carry on with my father's work. We'll figure out how to deal with Shangri-La later. For now we need to close ranks and mourn my father's passing, and allow the congregation to express their grief. Only once they've done so will we move forward with planning how to wipe the scum and their brat from the face of the earth." He looked around the room for any hint of dissention. Seeing none, he nodded as though it were decided. "Now, I need some time to pen a eulogy fitting for one of the greatest figures of our time. Does anyone have any questions?"

Elijah adjourned the meeting. By seizing the reins and controlling the discussion, as well as ending the meeting on the note he wanted, he'd effectively stepped into his father's position. Speaking as the bereaved son of the Prophet tonight, he would solidify that leadership in the minds of his followers.

Once that was achieved, he'd figure out how to destroy Shangri-La, but especially how to get revenge for the humiliation Julie had caused him – an embarrassment he would never forget, and that thinking about made him physically ill.

She would pay, as would the rest of her ilk.

Every man, woman, and child.

Chapter 44

Seattle, Washington

The morning fog had burned off and been replaced by a gray drizzle of cold rain that did little to warm Lucas as he rode, Art and Sam by his side, through the deserted streets of a residential neighborhood. The Chinese maps had shown two primary encampments, one on Harbor Island and the other at the Key Arena, adjacent to the Space Needle that towered above the city skyline.

Lucas couldn't fault the logic behind the choice of the arena for the main headquarters. The huge coliseum would comfortably house all the Chinese animals and troops with room to spare, and it was easily defendable, especially given the view from the Space Needle, which would enable spotters to see for miles in every direction.

What troubled him most was that the force the Chinese had sent would be woefully inadequate to occupy a sprawling metropolis the size of Seattle, which meant that there would be more ships on the way – it was just a matter of time. He'd shared his concern with Art while on the ship, but Art had been optimistic.

"Look at what happened with Artesia. Most of the squatters wound up joining up with us. When we free Seattle, I'd imagine the locals will rally and do the same, so instead of being an easy target for an invasion force, they'll be ready, equipped, and armed to the teeth."

"The question being why they didn't stop them this time."

"Probably because nobody but the gang that ran the place had any guns. Makes sense – if you're a smaller group, your only advantage over thousands is to be the ones with the weapons. But reverse that situation once we've liberated the city, and you have thousands with not only the Chinese's scavenged weapons, but whatever's in the national guard armory and the military bases. I'm sure the Chinese were thinking this would be a walk in the park – thugs who would run at the first sign of a serious fight. But face them off with an armed citizenry that has everything to lose by backing down and it's a different story."

They'd set off toward the downtown area from the North Queen Anne district. The homes nearer the rail yard had been abandoned and so were easily occupied for the day. They hadn't seen anyone since setting out earlier, sticking to the smaller streets. The area was dotted with the ruins of houses that had burned to the ground, and most of the windows in the ones still standing were broken out, the façades tagged with graffiti and many pocked with bullet holes from the months of looting that had followed the collapse. The district was a massive ghost town, and in spite of his familiarity with the devastation from the virus, the sight of miles of uninhabited dwellings made Lucas's skin crawl.

The idea had been to try to find some locals who could give them information about the Chinese, but so far that had proved difficult, and they'd been meandering down the streets for over an hour before they spied a lone man dressed in filthy rags pushing a shopping cart along the street, stopping at each house and going inside before returning with some find.

They rode toward him, but when he saw them, the man bolted away, moving faster than seemed possible given his physical condition and age. Lucas looked to Art and frowned. "Doesn't bode well."

"He's probably been surviving a long time by avoiding trouble," Art reasoned.

They continued past an elementary school and spotted two men pushing a cart toward a park, where there were six other food carts set up beneath tattered umbrellas to stave off the worst of the rain. A crowd of several dozen men and women stood beneath towering trees, munching on whatever was on offer. All looked up at Lucas's group as they neared, with expressions ranging from surprised to frightened.

They dismounted and approached the carts, and one of the men frowned at their approach. Lucas eyed him and then the food. "Something wrong?"

"You didn't hear? The Chinese said anyone with a weapon will be shot on sight."

Lucas adjusted the sling of his M4 on his shoulder, glanced down at the Kimber at his hip, and shrugged. "That right? Well, I'd better make sure they don't see me, then." He eyed the cook. "What is that?"

"Squirrel."

Lucas sniffed. "Any good?"

"It takes a few of them to fill you up, but with the glaze they aren't half bad."

"We'll try one each," Lucas said, indicating Art.

The cook removed three skewers of cubed squirrel meat and handed them to the men with soot-crusted fingers. "That'll be a round."

"Surprised they let you keep bullets," Lucas said, handing the man a cartridge.

"Not supposed to, but you gotta do what you gotta do, right?"

The man who'd stared holes through Lucas grunted. "If they catch you, you're all three dead men."

"You already said that," Lucas said. "They have patrols around this area?"

"Mostly they stay holed up in the arena. But you never know. Some days, nothing; others, they'll have men crawling a neighborhood. No rhyme or reason."

"The arena?" Lucas asked, sounding surprised to encourage the man to talk.

"Yeah. They had a bunch of us build a wall around the grounds. Took hundreds of men the better part of two weeks. They held us at gunpoint and gave us slave rations. A bunch of us got sicker than dogs and didn't make it." He spit near the base of a tree. "I thought it was bad with the gangs, but the Chinese have them beat."

"What did you build the wall out of?"

"Anything we could find. We stripped a bunch of the buildings around it and hauled rubble day and night."

"Are there a lot of them?"

"Must be at least...I don't know. Five hundred at the arena."

"Heard they had a base over on Harbor Island," Art said.

The man looked at Art's bandaged arm and nodded. "That's right. But the main base is at the arena."

"That where the bigwigs hang out?"

He nodded again. "They stay in the building next to it. The arena's for the peons. They got power and water over there. Had their own engineers to set it all up. Went out with a bunch of slave labor and pulled every panel for a half mile off the houses and installed them on the roof." He laughed harshly. "The joke's on them, though, with the weather like this a lot of the time."

"Nobody fought back?"

The man gave him a wry grin. "With what? The gangs confiscated all the guns early on − not that there were a lot of guns around. Remember, this is Seattle. We thought guns were the root of all evil. Not sure anyone's still alive who feels that way." He looked Lucas and his companions up and down. "Not from around here, are you?"

"Nope. Just passing through." Lucas paused. "They patrol at night, too? We're lucky we made it this far."

"Not that I've heard of. Too dangerous for them, I suppose. They're probably afraid someone will take a potshot at them."

Art nodded. "Makes sense. Still, I'm surprised to hear there are Chinese everywhere."

"Yeah, well, join the club."

"Why don't you leave?" Sam asked. "Or organize some kind of resistance?"

The man laughed again. "Leave and go where? Portland's supposed to be toxic. Canada sealed their border − not that I blame them. So that pretty much leaves here."

"Lot of other towns," Lucas said.

"Yeah. Heard about them. Regular vacation spots, aren't they? Prison gangs, cartels, and marauders running them. Might as well stay put. At least I know the lay of the land here."

"What if you had guns? You think this would have gone differently?"

His expression darkened. "Hell yeah. I mean, there's like ten thousand survivors here. You think we would have let anyone take the place over if we'd had a choice?"

"Sorry. No disrespect intended," Art said. "Just seems strange to have so many people letting a few push them around."

The man shrugged and moved away. "Life's that way sometimes. No telling, is there?"

The squirrel was edible, but they decided to try some of the other carts. One featured apple slices roasting with an assortment of nuts, and they each bought a bag. Lucas decided to pass on the stewed cockroaches. "Good source of protein," the woman at the cart assured them with a gap-toothed smile. "And cheap."

"Good to know," Lucas said. "Maybe later."

They climbed back on their horses and continued toward the arena, finally stopping when they could clearly see the needle jutting high above the city. "Sounds like we have to hit the arena at night, like we did in Salem," Sam said. "No point risking our necks riding around anymore, is there?"

"Probably not," Art said with a yawn.

"You boys head back. I'm going to nose around and see if I can get any more info."

"It doesn't sound like there are any surprises. They're dug in. If you take out the arena, you take out their command. The island will be a piece of cake if it's a small contingent."

"Maybe. But no harm in checking."

"You going to try to make it down there?"

"No. But I want to scope out approaches to the arena."

"If it keeps pissing like this, they'll never see us coming," Art said.

"Hope not," Lucas said. "See you back at the house."

He rode toward the arena, and the homes gradually gave way to multistory buildings, most with the same bombed-out look he'd seen in the larger metro areas he'd traveled through. It never failed to amaze him that a sophisticated society could be reduced to living like refugees in a war zone in just a few short years, but from what he'd seen of his fellow man, it was sadly predictable. Only the smaller towns, where a sense of community had existed and neighbors knew each other and helped out when necessary, had fared decently in the collapse. The larger cities, where everybody was a stranger and nobody wanted anything to do with everyone else, had been eviscerated and would never recover.

Lucas turned a corner and nearly ran headlong into a three-man Chinese patrol that appeared shocked to see a heavily armed rider on horseback in the middle of the city. They were raising their rifles when Lucas spurred Tango hard right and simultaneously brought his M4 to bear. One of the soldiers got off a shot that missed by a few feet, and Lucas fired a host of three-round bursts as he drove Tango through a collapsed picture window and into a storefront.

He was off the stallion in an instant and dropped to the ground. Bullets slammed into the brick façade by his head, and he squeezed off another burst that caught one of the soldiers in the abdomen and sent him staggering three steps before dropping. The others ran for cover, but Lucas was too fast and cut them down with two final bursts as they neared a doorway. Both pitched forward and their rifles flew onto the street, and then the area was silent except for Tango's hooves on the broken glass behind Lucas.

He stood, brushed himself off, and went to retrieve Tango, who was sensibly back as far as he could get in the gutted shop. Lucas took his reins and patted his nose, and murmured reassurance before he led him back to the street.

Lucas knew he had to get clear of the area before reinforcements showed up, and he swung up into the saddle just as five civilians in filthy clothes, their hair matted and long, appeared from one of the buildings. One of them pointed to Lucas and called something over his shoulder, and three more emerged from a doorway, one with a baseball bat in hand and one of the others with a pipe and a length of chain.

"Whoa there, fellas. Don't have any argument with you," Lucas said as the men moved to encircle him.

"You killed them Chinese," one of them said.

"That's right. They were trying to kill me. Seemed like a good idea."

A voice spoke from behind him. "Put the gun down and get off the horse, nice and slow."

Lucas twisted to see who was speaking and saw a man pointing one of the Chinese patrol's assault rifles at him.

Lucas held his M4 away from his body and eased out of the saddle, and then set the gun on the ground.

"Pistol too," the man said, motioning with the rifle.

Lucas complied with a frown. "Now what?"

"The Chinese made it clear that if any of them got hurt, they'd round up and execute ten for every one of them. You just condemned thirty of us to death."

"I didn't know. What was I supposed to do? Let them shoot me?"

"You're a damned fool riding around with guns here. You were asking for it."

"So…what's your move? You're the man with the gun," Lucas said.

"We should take him in," the one with the chain said. "Maybe they'll give us a break if we do."

"You mean turn me in to the group that invaded your country? To try to save your own skins? Let me guess – you all were hiding in your rooms when they landed and took over the city."

"That's enough of your mouth," the man with the rifle warned.

"Why?" Lucas asked. "What are you going to do? Shoot me? The Chinese will the moment you hand me over. And they'll probably shoot you for good measure, since you make it so easy for them."

The men looked less certain. Lucas looked around, hands raised, and shook his head. "Sad to see men willing to crawl on their knees.

Me, I'd rather die a free man than live like a slave."

"They're gonna come through and shoot thirty of us. We got no choice, mister."

"Of course you do. You can help me get rid of the bodies so they never find them, and take their guns and put them to good use. Or you can be yellowbellies and turn me in to the gang that has you living like animals."

The man with the rifle lowered it, and the men exchanged glances. "He's got a point," the one with the bat said. "What are we turning into?"

Lucas addressed the one who seemed to be having second thoughts. "I remember stories about France back in the Second World War, when a lot of them turned their countrymen in to the Nazis. Never understood how men could sink so low."

"But what are we supposed to do? Let you go and get shot ourselves?"

Lucas lowered his hands. "Like I said — make the bodies disappear. Nobody knows what happened. Maybe go find a new shithole to live in till it dies down."

"We could do that," the man with the chain said. "Not like there ain't a million places to lose a body or three."

Lucas allowed himself a half smile. "You won't be sorry."

He leaned down to retrieve his weapons, and the man with the rifle raised his again. "Hang on there. Nothing's decided yet. These idiots want to get their asses shot for bucking the Chinese, that's their business. I'm not going to."

"Now hold on, Len," the bat man said.

"No, you hold on. This guy's gonna get us all killed. I say we take him to the Chinese, and good riddance."

The men stared at each other, uncertain what to do. Lucas eyed the man with the rifle. "You're going to have to use that if you think you're going to keep me here."

One of the others scooped up another Chinese rifle and trained it on Lucas's head. "Len's right. Let the Chinese sort it out. This isn't our problem."

"Bad idea, pardner," Lucas said.

"Shut your piehole," the rifleman warned, "or I'll–"

A shot rang out. A hole appeared in the center of the man's forehead and his head jerked back. He fell, dropping the gun, and another shot caught the second gunman in the chest. He crumpled with a groan, and Lucas grabbed his Kimber and M4 and stared down the rest of the scavengers.

Art and Sam rode down the street, rifles leveled at the crowd, and Lucas holstered his pistol and pulled himself onto Tango's back.

"Took you long enough," he said.

"You looked like you were having fun. Didn't want to spoil it," Art said.

Lucas glared at the men. "You've got two choices. Leave your two dead here with the Chinese, and it'll look like they got into a fight. Or hide the bodies and git. I'd do the second, but it's your call." He sighed. "Sounds like if you stick around, you're worm food. Just a matter of when."

Lucas rode away, and Art and Sam covered the men until he rounded the corner, and then spun and galloped to follow him, leaving the locals with the most difficult choice of their lives.

Chapter 45

Barton sat at the oval conference table in the meeting room Snake used for his difficult discussions, staring at him like he was crazy. Snake had received confirmation from Laredo that his entire force had been routed, with only twenty men surviving and managing to escape the cartel's onslaught. They'd traveled east until they'd arrived at a trading post with a shortwave set, and radioed a report that had sent Snake into a rage.

He'd threatened them and told them not to bother coming back to Houston or he'd shoot them on sight, and then retired to his quarters for some chemical fortification before making some hard decisions. The loss of Laredo was a body blow, and as news spread, he could expect other towns under Crew control to come under attack by rivals. Snake and his men lived by the law of the jungle, and weakness would lead to a swift death. Losing a major trading hub to the Mexicans would shake the Crew's credibility to its core, and it was only a matter of time before other predators began circling; or worse, his own men decided that he wasn't a sufficiently strong leader and had to be taken out.

Which left him exposed and vulnerable. He had to do something dramatic to regain control or he wouldn't last a month. The question was what. Like many collapsed empires of the past, he was overextended with his fighters spread too thin, unable to supply them with reinforcements in time should they be attacked by a large group – Laredo had proved that, and it would be repeated until the Crew was no more.

"Are you deaf?" Snake bellowed. "They took Laredo from us like we're nothing, and we'll never get it back now. That was a big part of the territory's income. A lot of trade with Mexico now gone forever. Meanwhile you've been promising me to get the refinery live and for gold to show up, but you've done nothing." Snake glowered at Barton. "I lost Laredo because I didn't have fuel to run a couple of tanks and armored personnel carriers down there. I lost it because you screwed me over, and you're giving me nothing to work with."

"You lost it because someone has been feeding your enemies compromising information about where you're weak. I have nothing to do with that."

"That's a guess. You don't know it for a fact. And even if you're right, I'd still have Laredo if they'd leaked that I had armor headed to blow up some Mexican ass."

"Snake, I'm doing everything I can. I just relay messages. They told me the gold was on its way. I believe them. As for the loss of Laredo, we had nothing to do with that, and you and I both know it. So quit taking your frustrations out on me and start concentrating on your own business. Get your nose out of the pipe, for starters. It's making you weak and clouding your judgment."

Snake's eyes narrowed. "Who the hell do you think you're talking to?"

"To someone who's losing their grip and lashing out. Time to buck up and start acting like a leader, or you're going to be replaced."

Snake drew his Desert Eagle .50 caliber and leveled it at Barton. "Say that again."

Barton didn't blink. "You wouldn't dare. The Illuminati would cut you to–"

The big gun bucked in Snake's hand, and Barton's chair blew back two feet from the impact. He slowly looked down at the wound in the center of his chest, and then his eyes rolled back into his head, and he died without a sound.

"Yeah? Who's the big man now, punkass? Got any other 'observations' you wanna make? Piece of shit." Snake spit on the dead man and turned when the door flew open and three of his bodyguards entered with guns drawn.

Snake waved his pistol in the air and then slipped it back in its holster. "Our boy here and I had a disagreement. Get him out of here and make sure he disappears for good. Anyone asks, nobody knows what happened to him – he just went for a walk one day and never came back." Snake paused and looked each man in the eyes. "And if I hear anything at all about this from anyone, all three of you will follow him, you understand? Open your mouth and everyone dies."

They nodded and Snake pushed past them. He stopped in the hall and looked over his shoulder at them.

"Things are going back to the old days, where it's just the Crew. We don't take orders from anyone. We don't need anybody. We tell them how it's gonna be, and if they don't play ball, they wind up in a ditch."

The men nodded again, unsure of how to respond, and Snake stormed away, his arms twitching from the meth, his eyes wild, and the stink of flop sweat strong in his wake. In his quarters, he went right for his stash and stuffed a wad of marijuana into a pipe with shaking fingers to calm his nerves.

The Illuminati punk had been asking for it. Nobody talked to Snake like that. He should have known better than to disrespect him to his face.

Snake inhaled a huge hit and held it deep in his lungs. A part of him knew he'd set something in motion he could never undo, but the drug buzz numbed that part, leaving him to laugh silently at the split-second expression in the dead man's eyes when he realized he'd called Snake wrong.

Chapter 46

Seattle, Washington

Lucas surveyed the arena through his M4 night vision scope and watched as the soldiers at the main gate guard post scanned their surroundings with night vision goggles. They had a big machine gun on a tripod behind an array of sandbags, and there were four of them, all obviously alert.

The Chinese had discovered their ship earlier in the day, so they knew something bad was coming their way. But they had no idea what, or how many, or even why, which was an advantage Lucas hoped to leverage with the strategy he'd mapped out with Art. Rather than a frontal attack, they would need to lure the Chinese out where they were vulnerable, which was the initial part of his plan. If it worked, some percentage of the troops would fall prey to the militia's guns, and then the battle would begin in earnest.

"Ready?" Lucas asked.

Sam nodded beside him, his M16 equipped with a similar NV scope as Lucas's M4.

"On my count."

"Okay."

"Three…two…one…fire."

Both rifles fired in unison, and two of the soldiers fell. Lucas shifted his aim to the one on the left and squeezed off another shot, and Sam did the same with the man on the right, with identical effect.

"Now let's see if they take the bait," Sam murmured.

They scurried away from their hiding place, back toward the buildings that lined the streets near the arena. They made it a hundred yards and stopped. Lucas raised his radio.

"Anything?"

"Looks like they're mobilizing."

"Send in the first twenty and take out some of their shooters at the wall. Won't do for them to be too complacent. I want them worried and reacting, not thinking."

"Roger that."

Gunmen emerged from the buildings and ran toward the spot where Lucas and Sam had hidden. When they were in position, they began firing at the Chinese, their rifles popping and cracking to little effect. A few of the guards who were manning the wall fell, but most of the shooting was to convince the Chinese that the attack was with rifles and nothing else.

They'd moved into position at midnight as the cloud cover had blanketed the city, ensuring darkness; the drizzle rendered the spotter nest in the Space Needle blind. Lucas and Art had hoped that the Chinese would be thrown by their vessel showing up with nobody aboard but the dead, and would make a few stupid mistakes that would cost them the city.

If they didn't, the alternative was to lay siege to the arena in conjunction with a relentless barrage of round-the-clock shelling and starve them out. But that was less desirable, even though it would be effective, because it would require not one but two sieges – the other at Harbor Island – and ran the very real risk that another ship would appear on the horizon, tipping the odds drastically in the invaders' favor.

Art's advance group continued firing at the arena, and then, after a seeming eternity, the Chinese began shooting back. The occasional shots from the militia were answered with a cacophony of fire from the wall, and the men kept their heads down, waiting for the Chinese troops to exhaust their magazines.

Snipers in the buildings near the arena took well-targeted shots at the assembled Chinese, never lingering at a window for more than one kill before moving to a different one. There was no doubt the Chinese had rockets and grenades, too, and would bring them to bear if presented with opportune targets.

After ten minutes of gunfire, several of the militia tossed fragmentation grenades at the gate, and when they detonated, all twenty men ran toward it as the snipers in the buildings laid down covering fire on full auto. The Chinese retreated from the gate as more grenades sailed over the wall and exploded inside the perimeter, and then an officer screamed orders and the confused melee organized while the militia took potshots at them through the rents in the gate.

One of Art's snipers hovered the reticule of his high-power scope over the officer's shoulder blades and squeezed off a round that sent the man to his knees in an eerie kind of slow motion. The soldiers, clearly shocked by the execution of their commander right in front of them, broke into smaller groups. A sergeant bellowed instructions as they made for the wall.

"Have them pull back," Lucas said, watching from the second story of the building in which he'd taken cover.

Art relayed the order, and the militia emptied their magazines through the gate. He tossed a few more grenades and retreated, running in disorganized fashion toward the intersection from which they'd come.

"Come on…come on…" Lucas whispered, watching the action in the pale green of his NV scope.

The last of Art's gunmen were almost to the nearest building when the Chinese threw open the gate and hundreds of them poured through, urged forward by their squad leaders. They spread out like a plague of ants darkening the street, firing as they ran. Two soldiers pushed the dead guards in the machine gun nest aside and began spraying the buildings with large-caliber rounds, covering for the running troops.

Lucas ducked and crawled to the stairs behind him, and then bolted down and outside, where he kept to the shadows in a back alley, his boots splashing in puddles from the continuing drizzle. When he'd made it a block, he entered another doorway and climbed to the flat roof of a three-story brownstone and lay by the rim to watch the action below.

He estimated roughly two hundred Chinese had emerged from the arena to chase the advance group, which was fewer than he'd hoped, but there wasn't anything he could do about it now. He watched as the Chinese troops fell into the trap the militia had laid, and waited for the second phase of the assault to launch.

He didn't have to wait long. Gunfire roared from the building across from him as one of the Brownings they'd brought rained death on the Chinese infantrymen. Some tried to retreat to the arena, but more militia cut them off, boxing them in as still more of Art's gunmen appeared in the building windows and picked them off from above. Snipers took out the pair of soldiers in the machine gun nest, leaving the Chinese completely cut off from their headquarters and fighting for their lives.

The battle became a slaughter, with the Chinese suffering staggering casualties, the survivors with little cover and fewer options. When it was nothing more than a mop-up operation, the gunmen who had closed off the route to the arena turned and directed their fire at the gate, where another wave of Chinese was blasting away at them.

"Tell Henry to start dropping bombs," Lucas said into the radio, and picked off a few of the soldiers closest to the gate while he waited for the shelling to commence.

The first mortar round fell short of the arena and exploded in the midst of the second wave of Chinese troops.

Lucas toggled the transmit button. "That first shell is on target for the staging area. Shift the other mortars farther toward the building, but keep that one for whenever they poke their heads out."

"Roger that," Art said.

More shells exploded closer to the arena, and by the time the fifth one had landed, they were exploding directly on its roof. Lucas watched as troops came running out of the edifice, and called in another of Henry's shorter-ranged shells to keep them occupied.

Explosions from the street where the militia was finishing off the soldiers drew his attention, and he scanned the area for the source. He recognized the rhythmic thud of a grenade launcher like the Mk 19s they'd brought to the fight, but couldn't find the nest anywhere at the arena. He frowned as the grenades killed a dozen of his fighters in as many seconds, and then realization widened his eyes at the likely source.

To place the grenades that precisely, the launcher had to be firing from above.

And there was only one place that fit that description.

He confirmed his hunch through his scope and then lifted the radio to his lips. "I'll be over to you in a minute. Get one of the grenade launchers ready."

"They are. You want us to start hitting the arena? Remember, we've got limited ammo."

"No. They've got one in the Space Needle."

Lucas raced down the stairs and broke into a run toward the hotel Art was using as his command center – close enough to see the fighting through binoculars, but at a safe enough distance that he didn't have to worry about rifle fire. Lucas dodged and zigzagged as rounds blew chunks of asphalt from around him, and didn't slow when he'd turned the corner and left the fighting behind.

Art was on the third floor. Lucas appeared in the doorway. "Where are the launchers?"

"On the roof. They're using the elevator shaft for cover."

"Okay."

Lucas took the stairs two at a time and burst onto the roof, where Terry and a helper had the Mk 19 ready, with a belt of grenades loaded.

"What's the range on that thing?" Lucas asked.

"Couple of thousand yards. But it depends. Accurate? Maybe a thousand."

"How far away is the Space Needle?"

Terry squinted at it. "Damn. I don't know."

"Take a shot at the middle of the tower and see what happens. The drop will tell you the range, right?"

"Should. But the rain isn't going to help."

"Just do it."

Terry adjusted the launcher's graduated rear sight, leveled it on the tower, and squeezed the trigger. The launcher lobbed a handful of grenades at the needle.

They waited for the impact, and when it came, the area halfway to the top lit up with orange explosions.

"Well, I'll be damned," Terry said. "Pretty much dead-on."

"Great. Put a can of rounds into the observation deck."

"You got it."

Terry shifted his aim, and the launcher blasted repeatedly for a solid minute. The area beneath the deck exploded with blasts, and then the observation area burst into flames as scores of 40mm grenades detonated inside.

When the ammo can was empty, Lucas peered through his NV scope to survey the damage. The observation deck was in ruins, with fires burning, and the explosions from the militia position near the arena had stopped.

"Holy…" Terry blurted, and Lucas lowered his rifle. The tower was leaning where the steel support structure had been damaged by the grenades that had hit it. The observation deck yawed over in slow motion as though debating whether to give in to the pull of gravity, and then dropped to the ground below, trailing flames and debris.

"Woohoo!" Terry yelled, and high-fived Lucas, bringing a smile to his face.

"Good shooting," Lucas said.

"Thanks. Want me to go to work on the arena?"

Lucas shook his head. "No. We've got a lot more mortars than grenades. Save them for something special."

"Like?"

Lucas looked off into the distance. "Harbor Island."

The arena became a killing zone as the mortars destroyed any place the troops could hide, and when the Chinese tried a desperate sortie through the gates, they were cut down by the Browning and rifle fire from the militia. After an hour of devastation, the troops retreated to the far side of the grounds, and Art ordered three hundred of his men to rush the gate while another Browning, situated on the third story of a building across the street from the gate, laid down cover.

The fighters did as ordered, and the majority made it inside, where they used the numerous craters created by the mortar shells for cover, as well as the bodies of the fallen. Art instructed Henry to concentrate his shelling on the far side of the arena now that the building was a smoking crater, and the battle continued for twenty more minutes, with the militia decimating the Chinese, who had nowhere to go, another hundred gunmen having flanked them and cut off their escape over the wall.

When it was over, Lucas and Art waited for a report on casualties with grim expressions. The lieutenants called in one by one, and by the time they had a full count, they'd lost nearly a hundred of their men, with another forty-three wounded.

"Brave, every one of them," Art said.

"Dead's still dead," Lucas replied.

"But we still have four hundred fifty able-bodied fighters. You see any reason not to finish this tonight?"

"Absolutely none."

Chapter 47

Lucas led the men through the streets. He knew when they began taking incoming rounds four blocks from the Harbor Island Bridge that the remaining Chinese troops weren't going to go easily. Sam and Henry were at the head of another group a block to the east, and Lucas's radio crackled as the men scattered and he took cover.

"We're getting hit hard over here, Lucas," Sam said.

"I can hear from where I'm at. We're taking a lot of fire, too."

"They're in the buildings."

"Yep. Going to be ugly from here."

Lucas called one of the fighters with a rocket tube strapped to his back to where he was crouched, and pointed at a muzzle flash eighty yards away. "Think you can put that thing through that window?"

The man gave a grim smile and slipped the launcher free. "I can sure try."

"Do it."

The man sighted the rocket at the window, and then a round took the top of his head off and he fell against Lucas. Lucas pushed him away and squeezed off a couple of three-round bursts at the shooter, and then reached for the rocket launcher, sighted it, and fired. The projectile streaked toward the building and blew half the second-floor façade away, destroying the area where the sniper had been.

Another sniper opened up farther down the street, and Lucas pinpointed him with his M4 and put a bullet through his throat.

The fighting from Sam's street was far more intense than what

Lucas's squad was experiencing, where after several more rocket launches, the street appeared clear for at least that block.

Lucas radioed Sam. "You need a hand?"

"Negative. We're about done. But, Lucas? Bill…he didn't make it."

Lucas exhaled heavily. "Damn. You sure?"

"No doubt. Sorry."

"Make them pay."

"We're working on it."

Lucas called for Terry and his loader to join him, and when they were at his side, he frowned as he looked through the rain at the base of the bridge three blocks away. "See that rubble? I'm betting there's a nest there. Can you put a few grenades down their throat without destroying the bridge?"

"I'll do my best."

The Mk 19 was heavy, and it took both of them to set it on the tripod and load the ammo belt into the feeder. Another man waited behind them with their last ammo can of grenades, each container weighing sixty pounds and requiring its own hauler.

The launcher barked four times, and the grenades detonated at the rubble pile, sending chunks of concrete into the air with each explosion. A .50-caliber heavy machine gun opened up from the building alongside it, and the pavement around Lucas sprayed divots of asphalt on them.

"Move!" Lucas barked, and ran for a doorway on his right as the others followed with the launcher and ammo.

Mortar rounds exploded down the street, and Lucas radioed Art. "They brought out the heavy artillery."

"I can hear it. I'll have Henry set up wherever he can and start shelling the island."

"Sooner the better. Sam's group is getting hit hard. Bill bought it."

"Hell."

Art gave the order for Henry to find high ground and blow the bridge on the far side of the island as his first priority target, thereby making it impossible for the occupying force to escape.

"Once you've cut them off, take out all but one of the bridges on this side. Worst case, we'll wait them out."

"Will do," Henry said.

The firefight from Sam's street died down as more rockets found their targets, and Lucas's men continued toward the bridge, fighting tooth and nail each block as the area around them exploded with mortar rounds. The rain intensified as the blasts continued, and Lucas's group lost another seven men before they reached the base of the bridge.

Sam's fighters joined them and they did a quick count – crossing town and making it to Harbor Island had cost them sixty men, an expensive trek no matter how they looked at it.

After blowing the bridges, Henry's crew had shifted their fire to the buildings on the island that were the likeliest shelters for the remaining troops. The answering mortar fire stopped when a lucky round had taken out the Chinese squad. Lucas had Terry's men set up the Mk 19 at the base of the bridge, and positioned the two Brownings high in buildings where they could hit anything on the island.

The Chinese were smart and didn't give the militia any opportunities to neutralize them, but by the time the rain had stopped and the sun was rising, the war of attrition was taking its toll. Henry's shelling and the judicious use of the launcher and Brownings had whittled down the remaining two hundred soldiers to no more than a hundred.

Once it was light out, that number quickly got cut down to fifty, but the Chinese survivors seemed determined to fight to the last man. The militia obliged them, surging over the bridge in waves and searching building by building to eradicate the rest. By the time the sun was high in the sky, the shooting had stopped, and Seattle was officially free of invaders.

Lucas stood with Art at the bridge, surveying the damage, and shook his head. "Lot of dead."

Art shrugged. "That's war."

"Was it worth it? You know there's more where they came from."

"Only the locals can decide that. All we can do is arm them and teach them to fight. In the end it's their city, and they have to do the heavy lifting."

"Be a shame if this was all for nothing."

"It wasn't for nothing, Lucas. We did it because it had to be done, and we were the only ones who could do it."

Lucas stood silent for a moment, considering. "If you say so. Right now, it seems…pointless."

"I know. But it isn't. We're taking our country back. There's going to be a lot of blood shed doing it, but damned if we aren't going to."

"You think they want it back? Seems like most aren't willing to fight for it. Maybe it's better to let someone else rule over them if that's how they want to live."

"Well, there's only one way to know for sure. This will be our test case. If they want, they've got freedom. What they do with it's their choice."

Lucas exhaled forcefully. "You're right. I'm just beat."

"Same here. Let's find somewhere safe and get some sleep. It'll all be clearer in a few hours."

When Lucas awoke, it was late afternoon, and Art was nowhere to be seen. Lucas rose and took a sip from his canteen, and then walked to the window of the abandoned home they'd commandeered. Sam and Henry were outside, talking excitedly. Lucas approached them and tipped his hat. "Gents."

"You're up! Good. You need to come see. It's amazing," Henry said.

"What is?"

"We've had over two thousand men sign on with us since this morning. They're coming out of the woodwork."

"Two…thousand?"

"That's right. And there's more on the way. Looks like we have a real army now."

"Depends on what you mean by real. Or army."

"Art's going to make a speech to them in a little while. He sent us to wait for you to wake up. He wants you to talk, too."

Lucas shook his head. "Not my thing."

"Just a few words. That's all. You're one of the leaders. You can't pull a no-show."

"Watch me." He sighed. "I need to find a shortwave radio. I want to let Ruby know we're okay, and talk to my family."

"That can wait. You've got thousands of people waiting to hear from you."

Lucas adjusted his hat, and the corner of his mouth tugged with the start of a grin. "Then waiting a little longer won't kill them."

Chapter 48

Amber Hot Springs, Colorado

Arnold stared down at the valley, Eve clinging to him and Julie by his side, and then coaxed his horse along the last of the trail to Shangri-La. The guards at the valley mouth waved them through, and the townspeople stopped working to rush to them.

Elliot arrived with Sierra and Tim. Sierra let out a cry of relief and ran to Eve. Arnold hoisted her and held her out to Sierra, who took her in an embrace. Tears streamed down their faces as Sierra smothered the little girl in a bear hug. Elliot watched with a sympathetic gaze, and Arnold's party dismounted and handed their reins to the stable hands who'd come running.

"So you were successful," Elliot said. "Congratulations."

"Yes and no." Arnold gave him a short report on their escape. Duke's face fell at the mention of Ellen having lost her life, and he stepped away, his expression clouded.

"You had to kill this preacher fellow?" Elliot asked.

Arnold looked slightly apologetic. "He was a part of the riders who were chasing us. But, Elliot…he was nuts. I mean, stark raving. He was planning to gas everyone in his church that night."

"What!"

Arnold recounted what Eve had told them, and Elliot stared off at the tree line. "Madness."

"That it is. But it also means we have a serious problem. Ellen knew our location. We have to assume she told them. Which means we aren't safe here."

"You think they're hot on your heels?"

"I don't know. But we can't assume they aren't."

Elliot frowned. "We picked this place because it was defensible. Maybe it's time to stop running every time a threat surfaces."

"There are thousands of them, Elliot. Thousands. Even if they're lousy fighters, the sheer numbers…"

"I know. I'm just – everyone's tired of having to move just when we get settled."

"Not much to be done about it."

Elliot walked away, lost in thought. Sierra neared Julie and Arnold with Eve in tow. "Thank you so much. All of you. I…it was like a part of me died when they took her."

"Well, she's back now, so you can spoil her rotten," Julie said.

"If there's anything I can ever do for you, let me know. Anything at all. I mean it."

Devin smiled from behind Arnold and looked to Anne. "All I want is a bath and a hot meal."

Anne nodded. "Me too."

Julie took Arnold's hand and gave him a knowing look. "We've got some unfinished business to discuss, but a bath and some food sounds awesome."

"We do?" Arnold said, and then swallowed drily. "Oh. Of course. Right."

"Elliot!" a voice cried from the cabin Elliot used as his office. "Transmission coming in. It's Lucas!"

Elliot hurried to the operator, who handed him a headset. "He's on the air now."

Elliot lowered himself onto the tree stump the operator was using as a chair and sat forward to transmit. "Lucas?"

Lucas's voice rang in his ears. "Elliot."

"Where are you? Are you on your way back?"

"Took a detour." Lucas told him about Astoria, Newport, Salem, and finished with Seattle.

Elliot was speechless when he finished. "You…you're in Seattle now?"

"That's right. We drove the Chinese out, and we're putting the finishing touches on a self-defense force for the city."

"I don't understand. Is Ruby all right?"

"She's in Salem. We're going to head out shortly. Maybe tomorrow. But, Elliot? We have something like three thousand fighters, and about five hundred more in Salem. It's a big group."

"That it is. What are you planning to do with them, Lucas?"

"We'll need to talk about that when I hit Salem. But the mood is to return to Shangri-La and clear the warlords out of the cities along the way."

"That's…that would be amazing if you could do it."

"I'm not thrilled about it, but it looks like we can. We beat the Chinese three times, and they're an actual army. A gang like the Crew wouldn't be anywhere near as tough."

Sierra appeared at the door. "Let me talk to him."

Elliot welcomed her in. "Lucas, we had some trouble since you left." He gave Lucas a brief rundown on the recent encounter with the church. When he was done, Lucas's question was almost a whisper.

"Is Eve okay?"

"Yes, yes. Everyone's fine. Sierra's right here. She wants to talk to you."

"Put her on. I'll radio when we get to Salem."

"Will do."

Sierra took the headphones and replaced Elliot in the seat. "Lucas! Are you okay?"

"Yes. I can't wait to get home. It's been way longer than I hoped."

"Where are you?"

Lucas repeated his story.

"So…you're now the leader of some army?"

"Not exactly."

"That's what it sounds like. What about us? What happened to living out our days together as a family?"

"We will. I'm headed home after I pick up Ruby."

"That sounds like it could be another month, Lucas. At least. And with some army on foot...we might never see you again."

"Nothing's going to stop me from coming home, Sierra. Nothing."

The transmission broke up. Lucas's voice returned, but distorted. "Power's almost gone here. I love you, Sierra. I'll call from Salem. I swear."

"I love you too, Lucas," she said, but all she heard in her headset was static.

Duke approached Elliot, who was deep in discussion with one of his advisors. "I'm going to head back to the trading post with Luis," he said. "Nothing much for me to do here."

Elliot put a hand on his shoulder briefly. "I'm sorry about Ellen."

Duke waved the comment away. "Don't be. I was a fool. But there is the question of what's next. You going to move the town? If so, where are you thinking?"

"We haven't decided. But if we do, it'll be somewhere we can lay down real roots. I'm thinking it won't be Shangri-La anymore. Maybe that idea isn't realistic now, or even necessary. Perhaps we should find an abandoned town and settle there, and just be residents of the town. Normal people. Now that the vaccine's in wide distribution, the purpose of Shangri-La's largely over."

"I don't know. The idea of an enclave where everyone's trustworthy and living in peace, far from where marauders or others can reach it, has a lot of appeal."

"That's why I said we're thinking about it. I'll contact you and let you know."

"The trading post needs to move, too. We can't risk the church attacking us out of retribution. If Ellen told them how I led her to you, they'll come for us."

"That makes sense."

"Maybe we'll set one up in Colorado Springs and call it something different so they don't put two and two together. Luis's Trading Post has a ring to it."

"Let me know what you decide."

"You too."

Elliot watched the defeated trader mount up and ride down the trail with Luis at his side, and exhaled softly. Just when everything should have been going well, with the nightmare virus contained, the Crew threat eliminated, and a new home in the making, the world had thrown them curves, and the future looked more uncertain, not less, with every sunrise.

"Well, hell," he muttered, and then caught sight of Sierra walking from the cabin with Eve's hand in hers and Tim's clutched in her other, the sun shining off the children's hair like halos.

In spite of his dark thoughts, he smiled.

Perhaps everything would work out after all.

About the Author

Featured in *The Wall Street Journal*, *The Times*, and *The Chicago Tribune*, Russell Blake is *The NY Times* and *USA Today* bestselling author of over fifty novels.

Blake is co-author of *The Eye of Heaven* and *The Solomon Curse*, with legendary author Clive Cussler. Blake's novel *King of Swords* has been translated into German, *The Voynich Cypher* into Bulgarian, and his JET novels into Spanish, German, and Czech.

Blake writes under the moniker R.E. Blake in the NA/YA/Contemporary Romance genres. Novels include *Less Than Nothing*, *More Than Anything*, and *Best Of Everything*.

Having resided in Mexico for a dozen years, Blake enjoys his dogs, fishing, boating, tequila and writing, while battling world domination by clowns. His thoughts, such as they are, can be found at his blog: RussellBlake.com

Visit RussellBlake.com for updates

or subscribe to: RussellBlake.com/contact/mailing-list

Books by Russell Blake

Co-authored with Clive Cussler
THE EYE OF HEAVEN
THE SOLOMON CURSE

Thrillers
FATAL EXCHANGE
FATAL DECEPTION
THE GERONIMO BREACH
ZERO SUM
THE DELPHI CHRONICLE TRILOGY
THE VOYNICH CYPHER
SILVER JUSTICE
UPON A PALE HORSE
DEADLY CALM
RAMSEY'S GOLD
EMERALD BUDDHA
THE GODDESS LEGACY
A GIRL APART
A GIRL BETRAYED
QUANTUM SYNAPSE

The Assassin Series
KING OF SWORDS
NIGHT OF THE ASSASSIN
RETURN OF THE ASSASSIN
REVENGE OF THE ASSASSIN
BLOOD OF THE ASSASSIN
REQUIEM FOR THE ASSASSIN
RAGE OF THE ASSASSIN

The Day After Never Series
THE DAY AFTER NEVER – BLOOD HONOR
THE DAY AFTER NEVER – PURGATORY ROAD
THE DAY AFTER NEVER – COVENANT
THE DAY AFTER NEVER – RETRIBUTION
THE DAY AFTER NEVER – INSURRECTION
THE DAY AFTER NEVER – PERDITION
THE DAY AFTER NEVER – HAVOC
THE DAY AFTER NEVER – LEGION

The JET Series
JET
JET II – BETRAYAL
JET III – VENGEANCE
JET IV – RECKONING
JET V – LEGACY
JET VI – JUSTICE
JET VII – SANCTUARY
JET VIII – SURVIVAL
JET IX – ESCAPE
JET X – INCARCERATION
JET XI – FORSAKEN
JET XII – ROGUE STATE
JET XIII – RENEGADE
JET XIV – DARK WEB
JET – OPS FILES (prequel)
JET – OPS FILES; TERROR ALERT

The BLACK Series
BLACK
BLACK IS BACK
BLACK IS THE NEW BLACK
BLACK TO REALITY
BLACK IN THE BOX

Non Fiction
AN ANGEL WITH FUR
HOW TO SELL A GAZILLION EBOOKS
(while drunk, high or incarcerated)

Printed in Dunstable, United Kingdom

67100128R00154